FORGIVEN

A Novel

Maureen Sutlive Taylor, EdD.

Terns Press

Teresa – You have blessed me through Victor and now your friendship! Much Love – Maureen

Terns Press
Peachtree Corners, Georgia 30092

Copyright© 2014 by Maureen Sutlive Taylor
Book cover design by J. Chris Taylor
ISBN 9978-0991401895

CONTENTS

ACKNOWLEDGEMENTS

The old adage that no person travels alone can be easily transferred to no person writes alone. Because of this, I have many people to thank who have participated in some way to the production of this book. I owe a debt to my wonderful niece, Dr. Ashley Oliver Bufe, who read the roughs while starting in a brand new practice, pregnant, and working day light to sunset. She receives an A++ in her cheerleading efforts to rally me on.

My gratitude knows no bounds to Dr. Jan Meehan, my dear friend and colleague, who proofed this novel repeatedly, kept smiling, and offered brilliant suggestions all in question form. Thanks as well to Carol Sacca, who read and edited my work in its roughest form. Her encouragement supported me in some very doubtful times. I am also indebted to Katie Dahl Padgett, my English major friend from the University of Georgia (and former student) for combing through this work with enthusiasm and support.

Thanks to my friends and colleagues who continued to urge, cajole, tease, threaten and push me to the finish line: Clancey Goodwin, Danielle Walcott, Kathy Eichler, Cheri Griffin, Gretchen Runaldue, Dorothy Swindle, Cathy Capehart Wilder Sharp, and Terri Kittredge Andrews. You are forever more in my prayers.

Dedication

I am not sure that it takes a village to raise a child, but I am absolutely certain that it takes a family effort to get a book born, bred, and ready for reading. My long suffering family stood fast in support through every part of the story line, my random ideas, changes and more changes, and general roller coaster moods of a writer creating her first novel.

For my brother, Barry Sutlive – your perseverance and cheer while reading my rough draft of a romance novel and offering encouragement when I wanted to put an end to the book, kept me motivated in the right direction. May God bless you for your faith in me.

For Karen Sutlive Oliver –for your prayers for the right words and the truth of this book to touch others. Thank you.

For Greg Sutlive – for teasing me and finding other authors who could share the pitfalls of writing and getting published. Thank you for keeping me in check.

For MaryAnne Sutlive –for your support over the years as I continued my pursuit of writing this book. Your work ethic and "just get it done" attitude has always made an overwhelming task seem very manageable. Gotta love that about you.

For my wonderful son, Chris Taylor –you helped design and create the book cover, rescued me from cyber hell found in Windows 8.1 and Adobe InDesign, and continuously supported me in finishing this project. You are the best son, and I am grateful for your help and creativity.

Finally, for my mother, Anne Prescott Sutlive – for being my biggest fan; she wanted the story setting to be Tybee Island so others, new to

Tybee, might feel some of the joy she felt living with her memories of such a wonderful place. My mother did not live to see this book published, but I know she has been with me every step of the way. I dedicate this book to my loving family and to our precious mother who always said, "Dream for a while. Plan **it** all out. Then get busy and have something to show for it." Mom, I hope you think I do.

CHAPTER 1

───────~───────

There is no parallel universe, although the idea is grand. There is no avatar substitute when living grows too hard. There is no treatment for the realities of life that crash into the world like runaway trains on crack. Yet, there is a fragment of hope, thin as a baby's fine hair, that continuing could become a reality. Odds are slim though, at best.

The sun still clung sleepily to its space just below the horizon, and the fading crescent moon dipped as if sliding down the back of the sky. A palette of blues and grays spilled across the sky, and the sands were shades of blanched almonds. All the colors produced a serenity that belied the outside world. A stillness held everything at bay, even the emotions on slow boil just beneath the surface of Katie's fragile mind. She had retreated to the beach seeking healing and a chance to salvage what little was left of her nervous system. Her life had been a review course for the media saturated reality shows that profited off the lives of suffering souls. She knew in her heart that the only hope of healing would lie in the roots of her very existence, the place where it had all begun. Tybee Island seemed to be her last chance.

The starting point of her memory, the one that shows where it all began, was a blur. Katie just knew that being on the island flooded her with memories that hugged her and pulled at her heartstrings. If she closed her eyes, she had vivid images of her grandmother Dolly's first beach house, the one that sat on Second Street standing watch over the ocean. Dolly's was a big shell of a house, and each nook and cranny, every cot and double bed, was filled to overflowing with children, cousins and uncles, and then some whom Katie could not remember how they owned the right to a place to sleep. Although Katie was the only child of an only child, she was used to Dolly's brand of kinship, which was modeled after the old lady in the shoe.

One particular memory seemed to demand more attention than most. Dolly had invited Johnny Stapleton and his niece, Laura Anne, to the beach for an extended visit. Johnny, the best man in their wedding, was a newly appointed monsignor. Dolly believed in maintaining a close proximity to the clergy where a little holiness might just rub off. Besides, he was humorous and the fairest man she had ever known. Laura Anne, his precocious and horribly spoiled niece, wore two faces that changed when the timing was right. At the advanced age of fourteen, Laura Anne was showing distinct patterns of narcissism rare in such a young child. However, she was blonde and cool and a magnet for tweens who longed for a role model. For Katie, it was a love-hate relationship, but since Laura Anne was staying for the summer once again, Katie had little choice but to bite her lip and suck it up.

One hot, sultry night in early August, Laura Anne gathered her favorites for a trip to the local Tastee Freeze. The star of the menu, large vanilla cones dipped in chocolate, dripped in oozy streams down their shirts and smeared across sunburned cheeks and noses. Laura Anne magnanimously treated the entire affair dousing any flame Katie had been working on to diminish Laura Anne's status. Not until the next morning, when Dolly asked if anyone had taken money from her purse, did Katie feel vindicated, yet not brave enough to tell on the little blonde thief. That Monsignor thing and all was just a tad too scary for her.

Laura Anne was many things besides a thief and a liar. One night when forced to share a double bed with her, Katie laid on her side and listened to Laura Anne talk in her winsome way.

"You know, Katie, I heard my parents talking about you the other night, and they said you were an orphan. I really think that is so sad. They said you would have lots of problems growing up without parents."

Katie felt that gut-twisting wound, much like a sucker punch, deep inside her stomach. Nowhere to put that kind of pain, like the one that comes when a doctor adds a postscript to a cancer prognosis.

"Why would I have lots of problems? I still have Dolly to take care of me. And don't forget Cat."

"Sorry. Not the same as parents. And, all the kids at school will know you are an orphan. You know, that's kinda creepy living without a mom and a dad. But anyway, my parents, which I have two, say that Dolly is too old to raise you. They also said she's a religious freak so you're in for double trouble."

Actually, the pain from this kick was not as bad as the first. Luckily, it was too dark for Laura Anne to see Katie's face, but it might have scared her to death if she had. Katie's journey down denial lane, that curvy twisted road where emotions are shoved, shaved, and stuffed into meaningless little balls too slippery to catch, began that night. Only trouble is, in the darkness of their caves, they multiply and plot schemes to wreck your life when you least expect it.

Resisting the urge to bury herself under the covers, Katie hissed words to the bully in bed with her: "What about your uncle, the Monsignor? He's way holier than Dolly."

Laura Anne just giggled. "That's what I mean. My parents do not believe all that God stuff and they make fun of my uncle. I hate it, too. So I have my uncle and you have your grandmother. Two religious freaks. An orphan and a religious freak, that's what everyone will call you."

Silence stood by the bed and snuffed out any hint of a sound. Katie struggled to swallow that thick sob waiting to be released. Katie wanted to be strong and ignore all that Laura Anne had just spewed all over her, but it was a supreme challenge.

As if on cue, Laura Anne rolled over and whispered to Katie, "By the way, my dad started laughing and called you Rapunzel. You know, the girl locked away in an ivory tower – you have heard the story …so no one would ever find her. Dad said Dolly would probably send you to a convent school to keep you away from boys. My parents laughed so hard over that one."

Laura Anne giggled that obnoxious smirk that always defines the precocious child who spends way too much time with adults and believes all the "how adorable" lies they tell.

"By the way, Katie, if you tell anyone I said anything of these things to you, I'll call you a liar and swear I never said a word. Good night, Katie."

That sob exploded while Katie cried into her pillow, desperately trying not to let Laura Anne hear her. The cruelty of the words looping across the marquee of her mind crushed her. Over and over, it played until Katie was quite sure it was true. Why else would she say it? Katie was alone except for Dolly, and though she had never thought of herself as an orphan, she suddenly felt very alone in an ever-darkening world.

Katie had always believed that Dolly was the consummate reader of people. However, certain factors could blur the waters enough to drive her divining rod off target. As was the case with Laura Anne. She had tried to tell Dolly about Laura Anne's killer words, but she could not bring herself to repeat them. Suppose Dolly could not hide the fact that they were true? But no matter what Katie told her, Dolly would always say "forgive her and move on. Don't look back on what she said or did, just let it go." It did not make any sense that someone could be that hateful and not get in trouble for it. There just had to be some kind of justice. Hadn't there?

It would be a long time before Katie could put thought and word to it, but she knew she would have to listen to her inner voice, that part that warns, in a tingling, something's wrong kind of way. Just a knowing in the pit of the stomach. Almost like a radio station just off tune. But as soon as she came face to face with that feeling that the stars were marching out of step, she would grow much afraid and begin a lifelong pattern of pushing her feelings way down deep....deep unto deep...until the darkness.

CHAPTER 2

It had been a wide-eyed night. Memories of a love gone by tormented Katie's mind. Morning failed to bring new promises, but it did relieve her of the pretense of sleep. Dolly was still in her room, and the house was wonderfully quiet. Maybe today she would try to run, get out on the beach, and face the world again. For the past week, she had treated herself as a leper and stayed behind closed doors and blinds. The world had not been a friendly place, and she was tired of feeling like Pandora. She so desperately wanted to close the box and move on as if nothing had ever happened. But it all did.

With the sun just barely up, Katie threw some water on her face, pulled back her bed hair, and dressed for her run. She had always loved that magical feeling of setting foot on the beach for the first time each trip. For some, the beach was hot, with scalding sand, itchy beds, and peeling sunburn. However, to true beach lovers it was a mystical place where God called to you from the deep. So many mornings in Katie's life, she would feel called, Bible in hand, to talk to Him in the early mornings, before the chaos drowned Him out. For now, this visit was sans Bible, but Katie had not forgotten the times she had felt His presence here. The only thing that mattered now was to continue to ignore Him and try to make this run on the beach.

"Come on, boy. Let's go out." Katie knelt down and pulled the yellow lab to her chest. She buried her face into the thicker fur around his red plaid collar and breathed in deeply. She loved the feel of him, the way he puffed through his cheeks when he could not respond any other way. She loved the way he slept with his back to hers, and the whine he released when he would become uncovered during the night. She especially loved the way he knew bedtime, and would stand in the bedroom doorway and prance and paw until she came. He should have been a sheepherder.

Beau could hardly contain himself, as if he knew what was coming. He loved the beach as much as the other beach people did, and yes, Beau was a people. And a finicky people at that. As far as dogs go, he had to have been one of the most beautiful labs she had ever seen. Matter of fact, according to the public, those who had seen Beau hanging out the back seat window or pattering down the street, he was a special dog from a very special breed. There was no doubt about it that Beau was descended from royalty and not just because he was AKC registered. No, you could just look into his eyes and know that he had quite a story to tell.

Grabbing onto Beau's leash, Katie held her breath as she faced the wide sandy plain. The briny smell of the ocean charged memories from very long ago and seemed to strengthen her. Crossing over the long, bleached boardwalk bridging the fragile dunes below, Katie drank in the beauty of the morning beach. To newcomers, one might expect a photo op had prepared the scene, but to true beach people, this splendor was repeated each time the sun rose. Most mornings found shell seekers scouring the treasures tossed up from the ocean, but this morning the whipping winds and threat of angry weather kept most combers at bay. Only the purple sandpipers, pencil thin yellow legs moving at amazing speeds, darted in and around the tide pools surrounded by the granite grey boulders, left over from previous attempts at stopping beach erosion. A few hardy brown pelicans bobbed on the rough crests of the waves hunkering down while they waited for breakfast. A scattering of seagulls stood at attention near the water's edge; it was beyond hope that torn bread pieces or boiled peanuts would be breakfast fare this day. Katie had wished that more people had been out that morning. Not too many, but enough that she did not feel so alone. Impatiently, Beau tugged on his leash and pulled Katie towards the beach.

Katie looked left, toward the North End, to get her bearings. The lighthouse still stood proud and tall. It had been a site for play for most of the islanders, even the regulars who only came during the summer. The old light keeper was a displaced WWII sergeant, Howard

Hennessey, a gentle man trapped in the Hulk's body. After making some changes on his birth certificate, from fifteen to eighteen, Howard joined the coast guard. During WWII, the coast guard and navy worked as one, which meant, for Howard anyway, he would see the war up close and personal. His short stint in the war ended at Omaha Beach, Normandy, France. As part of the demolition crew, Howard was in charge of moving debris in order to clear a path for the soldiers to land. Coming under attack from the Nazis machine gun nests, he rolled behind a landing craft hoping to be spared. He was not to be so lucky. Shrapnel to his frontal lobe left some distortions in his ability to filter emotions and problem solve.

As a result, Howard found himself back on Tybee Island, damaged but not destroyed, and in need of a job. What better place than the lighthouse? To keep his military training in practice, he took it upon himself to try and organize the lives and play of the beach children. Marching, quiet on the lighthouse steps, history lessons on the Widows Walk, searching for secret Nazi subs off the coast of Tybee Island, or any one of numerous lists of items all the children knew by heart kept them on their toes and eager to hear more. And with each generation of children and although he was stern and for all outward appearances seemed gruff and grizzly, Katie loved the tales he wove about the sea, about the losses of war, and the victories in life. His victory finally came when a small, sweet bride promised to love and cherish him until the end of times. It proved to be the greatest joy in his life and a vow that only the Lord would separate.

Mr. Hennessey allowed his favorite beach kids, the old timers, to call him Sarge, a name that befitted him and his gruff ways. But Katie found it impolite to call an adult by his first name, or even his add on name. So she compromised and called him Mr. Sarge. The old vet had a habit of taking his morning constitutional, rain or come shine, just a few hours after sunrise. Many combers preferred the sunrise when the beach was still all but deserted, but Mr. Sarge liked to say good morning to the beach and its people. As always he smoked his pipe, keeping it nestled in the palm of his right hand, while he nodded to familiar and unfamiliar faces alike. He was deeply browned and weather beaten, but there was something so comforting about this big beast of a man, black shorts, always the same black shorts, Marine style haircut, Rugby shirt, and the pipe.

Mr. Sarge called his pipe W.C. which Katie failed to understand. W.C. of course was Winston Churchill and had Katie been born during the war, she would have known that. She had already learned that the war was now and forever to come, the only war that truly mattered. It seems Churchill only smoked cigars made by Alfred Dunhill Ltd. in England. On a brief leave in London, Mr. Sarge, as a fifteen-year-old man boy, equated maturity with pipe smoking. Thus the purchase of a Dunhill Bruyere pipe, which would be a part of him forever. Engraved markings down the stem of the pipe showed the patent number and the date the pipe was made. Old Sarge used to finger the markings as he talked. A slow, back and forth rub, no a caress. This pipe was something more meaningful than the rest of the world would understand.

Katie had a special affinity for Mr. Sarge. She knew that he reciprocated those feelings and he treated her like the granddaughter he had never had. Actually, she was the only one of the beach kids who was allowed to hold W.C., a most treasured gift. Katie loved the feel of the old pipe and loved that it had been to war. At her young age, Katie did not understand a thing about the war, but she loved the idea that Old Sarge chose W.C. from all the other pipes in the shop. There was always something special about being chosen.

She also loved the smell of Mr. Sarge's pipe. It had a buttered rum smell, or so he called it, that made her smile. Something about the billowy smoke and the wild aromatics offered her a sense of security. She knew it was silly, but not any sillier than someone loving a stuffed animal, or a blankie, or even a good luck charm. Katie knew at a very early age that she saw the world through her heart and her fingers.

Although Sarge had often times tried to quit smoking, he was unsuccessful. But it had just become a part of him as he carried the pipe like an appendage. He was never without it. It was a conversation piece and an opportunity for him to share his faith and his life. The beach kids all knew his wonderful stories by heart, and they knew his faith journey as well. Jesus was Lord and that was that. It was not a debate. It was not an argument. It was the gospel truth; the truth and he hoped someone would try to prove it otherwise.

Today Katie remembered him for the kindness he showed her in her youth. She remembered him putting two fingers in his mouth and whistling when the kids were swimming too close to the jetties or when the undertow was getting too strong. There were times when early morning tide pools were biomes of adventure. It would not be unusual to see Sarge laying down in the middle of the pool and searching for periwinkles with the kids. Did not matter at all that none of them shared his DNA. They were beach kids, and they all had a deep connection. Sarge was the self-appointed roving lifeguard who worked each section of the beach as he traveled back and forth from the lighthouse. Katie would find much later in life that she would need a touch of security from the past.

Shaking the memories that swirled around her, Katie and Beau headed out. Looking to the left, she decided to run towards the lighthouse. Freshly painted day marks in stark bands of black, then white, and once again black marked hope. For 74 feet the tower rose into the sky offering a marker that one was on the right track. And should a traveler stumble through the black night, a beacon of light would guide him safely home. Where had her beacons been? There had been no such markers available to Katie, and she laughed at the thought of the hundreds of lighthouses she would need to navigate in her tormented world. Katie had been lost like a ship in the middle of all the oceans. The memory of those times threatened to overwhelm her; the despair waiting to overtake her; the hopelessness of ever being happy again pounded at her unmercifully. Katie turned to start her run and tried to shake the negative thoughts that came unbeckoned. The exercise would help clear her head. Besides Beau was whining and straining to get started. He turned and looked up at her as if to ask, *what is wrong now?*

Buying time, Katie used the boardwalk rails to stretch out, ever mindful of her Achilles tendons that were too tight and too short. Suddenly, a quick movement caught within her peripheral vision drew her and Beau's attention to the fenced in dunes.

Oatmeal colored ghost crabs, black eyes bulging, scampered sideways through the warming sand. Tall sea oats swayed in the wind catching tiny particles of sand and dropping them to build the dunes.

Milky flowered morning glory vines ran in no apparent order across the piles of sand. She could hear the waves as they slapped along a freshly washed beach leaving foam deposits, opaque and tinged with the color of old tee shirts. As Katie moved towards the beach, the sand, blown into little dunes on the boardwalk, gushed and swished beneath her shoes. Standing on the last step, Katie panned the entire scene. She checked her pockets for two critical items, her iPhone and an Ativan. Fully armed, could she possibly leave the safety of the wooden steps bowing under the pressure of the eroding sand?

As she put her foot down, her breathing started to become shallow and her chest began to tighten. Almost fish like, Katie parted her lips and sucked in tiny breaths of air. That familiar tingling sensation slowly crawled over her body, a mixture of a cold chill and a hot flash. Now was the time to practice all she had learned. It was do or die time, but it was a first step, one of so many that Katie needed to make. As the panic levels began to rise, she remembered Dr. Martin.

CHAPTER 3

———————~———————

K atie began to revisit the first time she had met her therapist, Dr. Christopher Martin. He had a reputation for being the best anxiety specialist in the South. Patients were backlogged and staggered waiting for appointments, and from all that Katie had heard, he was worth the wait. Dr. Martin was a good-looking man who dressed the part. Katie perched on the edge of an olive drab sofa and did the once over as discreetly as she could. At just 36, he had already garnered the respect of his colleagues, published several peer-reviewed articles on treating anxiety disorders, and spent much time lecturing about outdated treatments for panic attacks.

As an added bonus, he was charismatic and warm. He appeared to be about six feet, ever so slightly tanned, not a gym fanatic, but a nice normal size. He was a man who was obviously comfortable in his body. And why not? Dressed in khakis and a royal blue Polo shirt, he epitomized ease and comfort. Just what a psychiatrist should offer.

And he had good teeth. They were real teeth, not cosmetically designed veneers, and not all the teeth were the same size and they were not artificially whitened ones that scream "I've been bleached" as soon as they walk through the door. No, there was something just wholesome and natural about Dr. Christopher Martin. Even his small scar that ran parallel to his upper lip added just a hint of the little boy tucked inside. His slightly mussed hair made you think he had just been caught napping on the sofa.

Sitting across from each other on matching couches, Dr. Martin began the new patient, two-hour session.

"Katie, you answered in your questionnaire, that you were a Christian. Would you like to start this session off with a prayer?"

Dr. Martin laid it out there so matter of factly that Katie was a bit shocked. *Prayer? Was he kidding?* She shook her head no, as if she were passing on fried rattlesnake.

"If you don't mind, I'd like to ask for the Lord's guidance as we start our work together." So in a man's whisper he began, "Lord, please guide me today as Katie and I begin our work together…Amen."

After the prayer, Katie opened her eyes to discover that certainly nothing had changed. Her anxiety was eating her up much like ants on a melting Hershey bar. There had been no miracle, and although Dr. Martin had not asked for one, Katie felt something should have happened. He had just seemed to know whom he was talking to and seemed so sure about asking for help. After all, he thanked God as if it were done. *Well*, she thought, *it did not take.*

Katie popped another Ativan under her tongue and tried to white knuckle it for the next twenty minutes or so. The drug worked quickly and provided enough relief that she could manage to sit miserably through the two hours of therapy. Dr. Martin went over a few of the questions on the medical form Katie had completed and asked a series of rapid-fire questions. Surely, he did not expect an answer to so many, yet maybe he sought her reaction instead.

Leaning back in his chair, Dr. Martin picked up his Flair pen and began. "Were there any childhood incidents that I might need to know about? For example, problems at home, one or more parents frequently out of the home. Anything along those lines?

Katie tensed. "Do you mean abandonment issues? Like maybe my parents left me when I was twelve or I had to go live with my grandmother? Could that be what you mean?" Her responses smacked of sarcasm and caught Dr. Martin just off guard.

"Certainly those are areas we will delve into. I see that those are painful areas for you."

"You have no idea. Next question."

"Have you been taking Ativan long? "

"Depends on your definition of 'long'."

"Okay, moving on. Have you ever taken an antidepressant to help with your anxiety?"

"Never knew that was an option"

"Katie, are these questions bothering you? You seem a little annoyed."

"Dr. Martin, I really don't mean to be so sarcastic and abrupt. I just want to get this thing fixed. Heal me. That's what I want and not a long conversation of why my life sucks."

"I see. Okay, just a few more questions and let me know if you can't bear it."

"Really, Dr. Martin, do I act like I can control my tongue?"

Chris Martin could not help himself. He leaned back into the sofa and just roared with laughter. This woman sitting in front of him was a sassy, defiant, and charming creature. He saw no victim mentality here.

"Dr. Martin. I can help you out with some of this. Yes, I practice avoidance behavior and yes, my family thinks I am a nut case, and yes, I have levels of anxiety that you would not believe. So, did I cover them all?"

"All but one, Katie. When did your panic attacks first begin?"

With a shudder, Katie pulled inside a little closer and made a conscious choice to go down that path again.

Katie could detach from the interview and retell every detail. She knew the answer to the day and to the minute, much the same way baby boomers know their precise locations when Kennedy was assassinated and later generations remember John Lennon's shooting.

"March 19, 2006. I was sitting on my bed at my grandmother's beach house, reading *In Cold Blood*, and trying to relax after a dreadful winter quarter at school. I had carried twenty hours, definitely an overload, and was in an experimental psychology class where the work was independent study. All the tests were oral. I played around and ended up taking all the tests, over the entire book, in three weeks. Made an A by the way. It did nothing to relieve my already full stress bucket. My dad's mother had died, my boyfriend dumped me, and I felt overwhelmed. I came to the beach for some peace on a long weekend, but I didn't find it. I had the most overwhelming fear that I was suddenly losing my mind; I wanted to run down the beach screaming for help, but I was too afraid to move. Panic covered my mind and body. My dad's brother is a doctor, and he was called to come over. He's the one who told me all about the joy of life long suffering with panic disorder."

Katie began to cry in spite of her best intentions, and with that, copious tears dripping quickly, she sank deeper into the plush down of the sofa. Anxiety felt just dreadful. It hurt. It made her want to vomit. It made her brain turn to mush. It made her feel weak and dependent, fearful of ever being alone. A terrible life spent on "what ifs." A demon's torment.

And in its passing, it left her depleted and filled with fear wondering when the monster would return. Overwhelmed by despair, Katie's tears caused her mascara to run in black rivulets down her face while she sniffed furiously to keep her nose from doing the same. She wanted to die. And she felt like such a fool. She always felt like such a fool – anxiety was a fool's disease...a fool's disease.

"Katie. Let's talk some about the increase in your panic levels. What is going on in your home life that could be precipitating some of this anxiety?" He picked up his pen, perched, and ready to write. Committing it to paper meant she had one foot on the yellow brick road.

"I suppose I should start with a question; is there anything in my life that is not causing me anxiety? My husband and I are having serious marital problems. Some pretty rough stuff has happened, and Scott does not understand why I cannot just snap my fingers and everything will be as it used to be. That's driving me crazy. I am bored to death and want to go back to work, but the anxiety is keeping me close to home. Sometimes I am so afraid of a panic attack that I'll turn around while I'm out and come home. I'm working on becoming agoraphobic and that scares me to death. So, can you see why I'm here?"

"Katie, nothing feels as terrible and hopeless as anxiety that's been hanging around for a while. But, we will work through this. And believe it or not, you are well on the road to recovery because you are not in denial about what is going on in your life. It will take some hard work, but it won't kill you. It might feel like it at times, but just remember, it's a process."

"Dr. Martin. At this point, short of torturing me, you can do whatever it takes to keep me from going over the edge. Because, I lay in bed at night, very often a husbandless bed mind you, and I pray for the white coats to come. I pray that this will someday soon end. I cannot stand the constant fear of a panic attack any more. My life feels like hell."

"Have you ever had any suicidal thoughts? Thoughts that you might harm yourself?"

"I know what suicide means and no, I don't want to kill myself. Although I am not going to church right now, I am Catholic and believe that suicide complicates death in a very serious way. But do I wish I were dead sometimes...sort of. Now you might want to ask me if I ever have thoughts of killing someone."

And with that, she started to laugh. Not a sicko laugh, but one that poked fun at the absurdity of her statement. It was touching to watch her smile through her tears. Watching Dr. Martin try to untangle her thoughts made her smile even more.

"Dr. Martin, I'm just kidding. I don't want to kill anybody, but sometimes when Scott, that's my husband, is being evil personified, I want my silver bullet and a stake!"

Chris laughed in spite of himself. A woman with a sense of humor in the midst of her anguish was not as bad off as she thought she was. Looking at her was a distinct pleasure. She was a certifiable mess, no doubt about it. But she came to him today searching for an end to her agony. And she dressed and coiffed as if everything was just fine. Here she sat, dressed to the nines and he simply could not take his eyes off her.

Before leaving the house that morning, Katie had decided that if she were sent to the funny farm, she would go well dressed. So she chose her favorite Ralph Lauren safari looking shirtdress, a chic, stretch-poplin outfit that hugged her body and showed off her best features. A pair of cork soled, tan shoes added a few inches to her height, and a contoured matching rope and calfskin, strappy belt hung at her waist. Her sleeves were rolled up above her elbows and the look was casual but classy. She had wanted to appear together, ready for anything, especially the straight jacket. Her intent would never have been to entice the good doctor. This was her first visit and he might have been a toad. Actually, Katie had lost all sense of herself and her beauty. Dressed to the nines or not, she was still a mess, albeit a very well dressed one.

To his amazement, Chris Martin was slowly losing his clinical detachment, and he was struggling to compartmentalize her. This woman, intermittently crying miserably and laughing through her tears, on his sofa, was an enchanting creature. Pretty to be sure, but with an energy and charisma he had never seen before. Most women, who sat on his couch so to speak, were a mess, just as Katie Stewart was. She was open and vulnerable, scared out of her wits, and dancing the "what if's" just as fast as she could... Yet, there was something so intriguing about her; those eyes were pleading for help and though her body screamed for sleep and relief, a steadying hand could raise her up, and bring her to wholeness once again. Chris found himself wanting to reach out to her. Wrap her in his arms and whisper words of encouragement. Mortified at these thoughts, Chris suddenly blurted, "Katie would you like a cup of coffee or tea?" in the most urgent voice. It startled Katie and she was almost embarrassed to have needed so much attention.

"I'm sorry – did I do something wrong?" Then Katie wanted to kick herself. It was her therapy session so why was she apologizing. She had struggled to keep peace for so long, that she had started to lose something that was quite important, parts of her very being. Oh, how she wished she could stuff those words right back in her mouth.

"Oh, no, certainly not. I'm sorry and I didn't mean to interrupt you. What an impulsive thought! Sorry. Really sorry." After a pause, Chris laughed and said, "Now, I really do need that coffee. And you?"

"Coffee with Splenda and real cream sounds wonderful."

"Real cream versus fake cream? Is that like a dream versus a nightmare?"

Katie laughed a real sincere laugh. "No, I just don't like the creamer created in the chemical lab. Real cream hits the spot unlike anything else."

As a handsome man and a doctor, Chris Martin turned aside many husband-seeking women. He had dated numerous females hoping to find that right one, who sought him not for who he was or the money he had, but for what he was inside, the man he strove to be. He was quite aware that there were an equal number of women seeking trophy husbands as there were men seeking trophy wives. He did not want one of them and refused to be the other.

However, warning signals were going off like horns blaring over rapidly rising waters. This woman had somehow gotten to him, her vulnerability merged with her strength touched him; his inner white knight wanted to rescue her, and it was all wrong. He drank his coffee too determinedly. He knew he would have to tread carefully and balance his feelings with his oath to heal and do no harm.

They talked some more and scheduled Tuesday mornings as their regular time. "Katie, here's my card and on the back is my personal cell phone number. If you need me for anything, just let me know."

Heading out the door, Katie suddenly turned "Dr. Martin, I just remembered. Next week I will be down in Tybee Island for Catherine's birthday. I am planning to stay for a week or two. So, now what should I do?"

Chris looked at her with an endearingly sheepish grin. "Tybee Island – your family lives there? I just bought a house there, right on Eight Place, last house on the street closest to the beach. Great house. Check it out when you get there. I didn't know you liked the beach."

Katie laughed. "Since this is only our first visit, there is a great deal about me you don't know. I'm afraid if I tell you too much too quickly, you'll send me away and never take me back."

Dr. Martin could only muster a twisted grin and think to himself, *hardly, what fool would ever send you away.*

"We live on 7th Terrace, just two short streets down from your house, and we are also the last house on the right closest to the beach. It is the big brick house sitting on two lots. My grandmother grabbed up the last lot and over built this hurricane proof house. She was always planning for the future. Her dream was to have lots of little grandbabies running through the house. She even built a nursery for them. The house has eight bedrooms. You've got to come see it when you come down next time." Katie was smiling. She was actually having a conversation and she was not angry or scared. What a wonderful feeling.

"Have you already given her some grandkids to fill up those rooms?" He felt like such an idiot asking that question. Was he now relegated to that freshman schoolboy with a crush?

"Not yet. But I do believe in miracles. Actually Dolly, my grandmother, prays a rosary every day for them."

Dr. Martin's receptionist had already buzzed twice to remind him his next appointment was impatiently waiting for him. This session had run over by fifteen minutes, something Chris had never done before.

"Katie, how are you on meds?"

"I'll need a refill before I return. Dr. Stiller, my internist, wants you to manage the meds now that I will be seeing you for a while."

"Not a problem. I'll write the script now so you can fill it before your trip. I'm going to add an antidepressant to help with the anxiety. Take as directed and preferably before you go to bed at night. Remember; call me if you need me. Practice your breathing exercises. And speaking of exercise, walk on the beach as often as you can, and watch your caffeine intake. It is probably best if you cut it out altogether. By the way, have a great trip."

Katie turned and put her empty coffee cup down. "I take it this was decaf?"

Katie started to go to Chris and kiss him on the cheek much as she would any of her close friends. She stopped herself and wondered what had possessed her. Chris looked a little surprised as Katie stopped in mid stride.

"Gotta run. Thanks again, Dr. Martin."

Just as Katie quietly closed the door, Chris noticed a book on his desk he had forgotten to give Katie. Jumping up he ran to the door and called to her. She turned around with a grin and waited.

"I forgot to give you this book I ask all my patients to read. It is by Corrie Ten Boom and it deals with forgiveness. This one is called *Amazing Love: True Stories of the Power of Forgiveness*. Have you ever heard of her?"

Katie walked over and took the book from Dr. Martin's hand. Then she started to laugh. "Tante Corrie has been haunting me for my entire life. Some day when we have more time, I'll share how important Ms. Ten Boom has been to my family. Funny, I have never read this book, but I will read it at the beach. The girls will be so excited to see I'm reading again."

"The girls? Reading again? Katie, I don't think I follow you."

"Never mind. It is too complicated in such a simple way. More over the next session and a cup of decaf. See ya later." And with that, she was gone.

As Dr. Martin sat behind his desk going over notes for his next patient, he could breathe in the citrusy sweet smell of her perfume. Not overdone, just a soft reminder that she had been there and had left just a hint of herself behind. He needed to shake her from his mind and get on with the rest of his patients. But he simply didn't want to. *Who are the girls?* He wondered.

There were to be many more wonderings, trips to the beach, and soul searching that would leave Chris Martin even more able to relate to his patients with high anxiety. As for Katie, her travail through panic would equal a climb on the north face of the Eiger.

"Never, never, never, never give up."

–Winston Churchill

CHAPTER 4

R egardless of Chris Martin's explanation of anxiety disorder, metaphors to define the beast, and chemical imbalances expressed in layman's terms, and of course the promise that it was not fatal, her fears were not allayed. How could she rationalize pure adrenaline, unleashed, and burning through her body leaving her drained and spent? Better yet, how could she explain that inside her home she felt safe, while outside she felt vulnerable and afraid? The anxiety hung around like smoke in a crowded bar, but it did not eat her up or immobilize her. Outside the monster took on strength and power and threatened her wherever she went.

Now on the beach, Katie forced herself to think back on what Dr. Martin had taught her, Katie did try to put into practice those procedures he had outlined for her for times just like these. She needed to focus on where she was. Here at Tybee, she needed to look around her and identify things she was comfortable with: the beach, the lighthouse, the smattering of people. But most importantly, she had to accept that life had dealt her a terrible blow and recovery might not be easy, but it could be done. Yet, she could not let anxiety ruin her already half-ruined life. She would have to face down the dragon, no matter how afraid she was, and she could not let him win. Not now and not ever.

Facing one's fear is a fear in and of itself. The very fact that you are afraid of what will happen and what you will feel, that terrible panic, makes you want to run away and hide, find a place of safety, and stay. *It just is not fair,* she thought. *Why can't I just be normal like other people? Why can't I just run on the beach without a second thought?* But in answer to all these questions she had asked herself and Dr. Martin, the same reply was always given, "It will pass, it always does. It is very uncomfortable, but it will not kill you. You are not on a continuum of insanity. Breathe and let it pass; let it float over you."

Yet, it was just so much easier said than done. Katie wished Dr. Martin were nearby now. She needed his reassurance and the safety she felt being connected to him. Just hearing his voice or knowing he was a phone call away seemed to calm her fears. She drew strength from him, but she knew something had crossed between them. Something intangible, but sweet enough and wrong enough to be real.

For now, the beach was still waiting. Ignoring the wild imaginations her mind carried with her everywhere she went, Katie pressed forward egged on by Beau. The ninety-pound pup was not easily ignored and had the power to pull her across the beach and into the ocean if he had been so inclined. The softly powdered sand gave way as she pushed off trying to get a solid footing. Moving toward the damp packed sand would give her the support she needed to begin her run, if she could run at all. The palms of her hands suddenly began to feel clammy and sweaty. She rubbed them vigorously trying to dry them. She hated that signal that her system was on hair trigger alert accelerated by the knot forming in the pit of her stomach.

"Breathe through your abdomen," she ordered herself through clenched teeth. *Breathe and think pleasant thoughts.* Yet the beach had suddenly become surreal and the silence was obvious and foreboding; she felt detached from it all. Everything was too sharp, too clear, too focused, like changing from a blurry scene to one too clear to be real. It provoked the most distressing feeling. This place that she loved, was so familiar with, so comforting, was now betraying her again.

Katie's legs had not turned to jelly as all the anxiety literature explained, obviously written by someone who had never had a panic attack. Instead they were like concrete, hard to move and inflexible. Concrete because they seemed so heavy, but unbending as if they were paralyzed. Paralyzed. God, how she hated that word. Paralyzing fear that makes you know you are going crazy. Loony. Mad as a hatter and drumming up images of insane asylums and hospitals. Surely, she was bordering on madness as none of this made sense, no sense because on the outside you could not really tell something was wrong, so no one would believe the emotional cancer destroying her desire to stay in a world that was so utterly unbearable.

That morning, after wrapping the safety Ativan in a tissue and tucking it down into her shoe, Katie was filled with a new confidence, albeit a weak one She headed towards the ocean with a safety pill as her companion. Surely, this time she would be just fine. Like other agoraphobes and those suffering from panic attacks, the fear monster was like a game of Russian roulette. Because a sufferer is no longer rational about something, it fears so much; logic has no entry into the equation. Panic disorder becomes a game of chance, maybe it would come and get you, or maybe the chamber was empty and you passed by unscathed. No. Never unscathed. Just say, it passed you by this time.

The fear had grown in intensity like a foreboding storm wreaking havoc over the sea. Fear like a shadow that is always with you. Fear that makes it hard to think, to breathe, to wander freely in the world, to drive on a freeway, to rest peacefully at night. Fear that drives you to know where all the exit doors are; fear that creeps over you and seeps in through your pours blanketing you in suffocating dread; fear that you can't reach your friends, and loved ones in case you suddenly go mad...suddenly go mad...just going mad. The fear of the fear of the fear- and the cycle continues. Always afraid.

The anxiety won again. The fear of *what if* choked her and made her dig deep into her shoe. Unfolding the tissue that held her meds, Katie now let the empty scrap of paper blow across the dunes, dancing here and there at the mercy of the wind. The pill sat melting under Katie's tongue as she watched the minutes pass agonizingly slow, waiting for that magic moment when she would feel the relief. Not total relief, but enough to steady her rocking world. Utterly defeated and hating herself for her perceived weakness, Katie thought of some means of escape. A thought that returned with alarming frequency. Now, as she headed back to the beach, tugging on Beau's leash, he looked up at her in disbelief. *No run? No walk?* The disappointment was all over his face, but it was not the first time he had been through this routine. She knew it would not be the last.

With a despondency that only a fellow sufferer could understand, Katie turned towards home and defeat, fatigued as if she had run a half marathon, hating herself for her weakness and her dependency on a drug. Dr. Martin had promised her she was not addicted, but she did need the meds and other therapy as she worked through this disorder. Holding tight to the promise, Katie knew that she would continue to declare her independence and keep trying. Well, she had just tried to do and could not do. Call it what you like, but Katie just failed one more time.

However, tomorrow, the next day, and the next day, she would try again. That self-imposed "now or never" and that pressure to succeed pushed her to test the waters, just the thing Dr. Martin had said not to do.

After a particularly rough session, he looked sternly at Katie and said, "Don't test. Don't try. Just do. Yes, you might feel dreadful, and you might have an anxiety attack, but you will get through it. Face your fears. The farther you run away from it, the stronger the fear becomes. Think of the Cowardly Lion in *The Wizard of Oz*. He was an old, growly bully who frightened everyone. But when he came too close to Toto, Dorothy overcame her fear and popped his hand. He was shocked, and he stopped his growling. I am not trying to diminish your very real fears, but I am saying that at some point, you will have to stand up to them and refuse to back down. Let the fear do its worst to you since you have already felt the worst fear, and it cannot go any higher. You survived it, however terrible it felt. It is just adrenaline that makes you so afraid. Face it and then go happily live your life. Not simple, but uncomplicated. Do it."

From the next boardwalk over, Katie heard someone calling her name. "Katie. Yoo-hoo. Katie." Katie turned in that direction and saw Catherine. Katie's oldest and dearest family friend, had called out to her, the words lost in the wind blowing more intensely now from the north. Earlier that morning the meteorologist on the weather channels had all but erupted into cheers at the storm brewing, spinning and turning on the big screen like some crazed red top. Storms this time of year brought chilling temperatures, dangerous winds and soaking rains. Houses were prepared for battle with the elements, and homeowners stocked pantries and bars with bread, milk, chips and potent potables. It was an event, not just a storm and not a hurricane either, but something that made your skin tingle in anticipation. Katie dreaded the thought of being trapped inside her house with nowhere to run and no place to escape. The mere thought made her feel dizzy. Panic disorders and nor'easters were the worst combination possible. Just ask Katie's mind, which had moved into full-blown "what ifs" at the mere thought of a situation she could not control.

Waving to Catherine, Katie motioned for her to come over. Beau started the dog shake that contorted his body in several different directions simultaneously. It was a marvel to behold. With his head down, he strained against the leash until Katie released him. In a flash, he was free, barking his greeting, running down the boardwalk and over to Catherine, nearly knocking her down. Giant buff colored mitts met her chest, just in the middle of her rib cage, and she roared with delight. Everyone loved Beau, and he loved everyone in return. Especially Catherine, who had the best dog treats and gave body rubs that surpassed the talents of the finest masseur,

Now Catherine was nobody's aunt, but in true southern tradition, everyone called her that. It just was not right to call her 'Mrs. Hamilton'. She was simply Catherine to young and old alike. She had no children of her own, and she had willingly accepted that fate. Instead, she doted on her dearest friend's granddaughter as if she were her own.

Katie watched as Catherine made her way down the wooden bridge, across the billowy sand and up the stairs toward her. Only slightly winded, Catherine opened her arms and invited Katie in, but Beau jumped between them as if the hug had been his. The light dusting of Beautiful powder brushed over Catherine's body enveloped Katie in old familiarity. Her embrace felt warm and secure, which helped calm Katie's racing thoughts. Catherine offered security and stability, and a knowing. Katie didn't have to explain just how crazy she felt as Catherine was well aware of the perilous tightrope her mind walked. Cat knew all about Katie's sufferings, her anxiety disorder, and had wept endlessly over the trials of her life. Wrapped arm and arm, the two women headed towards the screened porch to share a hot cup of tea and nestle in for a long morning chat.

Catherine had married James Bartholomew Hamilton, an esquire from a family of esquires dating back to the times that mattered in high society. JB's family firm was the most respected practice of attorneys south of Washington. As a matter of fact, they had, at one time, an office in D.C., but the firm had grown exponentially, thus losing some of the old south charm. Today, although JB had been dead for over twenty years, his name was still listed as senior partner. He deserved it and so did Catherine.

Catherine had been blessed with a silver spoon birth. She was the only child of Anne and Charles Brantley who owned textile mills up and down the eastern seaboard. Plants of this nature were not particularly popular with environmentalists, yet wildly loved by the town locals whose economy was supported by the Brantley's. Southeastern Textiles was a maverick of sorts in the industry as they set standards for pollution control. A sense of civic duty, often not seen by powerful landowners, was second nature to the family thus making them almost heroic to the people most affected by the mills. Plus, they had more money than God had and were nearly as generous with it. Bank cornerstones bore the Brantley name and several quite large streets were named for them. They had church pews engraved with their names and their family burial plots were something to behold. The grandest guardian angels made of imported Grecian marble, stood watch over the deceased Brantleys who had bequeathed all their earthly riches to the only child in the family, Catherine.

Catherine knew everyone in town and in many of the small towns surrounding Tybee Island. She had sold her in-town property and officially moved to the beach several years back. She no longer wanted her mailbox stuffed to overflowing with invitations to every wedding, baby shower, debutante ball or Junior League fundraiser. She knew she was in demand, not just because she was loaded and generous, a most unusual combination, but she humbly admitted that her name on a guest list added a certain sense of propriety. She was "A- listed" and she knew it, and now no longer cared a trifle about such foolishness. At 70, she had so many other fish to fry. Catherine had led a good life, had a strong Catholic faith and did her duty to God and her country. She voted Republican, straight ticket, paid her taxes on time, tithed regularly to the church and frequently invited the parish priest to dinner at the club. Her world was rocked when JB was killed in an accident where a teen-aged boy drank too much at his fraternity party. He ran a red light and ended JB's life. It changed hers forever.

Catherine Brantley Hamilton set sail on a course of despair several weeks after JB died. The numbness had worn off and the crowds had thinned around her. Her faith lay just beyond the reach of her fingertips and hard as she may try to reach Him, God seemed so very far away. She never once doubted that He was real or that He had somehow stopped being God or that He had even stopped being in control. But she was furious that she felt scalded, neatly boiled in oil, and He could not comfort her. She was furious at the drunk who killed JB, and she refused to forgive him. She could not justify the feeling. The right thing to do was the most painful thing she could have imagined. Defiance grew out of her refusal to obey God and honor what JB surely would have wanted. She could not see JB in heaven filled with joy and happiness. All she could see was a shroud of suffocating grayness that threatened her next breath. All she could feel was the despair that had become her constant companion, but an evil one who sapped the life from her and caused every movement to feel like she was swimming in sludge.

Yet one thing stood out as alive in the forest of all dead things. A magnificent Baccarat vase occupied space in the center of the bedroom mantelpiece. JB's best friend had sent him that vase as an intricate reminder of their personal and spiritual friendship. When JB left her, she brought it home from his in town office, hoping it would bring something to heal her. It did not. She cared nothing of forgiveness and despised the boy who had taken her best friend, the one she had committed to for life. A life that was tragically shortened abruptly ended, by an arrogant man-child not old enough to drink. Curses so vile were uttered against the boy. She could not speak his name. She certainly could not pray for him, and she certainly would never relieve him of the guilt he was rumored to feel. It seems he wanted to die. The coldness in Catherine's heart would have stunned her Christian friends. *I will hate him until the day I die*, she thought as she turned the engraved message towards the wall and away from her. It would be many a day before Catherine would fall to her knees convicted and horrified of her attitude so uncharacteristic of what JB had always preached and practiced.

JB was a fine Christian man. That was such a pat statement, but in Catherine's heart, she knew that JB was in heaven. No doubts as he had served God well; he had planned for his spiritual future; he knew where his eternal life would be spent. Yes, JB was a fine Christian man and evidence lay all around. The old adage "practice what you preach" was one JB held near. He found life worked better, when he let patience be his guide, but one thing really riled him up and it was hypocrisy. As a lawyer, JB had seen enough lying, cheating, and hypocrisy to last him a lifetime. He could blow steam over some of the lawyers he met who flew below the radar bordering on criminal activities. Well, some of them crossed the boundary, but they maintained such self-righteous attitudes. It made him wary and often sent him down on bended knees. Too many had walked the courthouse halls totally devoid of conscience or remorse.

This wariness usually served JB well making him a cool and accurate judge of character. Yet this was to be tested in a most unusual way. Several years before the tragic accident, by which JB's death was always referred to, the son of an old and dear friend, a son of a man of some great importance, found himself embroiled in a nasty political scandal. The young man, although well trained and superiorly educated in the finest halls, practiced an effrontery, which belied his well-bred formation. He was a most unpopular man whose past actions led many to believe in his guilt. Only his father believed in his innocence. On one particularly miserable day, with thunder and lightning acting out in a most disagreeable way, JB opened a package sent from the patriarch of this boy's family. A magnificent Baccarat crystal hurricane vase, a full lead crystal piece, lay in an opulently dressed box. The vase had a matching crystal stand hand engraved with the words "He will cast all our sins into the depths of the sea." Micah 7:10. A postscript was added, "No fishing allowed."

In future years, JB would retell this story numerous times. Steve Paulson was a devout Christian who sought the truth regardless of the pain or consequences. As a textile executive, he traveled the world seeking the newest trends in manufacturing. One summer he and JB attended a conference in The Hague, Netherlands. After an unexpectedly shortened session left the men with extra time on their hands, the two rented a car and drove to Haarlem to see the family home of Corrie ten Boom, a woman Steve admired greatly. Steve retold his story of the impact Corrie's struggle had on his life. Heading south on A4 Steve captivated JB with the most heroic of tales.

"After reading her books, I found my heart had undergone a profound transformation. I felt such a longing to hear her speak."

All of her books had a prominent place on his library shelves, and he quoted her frequently. It seems Corrie and her family had been Christian social activists involved in hiding Jews and others sought by the Nazi regime during World War II. Unfortunately, Corrie was caught and imprisoned, along with loved ones, in Ravensbruck concentration camp. Ravensbruck was a woman's concentration camp, actually one of the most infamous of the camps, which is quite a notorious concession. Death to the prisoners came in a myriad of ways: poison, beatings, shootings, hanging, or lethal injection. It mattered not the form, only that death came. It has been estimated that over 92,000 victims left this earth via Ravensbruck. Unfortunately, most of Corrie's family died, including her dear sister Betsie and her honorable and much adored father Casper.

The trip was to have a lasting impact on both men. As fortune would have it, Corrie was speaking in a nearby town convenient enough to attend. At the conference, a rounded, angelic looking elderly woman slowly made her way to the podium. Her gray white hair was pulled back in a soft bun and she looked like, for all the world, someone's well-loved grandmother. As she began, the entire auditorium grew silent. In a strong but well used voice, that particular to the elderly, Corrie began the story of her call to forgiveness. Several years after her miraculous release from Ravensbruck, contributed to a clerical error that read *Entlassan*, German for "released," Corrie was preaching to a crowd of thousands on God's call to forgive others as He forgives us. At the altar call, a familiar, but unwelcome face stood before her. A scar ran from his lip on the left side of his face, to the torn edge of his left eye giving him a perpetual sneer that was most frightening. It was ragged and raised, certainly the result of poor medical treatment. Corrie would always remember that scar as Betsie had said, "Corrie, we should pray for that man. Who knows what terrible things have happened to him over his life and what struggles caused him to be so cruel."

Of all the Nazi guards, this one was the last one Corrie ever wanted to see and would ever want to hear from. It was a look, a feeling, and a name she would never forget. One never does when one looks at evil in living form. If the devil can come in a million different disguises, this one of Gunter was his highest score thus far. Yet, that day he stood towering over her, smiling down at her, the top left incisor still missing, and thanking her profusely for her forgiveness of him and the terrible things he had done to her and to her dying sister. Corrie felt bile burn her throat and hatred filled her in a way that stunned and frightened her. This evil monster that had caused her such pain, dared to asked for forgiveness and assumed that he should have it.

Hearing the word of God in her spirit, Corrie prayed to live His word. She indeed forgave him and that event was to become part of her ministry until her death. Her closing words that day imprinted on the hearts and minds of JB and Steve. Corrie promised, according to God's word, that all people who repent and turn to the Lord would be forgiven. She promised that God would cast the confessed sins into the depth of the sea. Of course this brought great joy, yet her admonishment to all there, was simply, "Once God has forgiven and deposited your sins...no fishing allowed. What has been forgiven will always be forgiven...for you and for all others."

Prior to his conversion, Steve Paulsen had done some unforgivable things and had led a despicable life. As a new Christian, he willingly gave up his previous life's iniquities and redirected his life to live by Christian principles. Together, Steve and JB committed to a life of practicing forgiveness even where none was wanted and certainly was not warranted. This belief would be the premise of all future business deals, friendships, and foundations for raising their families. It would prove to be the bond that would hold them together until God decided otherwise. It would be a thread that tied JB to Catherine and Katie together in the time of their greatest needs.

Holding the vase in his massive hands, JB remembered the cords that bound them –no fishing allowed. He knew beyond a shadow of a doubt that Steve was calling him to a higher standard in defending his son: to ignore what God had forgiven and let sleeping sins lie. Throughout the long and tedious trial, where much trash and sins were uncovered, JB held true to his belief that he need not pull out his fishing pole. In the midst of the most damning evidence, JB held steadfast. In the end, the truth stood before the light and all was seen.

Catherine stroked the back of the vase, pushing it just a little farther away. The engraved message was too much to bear; too much honesty to be dealt with and a command from God she chose to ignore. It would be a while before Catherine could reconcile the promise of life everlasting with a seemingly never-ending life without JB.

At times like this, this period of a dry soul, a parched, barren soul that feels alienated by Jesus, almost abandoned, Catherine obediently turned to prayer. Faith was not a feeling, something she had preached to hundreds over the course of her life, but she wanted to feel Jesus. She needed to get something back when she prayed. If she turned over her bed pillow, she was certain to find a thousand prayers lying underneath. They were weak and ineffective as evidenced by the silence on God's end. Everything she had ever believed about prayer and Jesus was being challenged now. Everything was tumbled like balls in a bingo spinner. Everything was monochromatic, totally devoid of color and joy. In obedience to all that she had ever been taught, coupled with a strong will to persevere, Catherine picked up her rosary and began to pray. In between each decade, she talked to God. She begged the Blessed Mother for intercession; she confessed her transgressions, but she kept her heart closed. If only God could be a wizard and touch her with a magic wand making all of this go away. But He was not that and she knew that somewhere, far away and deep into to the trip, she would find Him again. For she understood that He had never left her or abandoned her; He held his arms open to embrace her as she once again had eyes to see and ears to hear.

"Oh, dear Lord. You promised not to give us more than we can bear. You promised that you would not break a bruised reed. But have you seen me lately? Have you really looked at how close I am to breaking?

Pour your peace into me, please, Lord. Give me the grace and strength to bear this."

As she fingered her beads, she meditated on the first sorrowful mystery, the agony in the garden of Gethsemane. Jesus had been abandoned, left alone to face the incredible torture of His body and mind. He came into the deepest realization that, for many souls to come, His suffering and death would be for naught. And Catherine began to cry and open up her heart to Him. She begged for his forgiveness and asked for the supernatural grace to forgive the boy, whose selfish act had taken JB away. She prayed for the ministering angels to go to him and for the warring angels to stand guard around him in prison. She prayed for that peace that surpasses all understanding. Finally, she prayed that he accept Jesus' forgiveness and use it in his life. "Give him a second chance, Lord. And give me one, too."

CHAPTER 5

A ll this made Katie something special in Catherine's life. Her best friend was Katie's grandmother, Dolly Prescott, who had shown her the simpler side of life. Dolly and Catherine, or Cat as her intimates called her, found a unique friendship that surprised people on both sides of the camp. Dolly was outrageous, funny and enormously charming, well-educated and from the middle of the tracks. She had been a dashing beauty in her day, and men had lined up to ask for her hand in marriage. Back then, just after World War II, marriage was much simpler than it is today. Why, in those days, no one had even invented "trophy wife", and only the wealthiest curmudgeon married a woman young enough to be his mistress. The death of both of the men lucky enough to marry for love, gave a once in a lifetime opportunity for true friendship to blossom.

Everyone said Katie had borrowed enough of Dolly's genes to be a near clone, but whatever fire or spunk Dolly had shared with her was lost; somewhere back in time, along a path of no return. For now, it was just fine with Katie. She no longer had the guts or desire to face the world or to love again.

Catherine raised her voice hoping to be heard over the wind. "Katie. Are you okay? Coming or going from your run?" Delighted to see Katie home again, Catherine called to her once more. "Are you all in one piece?"

Katie looked at Catherine and smiled a very weak one. "No. I am fragmented. Ah, I just was overwhelmed and turned around. I feel terrible about Beau, but my nerves are just shot. I want so badly to overcome this damn panic disorder, but it is the hardest thing I've ever had to do. I just hate it."

Catherine put her arms around Katie and pulled her close once more. "It will get better, and you will feel like your old self soon enough. Let God heal all the bumps and bruises, but it is not going to happen overnight. You'll get there, I promise." She pulled her white cardigan over her shoulders as they headed towards the house. "Where's Dolly?"

"She's at the post office. Let's go make some tea and see what the weatherman promises about the impending storm." Katie reached over and squeezed Cat after giving her a warm kiss. "What was that for?"

"That's for loving me even if I am so very peculiar at times."

"I love peculiar and have been described that way many a times. Now, I'm chilled so hurry with my tea."

Beau head butted Catherine right where the pocket of her pants fell on her leg. A secret treat, a beefy dog biscuit had been tucked away for Beau. A true retriever, he was not going anywhere until she shared her treasure. Cat, like everyone else, loved sweet Beau. He was all the very best of what labs could be and that made him practically perfect.

"She ran to the post office to get the mail and some stamps." Taking a tray into the kitchen, Katie saw a gray Yukon turn into the driveway. "Why don't you take a couple of throws to the screen porch and we'll watch the ocean for signs of the storm. Make that three as I see Dolly just drove up."

Katie watched her grandmother unload her mail from the car. Not much collected in her mail nest these days, but she loved a certain few magazines that wandered in each month. Now the wind had whipped her white hair into little tufts of curls giving her a boyish look. Stopping at the bottom of the stairs, she looked up to see Katie watching her. "Where's my puppy dog?" Katie laughed and shushed her grandmother, "He just robbed Cat's last dog treat and is now sleeping on the sofa. He's gonna come bounding out if he thinks you've got a treat." Dolly's deep blue eyes actually sparkled as she grinned up at Katie. It was always a dumb expression to say someone's eyes sparkled, but when you saw Dolly, she changed your mind. They were as pure as glass, not see through, but clear and strong. Maybe only a few people in the world could possess eyes that kind and beautiful.

34

Behind her smile and in reality, all Katie wanted to do was go lie down and sleep. Sleep, when it came medicated or not, was the best escape she had ever had. She was torn between sleep, abetted by the drugs, and the comfort of Catherine, Dolly and Beau.

"I'll get the heavy white mugs that are still in the dishwasher. They hold the heat longer."

Cat grabbed the three blankets and headed to the porch and the rockers. The screen porch had been Dolly's last project for the house before she proclaimed feat accompli. She had planned the porch to be a place for visiting with no mind paid to the elements. In the spring and summer, two enormous ceiling fans swirled warm to moderately hot air around just quick enough so it did not land on anyone in particular for too long. In the fall and winter, they were turned off and blankets of every fabric and design were stocked in closets for any number of guests. A stacked stone fireplace, and oddity for a screened porch at a southern beach, sat tucked into a corner as not to obstruct anyone's view. The view was sacrosanct. Not worthy of a genuflect, but certainly veneration.

The porch was screened in such a way that no one's vision was interrupted or disturbed. You could see whatever you wanted to see, and if you used the binoculars, you were touched by the magic of the porpoises playing chase in the water. Dolly had wisely bought up the small acreage of land just between her cottage and the beach, close enough to smell the brine and taste the salt. It was well worth it as her view was one of the best on the island.

Going into the kitchen, Catherine turned and brought out a silver tray with three teaming mugs of tea aboard. Catherine was not a snob about her fine silver and had shared most of what she had with Dolly. Dolly, ever practical, felt that every day was a special day and there was not any sense in saving the good stuff for the right occasion. She never understood that silver and salt air were mortal enemies. She did everything to her silver but run it through the dishwasher and that was only because it usually would not fit.

Dolly and Catherine had been the dearest of friends for some time. They were a perfect match and everything a best friend should be for another. Dolly had the wild and wonderful laughter, that laughter that comes from deep inside, a special place that makes a sound that calls others to it. She was wickedly funny and found humor in just about everything. She loved being on the beach, cooking meals for large crowds, pitching in to help anyone who needed it. Dolly rarely told anyone no.

There was great laughter and joy in her life now and as it had been for some time. However, her heart was smashed when Duncan Prescott had suddenly left her. It had been a beautiful, early spring day, the perfect day with cool weather and a nice breeze. The day beach people washed down the rafts, hosed off the chairs, and pulled out the coolers. With umbrella in hand and chairs in tow, Duncan and Dolly headed down to the beach to christen the new season. Sandwiches had been made and the Prescott's had planned to spend a good part of the morning soaking up the sun and visiting with neighbors.

The beach did not disappoint. Everything was awash in color and sun. The sea gulls, most impressive mischief-makers, squawked up and down the beach demanding a treat. Duncan pulled out his bag of boiled peanuts and threw a few to the birds. It did not take long before twenty or so birds hovered and landed, approached their chairs, voiced a complaint about their hunger, and took to flight again. Over the years, Dolly and Duncan had decided each bird had his own personality and knew exactly what humans were saying. Today would be no different.

After a nice long walk on the beach, a bit of splashing in an ocean far too cold to swim in, and a swig of beer to wash down the deli style sandwiches, the duo called it a day. An afternoon nap, sliding glass doors wide-open and ceiling fans spinning in their orbs, would perfect the day. After putting away the beach gear and hosing down their sandy feet, the couple shed their sandals and slid into bed. Both were deep sleepers and well-practiced nappers. Both knew that real beach people understood and appreciated the value of a nap. A good, hard, solid sleep in the middle of the afternoon fortified for you what the evening had to bring. At the beach, it could be unexpected, but welcomed guests having drinks on the porch and sharing tales. It could be the neighbor bringing in extra crabs he had caught down on the river eager to share the bounty. Or it could be just watching the rain, playing a little Scrabble, or passing the night with an Oscar winner.

The ritual of the nap was simple but necessary. Duncan always slipped out of his shorts, folded them and laid them across the chair by the door. Now he was down to his skivvies. No matter the weather, sleet, heat, or snow, Duncan stripped to his boxers to sleep. He had to pump the goose down pillows a few good times and flip them over two or three times. Finally, after a hard sock in the dead middle of the pillow, He would climb onto the right side of the bed and pull up a light cotton blanket just so it hit him about breast high. Then he'd pat Dolly on her backside, and call, "I love you the most, forever and ever, amen." Dolly always patted his belly and said, "No, I love you the most, forever and ever, amen." Then they would sleep.

During the nap, Dolly dreamed she was being chased by a motor boat. But the motor sounded like it was too deep and was struggling to make it to the surface. It made the oddest sound, a sound that you might make while blowing bubbles under the water and growling at the same time. It disturbed Dolly on the deepest level. She remembered trying to tell Duncan about the dream, but she was still dreaming, yet reaching for him, but could not find him. The sound was Annoying, would not go away, and called to Dolly pulling her from sleep. As she got up to wash her face and freshen up, she heard the sound again. Turning back towards the bed, she saw that the gurgling sound was coming from Duncan.

Dolly screamed and ran to his side lifting him by the shirt. His eyes were closed and he did not move, no matter how hard she shook him. Without letting him go, she reached across him to the phone and called 911. Whispering prayer after prayer, pleading with God to leave Duncan for just a little longer, Dolly felt the despair rising in her. She laid her cheek next to his and gently kissed him. "Duncan, please don't leave me. Please stay with me. Oh my sweet Duncan, how can I live without you?" She held him close, rocking him, and moaning, making a sound that she could not recognize. And in the midst, she remembered: *Eternal rest grant unto them, O Lord, and let perpetual light shine upon them. May they rest in peace. Amen.*

After an eternity, the EMT's arrived and in no time at all they had moved him from the bed and onto the gurney. And all the while, going against all that she knew to be true, Dolly watched his chest, under the white cover, urging it to heave and gasp for breath. Urging it to struggle to breathe to fight for life, not to give in. Dolly watched the ambulance slowly pull out of the driveway and down towards the causeway. It was not to be.

The autopsy found that Duncan's heart had been trying to quit working for some time. A massive coronary moved him from this plane to the next. Dolly was despondent that Duncan left her while she slept. She had wanted to say goodbye and thank him for a wonderful life together. They had been best friends, not in the silly "BFF" way people claim to be today, but it in that earnest, dig deep into the trenches friend, who never lied to you, no matter how painful the truth, who never let you down, and really loved you as a package deal, not in spite of the imperfections, but because of them.

However, despite the duality of losing their husbands and the common pains they shared, Dolly and Catherine were as different as day is from night, which probably made them an excellent match. Not a yin and yang sort of friendship, more one of a blending of all that was the essence of the other. Like an old married couple they had begun to finish each other's sentences and when not talking, they could whittle away hours just being together.

For now, the girls finished the puzzle and found they were a great team. If Dolly was always slightly unraveling, everything with Cat was smooth and even. She rarely seemed to startle and had a peace about her that made everyone feel welcome. Katie knew better than to mention it, as she had in the past, for Cat would say that it did "the peace that surpasses all understanding when you walk with the Lord." Katie cringed at the sound of that. It was the only thing that made her irritable around Cat. Katie had been raised a Christian and even became "born again." When the going got tough, she found out the hard way that her faith did not sustain her; she did faint and she certainly gave up the race. Her God had let her down and she wanted no part of pious platitudes. Still it pained her to have this small wedge between them although neither Cat nor Dolly ever mentioned it.

Cat at seventy was still lovely. Her hair had a slight curl to it that softly framed her faced. Eyes of emerald green sat in almond shaped spaces and cheekbones sat high and proud. Only Cat, at her age, could still have beautiful hair, a mixture of white and silver. She was regal even with the laugh lines and crow's feet. If Catherine were on the cover of *Vogue* then Dolly would have been on one called *The Girl Next Door*.

Nestling into the down cushions of the bisque colored twill sofa, with Beau taking up fully half of the couch, Katie sipped slowly, leaning back and allowing the tea to warm her inner most being. Catherine joined her in the trade wind rockers sitting side by side. A navy blue footstool sat ready by her feet.

"Did I tell you that Mr. Hennessey suffered a terrible stroke? His wife saw him lying on the Widow's Walk and called 911. Good Lord, he should never have been up there. By the time they arrived, a worker at the lighthouse had climbed up and brought him back down. He never did realize that he had gotten older and just should not be doing the things he did as a younger man. Looks like he will be in a nursing home for the rest of his life. Poor man. And poor Lizzy. She'll have a hard time with him out of the house. He is staying at Savior's Heart right there on the beach. We need to go down and spend some time with him. He is unable to speak now, and you know how he liked to tell a good story. Honey, he'd be just tickled pink to see you."

Katie was surprised how quickly she welled up over hearing about Mr. Hennessey's stroke. He had always been such a figure of strength and although through the eyes of a child, most men seemed strong, she recognized that her image of him had not changed over all these many years.

"I remember a bunch of the kids were playing down at the light house. I snuck up to the Widow's Walk and was playing where I was not supposed to. It had rained heavily that day and the walk was so slick. He had frequently warned us not to go out there since the metal was too slippery after a bad storm. Of course, I didn't listen, and I fell and nearly slid off the walk. It had started to rain again and I could feel myself losing my grip. Suddenly his two strong arms grabbed my wrists and he pulled me back to safety. He squeezed me so hard when he got me into the lighthouse. I remember his pipe sticking out of his mouth and he took little tiny puffs from it. I was so distracted by the smell and the puffs I hardly heard what he said. He was quite stern with me and gave me a frightening lecture. The whole time he had tears running down his face. Suddenly, he just grabbed me again and held me tight until both of us just started to giggle. I have loved him ever since. I got to hold his pipe. It was so silly, but I always felt so special when I got to hold the pipe. Isn't it funny how things have such sentimental value? Let's go see him tomorrow and then take Lizzy some of Dolly's coffee cake."

Katie moved to the empty rocker as Beau had stretched out and covered more than his share of the sofa. The girls laughed at how ridiculous it was that Katie moved rather than push Beau off the sofa. It never occurred to her to deny him his rest or excuse him from any type of gathering. Beau was family and deserved to be treated as such. Catherine reached out and patted Katie's hand, and continued sipping her tea and looking out toward the ocean. The heavy mugs warmed their hands and their company warmed their hearts. Katie's anxiety was held at bay, but lest one should ever forget, it hung in the wings waiting for another opportunity. Waiting, always waiting, hovering, watching, devouring, wanting to win.

"Looks like this storm is more than just the average autumn blower," Catherine surmised as she gently rocked pushing off with the tip of her toes. "The last really bad one we had was over two years ago. That one had quite a bite, if I recall correctly. Army Corps of Engineers came by and added those precious little picket fences to help build up the sand dunes. Without those dunes, we wouldn't be sitting here sipping tea," she laughed.

"I tried my hardest to get those engineers to do something about the erosion years ago. Why do people always wait to act when it's nearly too late?" Dolly stopped to rub Beau's belly and then pulled up her favorite rocker, the one with the licorice red striped fabric. She quickly fell into Catherine's rhythm. A few minutes passed as the girls rocked and listened to the wind whipping the sea into froth while Beau dreamed dreams and pedaled bicycles with his paws. Always on an adventure.

Katie put her tea down on the wicker coffee table and stretched, arching her back like a cat after a long afternoon nap. Her legs maintained the muscle tone she was so famous for even if she was a bit underweight. Goose bumps had traveled up and down her legs until there was not room for one more. The blue and white sailboat throw was just not warm enough as the winds began to whistle gently through the screens. Dear friends of Dolly's had made this blanket, the Four Weavers out of Dallas, and it had been very special to her. She used to show friends the intricate handiwork that was so impressive. She would tell them, "I feel like I'm surrounding myself with precious friends when I wrap up in this. And don't forget that friendship is just a tight third after Jesus and family." It was one of Dolly's favorite sayings.

Pulling off her headband, Katie released her warm brown hair, the color of chestnuts touched with golden highlights, from its running hairdo and let it hang gently past her shoulders. She had the good kind of hair, the kind that had tons of body and held a soft curl. Not a frizz in the bunch and it behaved in most types of weather. It had been gently tapered and now hung softly around her face. There was no doubt in anyone's mind that Katie was a remarkably attractive woman. Men had often commented on the fact that Katie was a perfect package. Her eyes were dark and smoky, almond shaped and intriguing. Many said her eyes danced, but Katie could never catch them doing that when she checked in the mirror. Her eyelashes were dark and thick giving the appearance of make-up even when she wore none. Her friends had always teased her about that. Katie's friends were loving and loyal, even though many wished they had a little bit more of that something special and Katie had a little less. Whatever Katie had, it didn't make her feel top notch, although she was eternally grateful that the pendulum did not swing the other way.

Taking the mugs back into the kitchen, Katie added to Cat and Dolly's memories of the storm and called out, "That was the October after Scott and I got married. He had gone on a business trip and I remember trying to come down here but was stopped by the bad weather. I was torn by trying to get here and yet too afraid to face the storm. Sounds like my motto for living…too afraid to face the storm."

Just remembering that autumn made Katie's anxiety level rise and, as with all people prone to panic attacks, she knew the level was rising up towards a full-blown attack. Changing her focus off Scott and back into the moment, as her therapist had trained her to do, Katie felt her levels slowly coming down. Do not think for a minute that she was ever without a level - that was how she gauged if she was having a good or bad day. If the elevator was too crowded her level rose to about a six. If the grocery store was noisy and had too many screaming kids running up and down the aisles, her level hovered near eight. But if she was all alone at the mall or- God forbid- the airport, the level could suddenly surge to ten and the world become surreal. The funny thing about panic attacks is that people on the outside really cannot tell what is going on inside of the suffering person standing nearby wishing for instantaneous death. Other than trembling hands and a ghoulishly white face, pale lips and wobbly legs, nothing else showed. All hell breaks loose but it is all in the mind. Just raw panic and adrenaline. A hormone gone bad. If someone could bottle this stuff up, it would put an end to criminals and their activities forever.

A shift in the wind Announced the storm was winding up. The ocean was only slightly frothy with white tips on the waves, but an old timer to the beach could feel the atmospheric changes. Katie could feel the pressure in her sinuses, Catherine swore her knees ached, and Dolly chimed in with her weather elbow. They laughed over the various barometric warnings they each possessed.

"Dolly, I was thinking that I really don't want to ride out this storm alone. I know the weathermen said it could be a humdinger, so I'd feel better if I could stay with you. Would you mind if I at least spent the night?" Catherine spoke without taking her eyes off the sea. It was not really a question, more of an acknowledgement as it was expected that she would stay.

"I would love to have you stay with us. We will watch a movie and make a wonderful dinner. Why don't you go back to your house and get your things. Oh, this will be a fun night. Let's check our stock and see what we need just in case we lose power. I really do hate it when the lights go out."

Once the new beach house had been built, Dolly put a perfectly tacky yellow bucket under each bed calling them her hurricane buckets. Each container had a lighter, a few packets of matches in a Ziploc baggy, several candles with little glass holders, a flashlight, batteries, a Swiss army knife, and a flare. As always, she was determined to be prepared at least for the things she could control. No one knew how the knife figured into the rescue plan, but it belonged to Dolly and that was good enough for everyone involved.

Sitting at the kitchen table to plan dinner, the girls laughed over the storm wish list. Because of Dolly's preparedness, sustenance was the major focus of this trip into town. If they lost power, then they could cook hot dogs in the fireplace or even roast marshmallows. "I can just smell them now. Marshmallows roasting on an open fire with lots of Hershey's chocolate. I haven't had S'mores in eons. What else should we put on the list?"

"Graham crackers and Snickers. And I've got that thingy where you can pop corn over the fire." Catherine giggled at the excitement she was feeling. She loved it when Katie was home. Katie had so much life about her and was always such a joy to be around whether she was fighting panic or not.

After checking the pantry, Dolly turned to her bookshelves to check on a recipe, a special treat she was planning. Next to her favorite cookbook, was a beautiful picture of her daughter Ashley and her husband, Michael. Dolly passed it daily without noticing, but today, with the storm brewing, she felt drawn to it.

"Your mom loved the storms any time of the year. Your dad used to hit the high tide when the waves were dangerous and far too strong to swim in. But he didn't care. He would swim out to catch a great wave and body surf to shore. More times than not, he would come up with a scrape from the force of the waves pushing him face down. More than once, he was caught in a wave and was tumbleweeded under the water. He came up laughing every time. I used to love to watch them play on the beach."

Katie loved hearing old stories about her parents. She remembered her dad teaching her to body surf and how much fun it was. They were so exhausted when they finished that it was hard to walk up to the beach house. Today with all the memories, Katie felt a wave of nostalgia pass over her. She remembered vividly the day her world, as she knew it, stopped spinning on its orb, and somehow found itself in another universe.

CHAPTER 6

W hen Katie was just barely twelve, she, Dolly, and her parents had left the restaurant, Le Mercherts, late one Friday evening. Somerville, just twenty minutes north of Tybee Island had decided to go upscale and away from the trendier atmosphere of other cities who occupied the last land before the resort beaches. It had been a delightful dinner as Katie's folks actually read the menu in French and impressed the sommelier with their knowledge of wines. They had promised to return and to talk up the restaurant to all their friends.

The highway back to the beach was dark with no moon to offer a hint of light. Many people had petitioned the county to put up some form of lighting, but the county lines, drawn up in 1893, made it a battle over money that no one would win. One side against the other fighting over a bill they felt was frivolous and cost prohibitive. Thunderstorms had threatened to show their ugly faces most of the day and into late afternoon. This was such a common occurrence that if everyone stayed home due to threat of storm, no one would ever leave the island. Yet this night the threat turned into a promise with grave delivery. The rains began just as the family left the island and continued to rage without end. On the way home, Katie's dad could see absolutely nothing ahead of him and rolling down the window was no help either. The marshes ran alongside the island road and with the torrential rain coming with high tide, he did not want to be stuck in the flash flood waters rising by the minute. He also did not wish to make contact with the Cabbage Palms that lined the highway. Trees that were three and four feet wide stood sentry over the marsh, and should an intruder get through, the fanlike leaves of the Saw Palmetto would at least slow the entrance.

Hydroplaning was also a concern. Without warning, a series of lightening cracks woke the sky followed by several sonic booms of thunder. Hail the size of Ping-Pong balls slammed into the car and covered the road in a matter of moments. It was frightening.

Ashley was very nervous. She loved the storms, but in a controlled environment, like on the screened porch at the beach. This wild, possessed storm was bellowing and threatening to plunder out of control. Michael Oliver had unbuckled his seat belt while trying to watch the road with his head hanging out the window. Ashley, ever the protective wife and mother, released her belt to check on Katie and Dolly in the back seat. Dolly and Ashley held hands and made a knowing eye contact for just a brief moment leaving Ashley to smile as her mother's lips fell into the familiar pattern of the rosary, which she said in times of need, happiness, or rejoicing.

"Katie, check your seat belt, please." There was an urgency in her voice that Katie had not heard before. Not understanding its source, Katie sputtered back, "Mom, I'm fine. You treat me like such a baby. I know how to keep on my seat belt. Gawd!"

"Hold on everyone, we're hydroplaning. Tighten your seat belts. Ashley, get your belt back on. Dammit, I can't see a thing."

Katie was startled as she heard the fear in her daddy's voice. Daddies were not supposed to feel afraid, and they certainly did not let things happen to their families. Katie closed her eyes and hunkered down in her seat. Yes, daddies were brave and they could fix anything, even terrible thunderstorms. She just knew it.

The storm intensified as if it were in a rage. The SUV swerved across the rain-drenched highway and threatened to flip over any moment. The tension in the car was palatable and someone began to pray. "Lord, we call on you in our time of need. Protect us from the dangers of this storm and…"

"Daddy!" Katie screamed. It would be the last sound he would ever hear.

The words were never finished as suddenly a wild, white-tailed buck darted across the road followed by several other deer of various sizes trying to leave the danger of the trees to the relative safety of the shorter brush across the highway. The deer and the black SUV made contact sounding as if they had entered a war zone. In less than a minute, it was all over.

Katie had no idea how many of them they hit or how many crashed into them broadside, but the carnage for both families was devastating. Ashley and Michael were thrown from the car and were lying close together on the highway. A doe had penetrated the windshield and was half in and half out of the car. Another deer had entered through the left back window and mixed its blood with everyone else's. It seemed as if time had stopped.

If anyone were listening, they would have heard the moans and cries from the victims, animals included. Ashley called out to Michael but got no response. Or at least she thought she did or at least had tried. Did her mouth move? Did any sound come out? Her body felt so trapped and so powerless. The rain continued to pour in angry slants that made it impossible to focus. "I have to get to Mom and Katie," Ashley moaned as she tried to move. Her legs were useless in moving her, so using her arms commando style she tried to drag herself towards the car, but she made no progress. At this point Ashley was flowing in and out of consciousness. That part of her, the innate mother, desperately wanted to get to her family. A severe laceration, truly a cut that nearly severed her scalp from her face, kept blood pouring into her eyes. The glass and the metal pieces pierced her arms and embedded in her hips and legs. *Have to get to Michael. Have to get to Katie. Dear God, where are they? Dear God, where are you?*

Just a few feet from Ashley lay Michael. He was technically alive but only in the strictest of terms. His strength that had always protected his family was slowly ebbing away. His laughter and his jokes lined up to leave along with his faith and his sense of honor and duty. All that made him father, son, brother, and husband, all that collective good that drew people to him like camels to water, all body systems were shutting down and his breathing was becoming shallower and shallower with each wave of rain.

Mercifully, the sheets of silver and animal blood covered the windows blocking the view of the damage from inside. Dolly and Katie were both knocked unconscious but had been saved from a far greater trauma by their seat belts. The car had spun out and was sent speeding down the slope leading towards the marsh. With an abrupt halt, the car came to rest at the base of an old gnarled tree. The engine cut out and a strange stillness hovered over the accident scene. Within minutes, sirens would break the blessed silence and start a journey of such misery, no one could have imagined.

The trauma center was radioed that a terrible accident had occurred. Two Life Flights were coptering in a young child, an elderly woman, and two adults with severe head trauma and other massive injuries. Dr. Barnes, head of neurosurgery, had just finished another emergency surgery and was headed out the door. Dr. Swenson, his partner, had called him and asked that he come to emergency, trauma one, stat. Ed Barnes half ran and half jogged the last corridor before coming to the frenetic activity of too much trauma.

"Hold on, Ed. I need to speak with you before you go in there." Putting his hands on his hips and lowering his head as if to pray, Dr. Swenson breathed out, "Ed, that's Michael Oliver's family in there, even Dolly. Devastating collision with deer and the weather. Ed, I don't think Ashley and Michael will survive."

Ed turned around and closed his eyes. He was blinded by his tears and was struggling to control himself. He would be no use to anyone if he couldn't pull it together. Going towards Michael's gurney, he shouted out questions in a rat-tat-tat beat that seemed to synchronize the entire room.

As head of neurosurgery, Dr. Barnes had seen a lifetime of destruction to the head. He'd seem some truly impossible cases beat the odds and return the patient to some semblance of normal living. He never gave up hope, as he had seen too many miracles to pull the plug on anyone.

Yet, the bloated, bruised, and bloodied face of his very best friend defied description. Michael looked like Massala in Ben Hur after the chariot race. No part of him was left unscathed. He was limp like a ragdoll and was now unrecognizable. Half of what would have been a darkly handsome face was left somewhere on the road. Deep gashes were engraved in his face and arms while blood ran everywhere. If Ed had not known better, he would have sworn a road bomb had gone off.

It was not to be. Life would end for Michael Oliver that night regardless of the medicine, the tricks, the tried and trues; he was in God's hands now and God was not going to let go.

Dr. Barnes hooked his foot around the legs of a rolling stool and pulled it to him, now sitting as close to Michael as he possibly could. He had been friends with Ashley and Michael for years. They had all been at the University of Georgia together, Ashley in Creswell and the boys in Russell as freshmen. Sophomore year they moved to rented, off campus housing and spent the next three years partying, studying, protesting, and just loving life. Ed would find his wife and soul mate while he was in med school at the Medical College of Georgia. A residency in neurosurgery took them both to Baltimore for a five-year stint at Johns Hopkins. The calling from Somerville was too strong, so Ed brought his bride home to family and precious friends.

The doctor in Ed Barnes took over as he moved into auto drive distancing himself from his best friend and focusing on the patient who was no longer there.

Calling the time of death, Dr. Barnes moved to the next trauma room to examine Ashley. The room was in a state of perpetual movement looking more like a MASH unit than a hospital emergency room. Too much time had been spent trying to tube her; too much damage and too much blood and vomit; they were trying to stabilize her for a CAT scan, hoping something could be done. Ed Barnes could not believe what was happening around him. He struggled desperately to separate himself from the memories of the past and the now. How could he start to lose it like this? Ashley, sweet Ashley, needed him. Michael was gone and Katie would be left all alone.

The CAT scan showed what everyone already expected. It was a death sentence, and she was almost there. Her head and facial injuries were some of the worst the staff had seen. The vascular injuries, if treated within six hours, might have healed. The air pocket behind the eyeball might have been workable. The shattered sphenoid bone, distal femur and tibia shaft fractures looked like someone had hammered them into large chunks. It was a miracle she was still alive. However, it would not be for long. Ashley's brain had been swelling at an alarming rate and her pupils showed no reaction to light. Her face had swelled to three times its normal size, and she no longer resembled anyone Dr.

Barnes knew. Opening the skull to allow for the swelling would have no positive effect on Ashley's life. She was quickly coming to an end on this earth and headed to an eternity with Michael.

Falling back onto the stool, Dr. Barnes slumped over and wept. A slow, heavy man sob tore the hearts of all the staff around him. This teddy bear of a man, who healed people, rescued them from the brink of death, was utterly powerless to stop the inevitable. Dr. Barnes called time of death at 10:42 and Ed Barnes shuffled off to Katie's trauma room. He did not think he had the strength to go there.

Katie awoke to the blaring lights of the emergency room trauma center. Although it was a summer night, she shivered under the flimsy blankets covering her. Slowly, everything began to hurt. At first, it was just her shoulder, but without warning, the pain began to travel like drunks on a roller coaster. Pain was everywhere she had skin, bones, or muscles. Tears rolled down the side of her face, and she desperately wanted to wipe her running nose, but her arm was attached to something on the side of the gurney. *Where are my parents*, she wondered.

Katie looked up as Dr. Barnes came into the room. He was a favorite of hers, the best hugger of all her parents' friends, and the one who always made time for her. She loved him like an uncle. "Dr. Barnes. Where are my mommy and my daddy? Where's Dolly?" Her lip had begun to quiver and tears were streaming down her blood stained face. "Are my parents hurt? When are they coming to get me? I want to go home. When can they see me? I'm scared." With that, Katie tried to curl into a fetal position, but her IV's were tangled and she could not move her arm. She looked so small and so fragile, vulnerable, too easily broken.

Katie's physical wounds would heal after a time, but the wounds of the spirit and soul, the psyche would take quite some time before healing took place. It would be a long and painful process for Katie and Dolly who were both saved from the physical trauma of human death; the emotional death, well, they were not spared from that.

There had been a great uproar over the loss of Michael and Ashley. They were well-loved, respected, and real pillars of their church. Like their ancestors, they had been civic minded and devoted environmentalist believing strongly in deer control. Michael had argued unconvincingly on many occasions that the deer herds around the island needed to be thinned out. The newly found fame of Tybee Island brought developers from around the United States. Developments meant more money, more jobs and more people. However, it also meant displacement of the natural habitat for the flora, and most importantly, the animals. Raccoons, opossums, field mice, and deer, found themselves in disturbed and diminishing habitats. Backyards and gardens offered food havens for these creatures, which, while it worked for one species, were undeniably a nuisance for the other. People were complaining about their yards becoming feeding grounds for the beautiful creatures while others complained of the traffic hazards they posed. More than one islander wore a deer dent on the hood of his car. At the next meeting, a vote was to take place on a special three-day hunting season that would alleviate some of the problem.

Instead, they were at a funeral and one of the saddest anyone could remember attending. Dolly and Katie held onto each other as they walked down the aisle to the first pew. The dreaded first pew where the survivors sat. Katie wanted to stop in the middle of the church and saw no reason to go up front. The coffins were there, great, black shiny boxes that sat hideously high in front of the altar, nested side by side, holding her parents. Why in the world would she want to sit by that? The pianist started the music, and Dolly felt Katie leaning heavily on her. The soloist began in a strong, clear, heart moving voice, singing of the power of God over the obstacles on this earth.

The entire congregation sat sobbing in the pews. No one was immune to the beauty of the songs and the solemnity of the occasion. The church was standing room only and filled with the young and the old, some singing brave and strong, while others warbled out the words. Most reached out to God asking for his grace to sustain them through this terrible time. Others said hello to Jesus for the first time in many, many years. Some knew Him personally, and found it just easier to rest in His presence seeking His peace, but it was easy for no one.

Especially Katie. She cried until she thought she would throw up. Her body shook in convulsions at the thought of her parents in those boxes and that soon they would be buried under the ground. She could hardly bear the thought. Dolly put her arm around Katie and pulled her close. She sang along beautifully with the words and cried nearly as hard as Katie. Dolly seemed to have a sense of acceptance that was far beyond the mind of a twelve-year-old girl. Katie was angry and terrified of what life had in store. Her mind raced into a thousand different places. *If Dolly dies, where will I go?* And it continued until Katie was feeling dizzy. She just wanted to leave the church, the people, the beautiful music, and the pastor. The one who kept wiping away his tears for Ashley and Michael. Their dear friend, who prayed with them, baptized Katie and had dinner with them at Dolly's most Sundays. How could he say there was much rejoicing in heaven over the return of her parents? *What about me? Where is my joy? So, God is all-happy with all the people He has snatched away from earth, and we are supposed to be glad that they have left this world? Why? Leaving this world means that they have left me behind. God, why would you do something that mean to me?*

A lone violinist sat waiting to play at the cemetery. The tent and chairs were all arranged before the family arrived. Dolly and Catherine sandwiched Katie and tried to hold her up. She was weak from crying and had the most devastating effect on all the people there. Everyone wanted to comfort her, but truly, no words could penetrate her heart this day.

Dolly and Katie were just too pitiful to look at with both shivering on this sunny day, drained and glassy eyed peering into the pits that would soon hold their loved ones. Katie had never felt so hollow and empty, much like the gaping cave waiting to hold her parents for eternity. It was then that Katie first felt the absence of the promises of her faith. There was no comfort, no Holy Spirit sent to minister to her; there was no peace that surpassed all understanding.

The floral decorations were magnificent. There were so many flowers that they tended to blend in with one another. A beautiful spray of shades of gerbera daisies, pink garden roses, larkspur and snapdragons caught Katie's attention. Her mother had always loved pink and some of the flowers were her favorites. Katie reached down, pulled off a baby rose, and pressed it to her face. It was soft and sweet and smelled just like her mother.

The other arrangements were equally lovely. Roses, lilies, iris, gladioli, snapdragons and carnations, in every imaginable shade, surrounded the tent and the gaping holes which would soon be filled with Ashley and Michael. Katie's rose was subconsciously torn in a several different pieces. It had gradually lost its smell and was no longer pretty and soft. It had browned around the edges and was wilting in her sweaty hands. It had turned ugly, she thought, and believed it was a prophecy of everything that was to happen in her life; it would start out beautiful, but soon it would turn out so very ugly.

The soloist came up next to the violinist and sang "On Eagles Wings," a favorite of many of the people there. Katie eagerly listened to the words hoping that something would make sense. The soloist sang, as an angel should, soft and strong. God promised to hold you up and lift you above the suffering.

Right then and there Katie's heart turned against God. This tremendous worship song, one that spoke so knowingly of God and His mercy, His redemption and protection, enraged Katie. Looking up at Dolly, she whispered, "He did not send angels to hold up my parents. A stupid stone didn't kill them, that car wreck did it. Where was God then? Where were His angels?"

Katie was getting louder and her voice was starting to overtake the singer. "Why didn't He guard my parents? I don't want them on wings; I want them back here again with me. He doesn't do anything He promises!"

Katie pushed away from Catherine who was trying desperately to calm her, and ran towards the river that flowed past the cemetery. She was quite familiar with the cemetery, as Dolly had taken her frequently in her visits to her loved ones. Dolly had insisted on fresh flowers and prayed continuously for the poor souls. While she had cleaned around the gravestones and did her praying, Katie had the roam of the cemetery, albeit a respectful one.

Katie had loved to come to the cemetery and read the old gravestones, some dating back to before the Civil War, but today she did not see them. She did not want to see them because now they were real and belonged to real families who probably still missed them. She was suddenly sorry she'd ever run through the graveyard and skipped over tombstones. She needed to get to the river and away from the entombment of her parents. The thought of people walking around her parents and thinking *Oh, how sad. A loving couple died together,* was enough to push her over the edge. She wanted her parents' gravestones to be covered so no one but Katie could read them. It was now suddenly so personal. Twelve-year-olds should not know anything about their parents' burial plots. It was just so wrong.

Katie felt a flash of heat brush against her body. Her hair felt damp and her hands were clammy, like dead hands. She turned away from the river and shifted her weight so she could lean against the giant oak tree draped with Spanish moss. Katie watched as the watchers, the mourners at the funeral, dropped flowers into her parents' grave. It was suddenly unbearable to think about them tonight, when it was dark and they were alone. Could they talk to each other? Could they comfort each other? Dolly had smiled when Katie wanted her parents buried in the same coffin. Now the thought of them buried and too far apart to touch crushed her.

She saw Dr. Barnes dropping a pink rose into the open grave. His wife seemed to hold him up as he started to stumble while turning away. He looked across several tombstones to Katie and he waved. A silly, hand up wave that had no meaning other than "I know you are there." Suddenly Katie began to scream, a horrible, blood-curdling scream from somewhere that no child should ever have to go. With her hands over her face, she screamed and screamed until everything went black.

Ed Barnes flew to her side and picked her up gently in his big bear arms. "Katie. It's going to be okay now. I swear we will never leave you. Katie. Shush now. Shush."

She was limp and drained, teetering on the edge of shock, and suffering far too much for such a young soul. After doing a cursory check, he knew she was bordering on exhaustion, overwhelmed by the adults going through the mourning and entombment process. It was simply too much.

Someone brought bottled water over and bathed Katie's sweet face. Her cheeks were the color of severe sunburn and her body poured sweat. Her dark eyelashes fluttered just a bit and she opened her eyes. From a scene in Pollyanna, Katie looked around at all the people who stood by. She suddenly felt so very shy around these dear friends of hers and her parents.

"Sarge, here, give me a hand with Katie. Let's get her to the hospital as soon as possible."

Dr. Barnes and Mr. Sarge picked her up and moved her away from the tree. The wind blew the old moss so that it tickled her arms as if offering some sort of condolence. Dr. Barnes decided a trip to the hospital was the wisest thing, and Katie started to cry once more. She protested quite loudly that she was fine and had just been killed by sadness. They all knew her only escape that day was to faint. In her mind, she might not have known it, but certainly, the messages from that broken heart let the brain know that they were in trouble.

"Please take me home, and I'll promise to go take a nap. Dr. Barnes, I just can't go to the hospital again. Please take me home."

Barnes hesitated for a minute and then decided he would go back to the beach with them for a while. Cat was having a reception at the club after the burial and she agreed that Katie could miss that. Mr. Sarge, puffing on his pipe, had been heartbroken by all that had happened to Katie. He was terribly fond of the Olivers and was devastated by their passing. Dolly and Cat had always been so good to him and his wife and invited the odd couple to every function they had. Sarge was definitely dancing to his own beat, but Dolly appreciated the extra kindness he had always shown Katie. Little did Dolly know of the reciprocal nature of their relationship. He would have stolen her in a heartbeat if he could have.

"Katie girl. Would you like to carry W.C. for a while?" It was so dear hearing that come from Sarge. "No thanks, Mr. Sarge. You keep it. But if it's okay, can I come hold it when I'm feeling better?"

"You sure can, honey. And we'll go crabbing and bring Ms. Dolly and Ms. Cat a whole bushel of crabs. Does that sound good to you?"

In a barely audible whisper Katie said, "Thank you Mr. Sarge. I can't wait to go crabbing."

She turned and buried her head in Dr. Barn's dark blue suit jacket. She grabbed onto his lapels and did not let go until they got to the beach. His wife had to drive but did so very carefully as she was blinded by the tears over Ed's suffering mixed forever with Katie's in that scary place of unimaginable pain.

It was then that the nightmares began. When others deigned to protect you fail to do so, the mind takes over and does mysterious things. For Katie the mystery came in the form of nightmares. Nightmares that came like legions of Roman soldiers, marching now, then kneeling phalanxes, never stopping, from the highest crest their armor shone in the blood red sun and they refused to be stopped.

The nightmares from all the worlds' dreams were bound together by their tails bucking like wild horses refusing to be tamed. Something out of Stephen King's mind, sinister, palpable evil, viscous, alive.

One came more frequently than the others did, and it was always a small kitten nestled at the end of her parents' bed. Katie's dad would move his foot and gently push the kitten over to the side. The black and white faced cat would awaken and stretch that great arched back stretch, sending the rear end up high into the air. The eyes were slits and the face appeared to smile. The purring was gentle and soft like a lullaby. Suddenly the furry kitten began to morph into a hideous rattlesnake coiled and ready to strike. The lullaby had ended, and now the threatening rattle superseded it. The rattle amplified until the bed began to shake, and the parents clutched each other. It struck repeatedly until their bodies swelled turning black and bulbous, skin tearing and ripping from the pressure of the poison coursing through their bodies. Only Katie's screams could finally silence the hideous rattling.

She would wake up from these dreams drenched in sweat. Her nightgowns would cling to her small body and sweat would have curled the hair around her face and neck. She desperately wanted someone to hold and comfort her, but she always woke up alone. A long time had passed since she had crawled into bed with Dolly. She was just too old, she would tell herself. She was just getting too old to be afraid all the time.

CHAPTER 7

D olly called Katie out of her reverie. "Katie, have you finished your section of the grocery list? I do not want to fight traffic and come home wishing we had thought of something else we should have thought of, and did not. Let's finish this and get on with it."

"I thought of something, a must have; grits, eggs, and corned beef hash. That finishes my contribution. Wait, Coke Zero, and now I'm done. So let's combine our lists and get going. I'll drive." Katie always liked to drive. It gave her a sense of control, that wheel in her hand, which she could turn around any time she wanted to. Somehow, her anxiety levels were much lower when she drove, but only when she was not driving alone.

Katie's enthusiasm was waning and she offered a weak smile, the curvy crooked kind that showed only a modicum of effort and success. The rain had begun to blow from the north sending a delightful, but chilly breeze whistling through the screens encasing the porch. Some of Dolly's friends had teased her about having a fireplace on the porch, but she had lived most of her life at the beach and knew there would be many nights that would demand a fire. She used to say "God confounds the wise." Katie never understood the meaning of that.

"Time to run to the market and see what the scavengers have left. If we have to go into Somerville, I would like to go once rush hour passes. The drive back to the beach can take forever. You take the Suburban so we can load firewood if we need to. Who knows, if we hurry we can be back in time to watch a good movie."

"I need a comedy! Nothing sad, sexy or subversive," Katie called as she hurtled down the stairs.

"Sheesh- what's left?" Catherine called to no one in particular.

The ride into town was worse than any of the three women had expected. The winds were increasing in intensity. They whipped this way and that and played havoc with the saw palms that ran along the highway. Katie was now getting edgy and quick tempered. The storm was unnerving in the best of circumstances, but the memory of the accident that took her parents, sprinkled heavily with her free-floating anxiety, and she was a train wreck waiting to happen. The cars lined up single file, bumper to bumper. Katie had to suppress the urge to run over them or at the very least travel the shoulder. Police cars with blue lights flashing made her think twice. The parking lot looked like a free for all, and Katie dreaded the thought of all those people pushing and shoving and bumping into her. She debated inwardly about staying in the car while Catherine and Dolly shopped, but the expectant look on Cat's face as she opened the door left no doubt what Katie was to do.

It was worse than expected and Katie experienced various levels of anxiety while in the store. Although she fought the temptation, she checked her watch to see if four hours had passed since her last Ativan. Katie counted on her fingers, three-thirty to four-thirty, four- thirty to five-thirty, five-thirty-to six-thirty, six- thirty to seven-thirty. It was seven-twenty-five and Katie swallowed her pill. Like skimming the fuzz off a Diet Coke, the pill had the same effect. The panic was still there only manageable.

Cat had noticed Katie's anxious demeanor and offered up a silent prayer for her. She had read everything she could get her hands on about panic disorder and found it not to be an easy read. She knew that Katie was suffering the scourge of the damned, but she was powerless to help. The research had implored friends and family members to understand the condition and be supportive.

Keep the patient from becoming house bound. Look for signs that they are avoiding situations and places. Encourage them to talk about their feelings. Do not make light of their feelings. They are the ones suffering, whether you understand it or not. Do not ask for explanations or look for a root cause. Be the support they need.

"I'm ready to get out of this mad house if you are." Cat called out to Katie as she maneuvered her buggy into the shortest line available. Dolly had walked down to the drug store to pick up some prescriptions, so she had escaped the madhouse. The store was heavy with people, rain and the indescribable smell of sweat. The humidity had swooped down on them and made every one hot and sticky. The air-conditioning was on overload and seemed to be straining to stay alive. It had long ago given up the battle to cool the air.

Katie resisted the urge to ram her buggy into the next people who excused themselves, ran their buggy up on her heel, or reached over her to grab the last loaf of bread. It was ridiculous. She wanted to climb the shelves and scream, "It's only a storm and not the end of the world!" She chose not to and soon found it was to be a wise decision. Out of her peripheral vision, Katie felt tiny excitement stings as she caught a familiar figure walking down the aisle. Spinning around she found she was correct; it was Dr. Chris Martin, and he was quickly walking towards her.

"Well, hello there. This is quite a madhouse isn't it?" Then he just stopped in mid-sentence and looked at her. Blinking and sharing his crooked smile. "How long have you been at the beach?"

"I came down a week ago. Some pretty rough stuff happened at home, so I am taking a break here at the beach. So far I've made the right decision." She smiled back at him while making direct eye contact.

"That's nice to hear. I mean, it's nice to hear that you're happy at the beach, but I'm sorry about your home problems. Say, how's the therapy going with Dr. Schladenhoffer?"

Katie just stood there as if someone had literally wiped the smile off her face. "It's going great, and I'm so much better. He's quite a therapist. Look, I have to get the girls out of here and back home before the heavens open up. Maybe we'll see you later. By the way, how long are you staying down?"

"In and out mostly. No real time set as of yet. A good deal of travel and then back to the beach to regroup." He could not have been vaguer. As Katie turned to break the conversation, Chris Martin called out, "Are the girls here in the store? I've always been so curious about meeting them."

"Maybe later, Dr. Martin. Gotta run." With that, she was gone to find the infamous girls and head home to face the storm. After checking out, the girls ran to the car laughing as the rain soaked them thoroughly. It was a nightmare - horns honking, breaks screeching and cars swerving dangerously around one another promised that the trip home would be delightful. Everyone just seemed mad.

Cat and Dolly noticed instantly that something had ratcheted Katie's irritability to record heights. She was moving in long strides as if someone were chasing her. She snapped at both of them and urged them to get in the car. No, not an urging, it was more of a command. Exiting the parking lot looked like an old *Saturday Night Live* skit about bumper cars on drugs. Katie's behavior was more than Annoying.

As good-natured as Cat was, what she found to be more Annoying was the profanity that had found its way into Katie's vocabulary. Cat frequently quoted Dolly when it came to the use of foul language. "It is a poor vocabulary a person has when curse words are the only adjectives they know." Seemed to Catherine that Katie's vocabulary had gone to hell in a hand bucket.

Slamming on breaks, Katie swerved to the left narrowly missing the Quick Trip gas station sign. "Stupid idiot! Move out of the way. Where did you learn to drive? Move out of the way!" A string of progressively worse profanity followed this.

"What a trash mouth! Katie, what's the matter with you?" Dolly shouted from the back seat. "And what, you want the sign to move?"

"Nothing's wrong with me. Can't I just be stressed from all of this? Ok, I'm sorry girls, but I'm crawling out of my skin, and I just need to get home. I'm really sorry I sound like a sailor."

"I'm sure glad Beau isn't in the car to hear his mother speak such garbage. He'd be ashamed."

Everyone laughed at that and the tension seemed to settle to the floor. One could still step on it, but at least it was not threatening to suffocate them. Katie did promise to watch her language.

Catherine's hand had risen to her mouth as she tried to cover her gasp. Do not be mistaken, Catherine had let a string or two loose on occasion, but this was serious profanity. It was not just that her mouth had taken on a filth of its own; it was the fact that she was absolutely unaware of the toads and lizards oozing from her mouth.

Reaching over to pat Cat's hand, Katie apologized once more. "Ok, I'm guilty as sin and I've been officially reprimanded. Before you two hang me, please keep in mind that I cursed, some pretty rough cursing, but I haven't murdered anyone, yet."

The girls all laughed and fell in line behind the miles of islanders heading home. By now, the weatherman promised the storm of the century, but no one believed him. He was always exaggerating the length and breadth of the storms that visited their section of the coast. An odd shaped coastline had protected them and had provided them with a natural harbor. Most of the damage from previous storms had ravaged other towns, but he was insistent that this would be "the one". Maybe he would be right this time as the temperature had begun to drop rapidly and a chill had settled in the cottage. It seemed that the ocean was a little too warm and the air a little too cool. The combination could ignite dynamite. Katie offered to light a fire while Cat put away the groceries. Both girls, now clad in pajamas and robes, met back in the den and the comfort of the fire.

"Surprise!" Cat called out as she uncovered a tray laden with hot toddies and chocolate cake.

Katie began to laugh. "Are we going to drink our way through the storm? You know I love these things, and I haven't had one in years. I don't know if you or the Toddy is the best medicine for what ails me."

"This is an old family recipe, and I will pass on the secret to you one day. Sip it slowly as it has quite a kick. Katie knew by heart and taste the old family recipe. A Hot Toddy was the undisputed cure of all that ailed you. Catherine's recipe was an old standard with a familial twist. Katie could see the dusted ground nutmeg adrift on the drink covering the bourbon, honey and lemon that brought miraculous cures. A rusty colored cinnamon stick gave the drink a sense of sophistication while providing a fragrant stirrer.

Feeling the soothing warm of the toddy tingling over her weary shoulders and down her arms, Katie finally began to relax, as much as was possible. She closed her eyes and listened to the sounds of fury, unabated, and wild like fighting stallions over their herd. However, she was not afraid. Moving out onto the porch, letting her blanket slip behind, Katie felt as if she could walk out on the sea. She wanted so desperately to be razed by the sea in hopes of a new Katie growing in the space she once held.

The lightening shocked the sea and looked as if the interior of the sky body had been illuminated. Rivers of veins and arteries were ignited, and glowed a sharp, crisp, white light. Then darkness. During the whole storm, that raging mess of angry sirens, the moon had not moved from his spot. The stars, although invisible, were still there holding tight to their places. Katie wondered what they were thinking; were they afraid of the storm? Or, because they could see each other above the clouds, did they even know what was happening? For a moment, Katie wished she could be up, looking down, away from the fury surrounding her now.

Suddenly, an enormous crack of thunder, then lightening drew her attention to the horizon. It looked much like the start of a firework display, but without the accompanying excitement. The moon was suddenly visible, all fat and jolly and round. A vague tint of gray had been dabbed around the edges, but the rest of the old man was startling in his whiteness, contrasting the blue black around him. Katie saw the path that led over the sea. For just an instant or two, Katie ached to trust and walk over that path. At this point she didn't care where it ended; she just didn't want it to lead her back here.

Over the next few hours, everyone on the island breathed a sigh of relief. People were taking down from the ready. The storm had been a tease, a trickster, a wanna be. Somehow the storm had veered left finding the water temperatures not appetizing, causing her to dwindle not grow. Storms like to be dragons pouring smoke, not summer showers needing a rainbow. Tomorrow, the meteorologists would be apologizing for the near miss and quote some scientific reason for another dodged bullet. Many people had heeded the warning and evacuated the island. Next time they may not be so inclined.

Katie flipped the damp cushions and covered them with throws. Grabbing a pillow from her bed, she hopped onto the day bed and watched as the diminished clouds were blown off the scene. They should have been ashamed of scaring everyone so much, and then failing to produce. Such were the unpredictability of summer storms at Tybee Island. But would they always be this lucky?

CHAPTER 8

Katie Oliver had been teaching middle school for about four years. Life had become pretty boring and the thought of a handsome knight in shining armor riding down the concrete halls, now filled with hormonally possessed children, just wasn't something her vivid imagination could envision. She sighed heavily as she went through the morning routine of checking mail and printing papers for the day's classes. She was a popular teacher with faculty, parents, and students alike, but this year she seemed to be out of touch with school. Maybe she was getting burned out or maybe she had chosen the wrong profession. Something just seemed out of kilter this year, and she just could not put her finger on it. It was a dilemma that would not be resolved today.

Elizabeth Hemming, Katie's best friend, college roomie, and closest confidant and teaching fellow, called out from the slate gray mailboxes overwhelming the tiny teachers' lounge.

"Hey, tomorrow night is Tom Harrison's political rally. He's running for county commissioner and I hear plenty of eligible bachelors will be there. Let's go."

Elizabeth's voice was more of a statement than a question and Katie knew it would be useless to put her off. Tom had been a fraternity brother of Elizabeth's ex-love Evan McLaughlin and they had all spent hundreds of hours on and off campus together. Evan was a gentle giant who adored Elizabeth and had suffered deeply when she called off their relationship. Elizabeth had been remarkable in her ability to see clearly regarding the relationship; there would be no divorce in her life so waiting for the stars to align, and an approval from the Lord, was just fine with her. What a shame Katie possessed none of the maturity Elizabeth had. In the meantime, Evan was the guardian, the steadfast soldier, the one who would wait until the end of time for his dream to come true.

"Sure, sounds like great fun," Katie responded halfheartedly.

"We could go by my place after school and freshen up and then go to the party together," she continued.

"Elizabeth, I said I would go," Katie said with more than a trace of irritation in her voice. Peeking around the corner of the shelves Elizabeth eyed her friend suspiciously. "I know you did, but you gave in without a struggle and I didn't feel like I got to say enough."

Both girls squealed with laughter, sadly a laughter that sounded way too much like silly seventh grade girls.

Moving around the corner of the dividing shelf of mailboxes, Elizabeth grumbled, "Did you just hear us? We are going to need some serious therapy if we don't start hanging around adults. Slap me hard if I start talking like I'm texting or call the first man I meet 'dude.'"

Katie and Elizabeth promised to talk more tonight and plan outfits for their big girl date tomorrow night. Katie, however, rehearsed a hundred different ways to get out of going to the rally without ticking Elizabeth off forever. Everything she practiced sounded hollow and extremely immature, so she sucked it up and planned to go. She didn't know why she was hesitant about attending parties and such. She just always seemed to have an odd sense of being uncomfortable. She pushed the thought out of her mind.

There was excitement in the ballroom at the Hilton that night. Everyone was dressed in Sunday best and finer, some even going to the ridiculous with formal wear, but Katie and Elizabeth were just perfect. Elizabeth wouldn't have let it be any other way. Elizabeth was an Emily Post clone who knew every right move, even when to curtsey to a queen. It was just her temperament and her brilliant mind; she never forgot a thing, which could be good and bad. She was also an exceptional judge of character, which too could go either way.

"I am twenty-seven years old and seeing all these available men makes me feel just as hormonal as our kids at school," Elizabeth whispered to Katie.

Elizabeth's lips edged her cocktail as if checking it for poison. She would never know what it tasted like because she simply didn't drink. She didn't mind if you did, she just didn't want someone to get into a serious conversation over tee totaling which often included drunks and born again Christians who often quoted scripture out of context, another thing that drove Elizabeth wild. So, she pretended to sip cordially and no one was the wiser. As they both took a sip of their drinks, a real and a pretend one, the girls burst into laughter as they realized they had slowly backed themselves against a wall. Swaying to the sounds of sixties soul, the girls scanned the room.

"I have never been a wall flower and I am not about to start now!" Elizabeth shouted as she grabbed Evan's hand and dragged him to the dance floor. He went willingly and still carried a flaming torch for the love of his life. As they moved around the dance floor, Katie turned to watch the crowd. A group of men laughing loudly drew her attention, and she meandered in that direction. With the slightest buzz from her cocktail that Katie was not sipping, she smiled bravely and coquettishly at a handsome man in a navy three-piece suit. She was a sucker for a man in a suit with a vest, and if he was this cute, the better. Scott Stewart bestowed upon Katie a million dollar smile. If it could have been filmed for a commercial, it could not have been more perfect. She responded with her own beautifully, orthodontically treated teeth and the mating dance was on.

Scott Stewart was a brilliant businessman whose primary business was as Certified Public Accountant. He was in partnership with four other men and had several underlings trying to suck up to him daily. However, he knew being a bean counter would not sustain his lavish lifestyle without tying him to a computer and the office for hours he was not willing to give. He dabbled here and there in other ventures and was gentleman enough not to discuss the vulgar side of money, of which he seemed to have plenty.

Without a word, Scott walked over to Katie, and like Cary Grant out of some sophisticated movie, held out his hand for her to dance. Within minutes, they had exchanged the pleasantries of name, job, family and friends. The conversation flowed easily and a comfort settled between them as they moved across the floor. Scott was a southern boy, attended a southern university, inherited a small sum from a semi-famous grandfather, and was an only child. He admitted to being rather spoiled but had hoped to grow out of it in the very near future. Though his family credentials were meager, Katie was delighted at her new find.

The band was wonderful and to Katie's great pleasure, played sixties melodies. She hummed and sang right along with the music while Scott led her in the shag.

"How in the world do you know these old songs?" Scott shouted as he took her hand and spun her around once.

"My mom and dad used to shag to this music all the time. At night, instead of watching TV, they would put in a cassette and dance across the den floor. They loved this old music. People tease me about being old fashioned or too sheltered, but I know this music changes my moods. Makes me smile while I dance. Fills me with chills. " Katie slid her feet as she forced them to stay firmly planted.

"I had a wild uncle who had a tendency to live in the past. He worked in the present, quite successfully, but after hours, he unwound to these sounds. Ah, but he was great. He still had all these singles that reminded him of beach parties at Pawley's Island. My Aunt Dell learned how to shag by practicing with the doorknob as a partner. I love to shag and I love this music. I can't believe you know it!"

Katie felt as if she had just heard straight from heaven. If she had laid a fleece before God, it could not have been answered in a more perfect way. If she had been clever enough to put God to the test, in a million years she would not have thought to pray, *Lord, please send me a sign showing me who my husband is to be. If he is the right one, let him love beach music.* The wick as pure as the driven snow, a true virgin wick, was about to be lit.

"When my uncle died, Dell sent me an old reel to reel recording of all their favorite songs. Whenever I am in a bad mood or just need a lift, I play these songs. I just can't believe someone gets this as much as I do."

Scott and Katie had no idea the music had stopped and people had moved off the dance floor. Softly, new words floated across them and Scott began to sing an old Drifters favorite to Katie, the beautiful one about magical moments. It hit the spot.

They danced and danced until the music slowed hinting that the night was ending, Scott pulled Katie so close to him she could hardly breathe. She did not care. She loved being in his arms. He would lean down and kiss her forehead and she would smile and nestle in closer to him. At a tall, six feet two, Scott seemed larger than life. His strong arms felt safe and protective around the feminine curves Katie possessed. Her face rested just below his shoulder and she could hear the excitement beating in his chest. That knowledge made her giddy, this power she had over him and should have warned her of her alarming immaturity. She was exciting him and she loved it. Suddenly, Scott pulled her behind the maroon curtains leading to the balcony, and hiding behind them, kissed her with a passion found only in her dreams. Pulling away from his embrace Katie blushed and felt heat rise to her cheeks as well as to every other place in her body that possessed a nerve ending. Her upbringing told her, urged her even, to at least act offended or at least a little hesitant. It was beyond her ability.

Reading the uneasiness about her, Scott cupped Katie's beautiful face in his hands and kissed her softly on her eyes, the tip of her nose, the lobes of her ears, and when she could hold her breath no longer, he brushed her wispy bangs to the side and pressed his lips in a lingering kiss right in the middle of her forehead. As if that was not enough, he gently lifted her cashmere sweater, just above her waist and softly caressed the bare skin at the base of her spine. Katie thought she would die right then and there. This is what Dolly and Catherine would call making love in public, but what Katie and Scott had in mind would be scandalous to the two older ladies.

"Scott, this is ridiculous, I don't even know you. This is not right. Please stop." Katie faintly protested. Scott kissed her even as her lips moved to say stop. "I don't want you to kiss me like that again," she stammered in a deep, breathy voice. She need not have wasted her lies. Scott knew that she felt the fire burning in her just as much as he felt the fire creating a burn that he never imagined. Scott had been with many women, even some he had professed to love, but never, nothing close, had ever exploded inside of him the way her body against his caused him to feel. It was addictive, and he had to have more. A little rougher this time, he held her wanting to squeeze her until she was one with him. *What madness had possessed him?* He wondered. His brain was thick and his breathing labored. He released her only to catch his breath and once more kissed her deeply with an intensity that exhilarated and frightened him all at the same time. Her innocence and welcoming arms inebriated him and he knew that, if he were not careful, she could possess his soul. Scott knew that their chemistry was something magical and only the powers above could keep them apart. Little did they both know, that without calling on the powers above, they were headed for trouble.

In the ladies room, Katie grabbed Elizabeth, pulled her into a cubicle, and slid back the latch. Holding onto her hands, she whispered, "Scott is going to take me home. Oh, Elizabeth, he is such a dream, and I feel like I am falling in love with him!" She gushed like a schoolgirl, eyes all dreamy and voice all whispery and soft.

Elizabeth's eyes took on a menacing glare as if she had just come up against evil. "Katie, you just met the guy. Plus Evan said he was a real player. He thought you should be careful because Scott had left a string of broken hearts across Atlanta."

"Oh, pooh, Evan's just afraid you might think Scott's cute and give him a try. Evan has never gotten over you, and it is so obvious. Anyway, what would Evan know about a guy like Scott?" Instantly Katie knew she had offended her friend.

With a glint to her steely gray eyes, Elizabeth said, "Go ahead and make a fool out of yourself. You are so naive about boys, and you always have been. Evan is in a class so far above Scott that he shouldn't know anything about him, but you know how rumors fly. And another thing, you were hanging all over Scott on the dance floor and more than one person raised an eyebrow."

The last words hissed out of Elizabeth's mouth like a slithering snake. She was furious with Katie and had every right to be. Elizabeth had really loved Evan, but was more than afraid to make a commitment so putting space between them seemed the practical thing to do. Both had suffered over it, but Elizabeth had been hesitant to rekindle the relationship. Obviously, being in his arms tonight had flamed a spark she thought long extinguished.

"All I can tell you, girl, is that I am shocked at how you threw yourself at him. You were high as a kite and your feet are still not on the ground. Lust not love, Katie. Remember that. Evan will gladly take me home, and I'll see you at school tomorrow. I'm sorry for your sake we came tonight." With that Elizabeth let the bathroom door slam behind her as she hurried over to Evan and without a second look, turned and walked out through the hotel lobby.

Katie was so confused. Everything had happened so quickly tonight. Her feelings for Scott were real, but she knew they weren't just lust. Girls like Katie were not eaten up with lustful feelings. Surely, Elizabeth was just jealous. Tossing that comforting thought to the wind, Katie grinned as Scott grabbed her hand, kissed it sweetly, and pulled her toward the exit. *That was not lust, just a sweet kiss on the hand.*

Driving into her driveway, Scott, unusually at a loss for words, hesitated before turning off the car. He just was not sure what to do. His voice startled Katie as he broke the silence. "Katie, I don't know what has happened to us tonight. I can't explain it, and I sure as hell don't understand it. But, I do know that something is going on between us, and if you are willing to give it a try, then I sure am." Scott's words tumbled all over themselves, but Katie knew exactly what he meant. She felt the same way.

"Let's sleep on it tonight and see how we feel in the morning." Katie smiled up at him, knowing full well they both would feel the same way.

He grabbed her and hugged her so hard, she squealed. It hurt just a little, and she told him so. His heart melted and he felt an unfamiliar surge go through his body. She was potent and dangerous, not in a way that he could fear her physically, but he could fear what she could emotionally do to him. He held her hand and found it difficult to concentrate. *My God, if holding her hand does this to me, I am ruined,* he thought to himself. He felt wild and out of control. *She was so sweet, so pure and when she looked at me through those milky brown eyes, I was hers.* Scott's mind raced with the thoughts clouding his judgment. Where was the cool player that all the girls wanted, loved and then hated? He had been a master at heartbreak, but suddenly he feared for his own safety.

Scott walked Katie down the sidewalk and up to the front door. It was almost awkward the way they stood at the door, hesitant to embrace. Scott wanted to tell her how much he wanted to make love to her, but he knew that might slam the door shut on their budding relationship. She truly was not that kind of girl, and he could not believe she was suddenly wrapping her arms around him, speaking to him through her actions.

Finally, he backed off and stepped away from her. She looked sleepy and her hair had a mussed look to it. *She must be beautiful in the morning as she shakes the sleep from her body.* Scott was appalled at how ridiculous his thoughts would sound if spoken aloud. He had never felt so foolish in all his life. *Damn.* She just stood there, staring at him with wide-eyed innocence, hiding the passion he had so lightly tasted. His heart beat for more. With that final thought, Scott turned and sprinted to the car, shouting goodbye over his shoulder. He could not bear to look at her one more time. He peeled out of her driveway like a lovesick teenager. Embarrassed as he was, he relished the feelings.

Later that night, Katie lay under the covers and relived the evening in its entirety. Ok, not the part about Elizabeth, but every moment that Scott had been in her life. His kisses, his touch, his sensitive fingers finding just the right spots to send shivers throughout her body made him even more wonderful. She rehearsed the night over and over again. Sleep would not come, and she did not care. But the thing that made it, cemented their future together, was at the front door.

Everything about him was right, even the way he smelled, the touch of his fingers running up her spine, the knowledge that he could be it, the man, the one who could take control of her life so she could finally resign as boss and sole proprietor. She was swimming in shark-infested waters, and she did not seem to notice or care.

CHAPTER 9

The weeks passed and Katie and Elizabeth found themselves deep into teaching, testing, and controlling pubescent teens. With long days and even longer afternoons, the girls found little time to socialize. A rearranged schedule meant their lunch times were changed and reassigned committees kept them as far apart as possible. Emailing a thought back and forth was as close as it came to real communication.

Beachgirl. – loved your outfit this morning. Great jeans – new sweater? Buy more. Going to Chastain this Friday for concert and have 2 extra tickets to see James Taylor. YES! James Taylor. Can you believe it? Evan and I are going together. Please ask Scott and ya'll come. 'Lizbeth

'Lizbeth...here's my answer cause I love James Taylor – OK you can't hear me singing but just think about the earth moving! I can't wait. Bring it on, JT.

Meet you at Chastain at 7. Same dinner menu as always. Got new tablecloth –you bring candle holders. Beachgirl

"Great news! Chastain caters. BRING NOTHING but you and Scott. 'Lizbeth

Elizabeth had just hooted over Katie's username, Beachgirl, and had teased her unmercifully about it. "Look. If it was good enough for Meg Ryan to be Shopgirl, then I can certainly be Beachgirl. And look how things ended up for her!"

The Chastain Amphitheatre was a fabulous place for a concert. Elizabeth's seats were for the tables right down front with all the other more fortunate ticket holders. Once the sun went down, the entire place would be covered in the glow of candles, awash with flowing wine, and people singing and swaying to the music. It was a perfect combination for a Friday night in Georgia.

Elizabeth was right and Chastain did cater a fantastic meal. Spicy Ginger Glazed Grilled Shrimp, Mango Black Bean Salsa, Red Pepper Sesame Vinaigrette, Fresh Cilantro and decadent desserts. A few bottles of Sauvignon Blanc capped the night.

And James Taylor did not disappoint. With his smooth, soothing voice and beautiful melodies, the crowd was pulled to its feet over and over again. The early fall night performed as if on command. Unusually cooler temperatures created the perfect weather and the sky held the full moon and more than a handful of stars.

Scott stood behind Katie and wrapped his arms around her waist. He sang softly in her ear and rocked her gently to the music. James Taylor serenaded them with rainbows of gold and dreaming of love.

Never had Katie felt such love. She trembled at Scott's touch and longed to be one with him. Not just in a sexual way, she wanted to be a total part of him. This much joy frightened her, and she could not believe she could be this happy. She turned around in his embrace and snuggled her arms under his shirt feeling the muscles of his back and the drinking deeply of his smell. She could drown in these feelings.

Scott, too, was adrift in emotions so strong he felt nearly overwhelmed. He could not believe how much he adored this woman he held so tightly; this woman he wanted to protect forever and always; this woman blending in with his very being. He could not express it and felt so terribly close to tears. How could he ever leave her again? And dear God, how could he ever live it down that he was crying out of sheer joy and happiness?

Nibbling on the top of her ear, Scott whispered, "I love you so much, Katie. Be with me always. No matter what comes our way. Just promise me you'll never leave me. I hurt I love you so much."

Katie pulled back and reached up to cup his face in her hands. She smiled at him, this smile that came from somewhere deep inside her, a place where no smile had ever come from before. "I love you, Scott. I will never leave you, and I will love you always. No matter what."

"Say it again. No matter what."

"No matter what. I promise you, forever." Looking into his deep blue eyes, she saw they were swimming in tears, which in turn made her cry. They held each other and rocked gently to James Taylor for the rest of the evening, oblivious to the world around them.

If Katie and Scott had not been on another planet, aided and abetted with a nice, fine wine, they might have noticed that they were not alone. Evan and Elizabeth laughed, sang, and held hands throughout the concert, but they got nowhere near Nirvana like Katie and Scott did. Yet, something did cement them together that night. No, they did not soar or tremble at each other's touch, but they rekindled a tamer fire that brought them far more comfort. Both were terra firma people.

Elizabeth, that excellent judge of character, was initially heartsick over this relationship. At first, she did feel a pang or two or three, maybe four of jealousy - who would not? Katie was hysterically happy for the first time in years. She was in love and it transformed her whole life. She dove deeper into her teaching and possessed this amazing energy. Not surprisingly, Elizabeth was concerned. She liked Scott, in spite of his reputation. Maybe all those rumors were just that. Maybe she was seeing a side of him that Katie saw. Whatever it was, she smiled when she saw him and actually looked forward to spending time with the two of them. It was nice to be wrong about something this critical.

The love lives of both girls progressed nicely while they balanced school, their friendship, and their men. Wednesday rolled around, and as inked on the calendar, a standing dinner date for Katie and Elizabeth. This time they would meet having sworn that neither one could cancel once again.

This time the girls met in a quaint restaurant just down the block from school. Elizabeth loved Chiamare and the fabulous Italian food they served. She was a fan of the lasagna with spinach pasta sheets layered with ragu, dusted with nutmeg, and covered with a béchamel sauce. Katie ordered spinach with cannelloni, touch of basil, and a dose of parmesan. She sipped happily as Elizabeth shared what had transpired in her life since Evan had come back into the picture. Katie nodded at the appropriate places, but in reality, she couldn't wait until her turn so she could talk about Scott. It had only been eight weeks and the relationship was moving much too quickly.

"And then he stabbed me," Elizabeth said as matter of factly as if she were talking about the weather. She paused waiting for a reaction from Katie. Her friend just smiled, took another big sip, and waited for her to continue the story.

"He had stabbed several girls before, but they were too afraid to tell on him. Some of the girls had even died, but they wrote his name on the wall using only their index finger and their own blood."

Katie smiled.

"For goodness sake, Katie. Are you even listening to me? Where are you?" Elizabeth demanded slamming her hand on the plate in front of Katie rattling the silverware as it came down.

Sadly, Katie had not heard a single word Elizabeth had said. She was embarrassed to admit it, but she stayed in a fog, a love fog as Scott had dubbed it. Katie reached out for Elizabeth's hand and apologized. "Elizabeth, I know that I have been a terrible friend. You and Evan have gotten back together and I haven't even bothered to ask about it. I am so sorry to have been such a crummy friend. Elizabeth, I have never felt like this before. Oh, I know people always say that, but for me it is true. Since my parents died, I have felt so scared that I would end up alone. Just not complete. You have all your brothers and sisters to talk to; I only have Dolly and Catherine. Elizabeth, Scott erases all those negative feelings. He gets in my soul and into my mind, and I feel like I belong to someone. I need him so much."

"Katie, I do understand how you feel. I just do not want you to mistake a feeling of need and a need for security, to trick you into thinking you are in love. You know Scott's reputation."

Katie rolled her eyes and continued, "Scott's changed since we started dating. We have talked about all his past girlfriends, and they meant nothing to him, not compared to how I make him feel. None of them was a serious relationship. He wants me; Elizabeth, ME... is that so difficult to understand?"

"Don't be ridiculous. Would it be too hard to imagine that any man would die to have you? That's what I do not get. You could have just about any man you want, but you have not been interested in any of the men you meet. Finally, Scott comes along and you flip over him. It's not too hard for me to imagine him wanting you, but I don't see why you want him."

Elizabeth saw that reasoning with Katie about Scott was not the right approach. "I understand that you guys think you are in love and that's fine. I believe you do really love each other. Just slow down a little bit. Nothing is gained by rushing into things. By the way, are you guys sleeping together?"

"I knew you were dying to ask that, Elizabeth, and the answer is no, even though you may not believe it. I told Scott I wanted to wait until we were married, and he supports me in that. Don't get me wrong, it hasn't been easy, but we stop before we go too far. I just can't tell you how wonderful he is. How many men Scott's age would say okay to waiting to make love? Not very many I assure you of that. You know how Evan smells and it makes you feel all warm inside? Well, Scott knows I love to put on his shirts after he has worn them for a while. So the other night, he was going out of town after our date, and left me a surprise. I had gotten into bed and was just a bit down since I wouldn't get to see him for a week. When I snuggled under the covers, I felt something by my feet and it was Scott's navy blue polo shirt. The note attached to it said he left it for me so I wouldn't be lonely. Isn't that just the sweetest thing?"

Elizabeth just looked across the table at her dearest friend who had surpassed all reasoning. She was done for, cooked up and ready for serving. All she could do now was pray for her and Scott, pray for the patience and the wisdom to do the right thing. "I give up. If Scott is what you want and you think he's the right one, then I am happy for you."

"Oh Elizabeth, I knew you'd come around." Katie squealed as she threw her arms around Elizabeth's neck. "Will you be my maid of honor?"

"You're planning on getting married?" Elizabeth asked incredulously.

Katie put her fingers over Elizabeth's lips and pressed. "We've talked about it, but nothing definite yet. But, I want you to be a part of it. You're my dearest and bestest friend. Be happy for me please. This is all that I have ever wanted."

"Fine. Now what do the girls have to say about all of this?' Elizabeth asked, a little sterner than she had meant to.

Katie pushed away from the table, leaving her money on the bill. She hugged Elizabeth again and headed toward the door. "I haven't told them yet," was all she said and Elizabeth felt suddenly sick. The sentence spoke volumes. Why hadn't Katie told them? It sat heavily on Elizabeth's heart.

CHAPTER 10

Katie slept soundly buried under the down comforter. The window was open and letting in the thirtyish-degree winds that blew in the winter weather. Down pillows held her head and an intruder might not be able to find her if he gave just a cursory look. A deep knocking on the door pulled Katie from her sleep. Throwing on her robe and shaking the sleep from her hair, she looked through the peephole and saw Scott standing there, shivering in the wind. "Hurry and come in before you freeze to death. Scott, what are you doing here at 5:30 in the morning?"

"I don't feel good so I came over to be sick in your bed. I think I have a fever," he moaned.

Brushing the back of her hand over his forehead, as Dolly had done to her many, many times, Katie Announced that he had no trace of a fever. "I didn't say I had a fever, Katie, I said I don't feel so great and I needed to be nursed by you." He laid his head on her shoulder and sighed. "Can't we talk about this later? I just want to go back to sleep."

Katie was filled with a thousand emotions. She felt needed like a mom, like a nurse. Why, Scott had come to her when he felt bad, he wanted to be with her. She fairly floated back to the bed. Scott had already jumped under the covers but not before stripping to his polar bear boxers. That sudden burst of energy surprised Katie, but the grinning Scott, the man she adored, needed her, waited for her, and she crawled gratefully into his waiting arms.

Scott was miraculously healed in a matter of moments. It seemed that Katie's warm embrace banished any trace of illness and filled him with a heat that caused him to kick off the covers. Suddenly Scott was on top of her, pulling her breath from her, pressing into her with a hunger that momentarily frightened her. And just as suddenly, she closed her eyes and gave into him. It was too early in the morning, her body was too sleepy, warm and her resistance was down. He must have spoken the magic words, enacted the spell perfectly. The walls came tumbling down and she gave everything she had to him. Scott did not realize it at the time, but she had surrendered herself to him, mind, body and soul.

Katie's mind swirled around her running parallel to Scott making love to her. No mind could contain all the emotions she felt. If was if she was having an out of body experience. She loved being with him like this. She felt scandalous, hot, warm, loved. But another part of her sat watching off to the side, horrified as if some secret had suddenly been unveiled. She felt as if she was watching something ugly, but her body felt so beautiful. The torment was tearing her in two. Scott, on the other hand, was blissfully happy, kissing his love and promising her the moon. It had been more wonderful than he had ever dreamed.

Rolling onto his back, wearing the most ridiculous grin, Scott breathed deeply, exhaling and thinking of returning to sleep, with Katie tucked neatly into the crook of his arms. Something from a magazine article, everything was just right. Or was it? Katie suddenly pulled away and curled up in a semi fetal position. Gentle sobs shook the bed as she tried to calm herself. But it was no use. It was if someone had split her body in two distinct parts, one loving Scott and being so close to him, and the other hating herself for giving in to him. Guilt clung to her like a thick, wet blanket. She didn't want to move and refused to answer Scott's calls.

"Katie, what's the matter? Why are you crying? Did I hurt you?" Scott moaned over Katie whispering the words through her hair.

It reminded her of some sleazy movie when the stud, puffed up with his manliness, wonders if he'd caused some physical pain. How could Katie tell him that she wasn't physically hurt, on the contrary, she was physically fine, great, wonderful, the best she could ever remember feeling. Yet, inside, everything ached. It was too archaic to say how she felt, not words that any modern woman would say. How could she tell Scott she felt sick? How would Scott respond to, "Scott, making love with you was the best thing in the world. Words cannot express it. But if you will excuse me, I need to go throw up."

Scott slid his bare arms under Katie's back, scooped her up and laid her across his chest. Watching her cry like that was killing him. "Baby, what's wrong. God, please tell me, please, I can't stand to see you like this." *How was she going to tell him? Now I hate you and me.*

Katie felt Scott leave the bed and return just a few minutes later holding a glass of chilled wine. "Here, have a sip of this and it will make you feel better." *Straight out of a romance novel,* she thought. His words were so slick. *Like a glass of wine could erase what I just did.*

Pushing her hair off her tear streaked face, Katie rolled over onto her back and then draped herself across Scott's lap. Tracing the outline of a white polar bear, she avoided Scott's face but began to speak. "I didn't want to make love, Scott. I wasn't ready."

Poor Scott, he did not understand where Katie was going with this conversation. He interrupted her next breath saying, "Oh, baby, you were so good. I mean we were so good. It just felt so right and so terrific. You were ready, I swear you were!" Tensing up and pushing off his lap, Katie purposely planted an elbow in his nearly perfect six-pack. Before she could speak one word, Scott recognized his own need to throw up. One look at her face and Scott knew he had stepped in it deeply.

Scott had never met anyone like Katie. She was pure and innocent, sweet, good and kind. Yet at this moment, her eyes shone like a woman possessed. His exhilaration declined as rapidly as his self-esteem. The room felt tight and stale, and he was suddenly very uncomfortable. *What had just happened?* he thought trying desperately to gauge his next step. Women adored him and he knew he had a reputation for being great in bed. Why women had called him and offered a romp in the hay without needing the pre-mating dinner and a date. Girls groped him and suggested sex often on the first date, so what was wrong with this girl? No girl had ever cried after a lusty round of love making so Scott was completely thrown off guard by the steely-eyed glare of the woman he so desperately loved.

"Katie, for God's sake. What did I do? Why are you acting this way? You're making me feel terrible." Scott sounded sincerely contrite, and Katie felt her heart soften. She was hopeless over this fool sitting in her bed, in her room, on her new down comforter wearing only red and white boxers and a most pathetic look on his face. "Help me to understand this, Katie. I just feel awful."

Taking her hand Scott kissed it and felt tears coming to his eyes. His vision was blurring and he knew in just a minute he would be blubbering like a fool. If his friends could see this scene, he would never be able to show his face in town again. "Katie. I love you. Help me find you again." *How can this woman move me this way?*

With that, he opened his arms and beckoned her to him. Reluctantly, she slid closer and looked into his eyes. "I can't make you understand this, Scott, but I didn't want to make love. I thought you were sick so I let you in. My guard was down, and I was vulnerable. I think you took advantage of that." Her words were measured carefully, and their meaning was beginning to sink into Scott's totally male mind.

"Of course I wanted you, I have dreamed of nothing else since the first night we met. I wanted our first time together to be on our wedding night. You know I am not a virgin, but I am not a wild thing either and I can count the men I have been with on two fingers. You, on the other hand, need an abacus to count your trophies. I did not want to be another notch, a fun romp, a sexual release. I wanted to give myself to you on that special night. Now, I am just like all the others. It just is not how I wanted it to be. I wanted to give myself to you. I didn't want you to sneak up on me." Tears that had been brimming slowly escaped and ran in steady streams down her beautiful face.

Scott's heart hurt. Never, in his entire life, had he felt such deep love for a woman. Katie had a hold of him, and he loved it. He loved her, and her thoughts no matter how crazy they seemed to him right now. Her words were speaking of things other than making love. They were a way of showing him who she really was. He could not believe the intensity of his feelings for her at that moment. He felt as if he could not catch his breath. He grabbed her and kissed her softly, fearing she might break if he held her too hard. In his arms, she softened and nestled in close, and they found their way back under the covers and in a darkened room.

Burying his head into the base of her neck he whispered, "Katie, I'm so sorry, honey, and I swear that I will never do this to you again. I didn't know how much this meant to you, and I feel awful. We won't make love again until we get married, I promise." At the time, Scott meant every word of it. It would just be the first of many, many promises he would make and never be able to keep.

For true love is inexhaustible; the more you give, the more you have. And if you go to draw at the true fountainhead, the more water you draw, the more abundant is its flow.

– Antoine de Saint-Exupery

CHAPTER 11

The sky, now bruised and angry, darkened as the clouds bullied their way over the sky plain. Surely, some wind machine was blowing the clouds from underneath, as they truly were those billowy types that are often talked about in fairy tales. The kind of clouds that warn of impending danger, usually the evil stepmother, but always something evil nevertheless. At times, they moved as if in fast forward motion and at others, they appeared to churn inwardly. Hardly surprising that ancient tribes feared the ominously brewing sky. It was a warning, but a warning of what?

Katie poked the fire and heaped a few more logs on the fading coals. Sitting by the fire, the girls rested after unloading groceries and putting them away. Because of the harried trip, the trio enjoyed their toddies longer than usual. That and just propping up their feet and resting a bit was all the three of them needed.

Catherine slowly sipped her drink, closed her eyes and sighed deeply. "You know, it was a day like this that Dolly and I first met Scott. You two came home for the meet and greet; we knew you were serious, but we had no idea you had discussed marriage, much less had gotten engaged. When that beacon of light entered the room before you, I knew you were a cooked goose. I haven't seen an engagement ring that beautiful…well, I guess I never had."

Looking down at her hand that still wore that magnificent ring, Katie let her memories take flight with Catherine's. She remembered the day Scott proposed and how utterly surprised she had been. Although the couple had talked in generalities about marriage and babies, they had never crossed that magical line into commitment.

Katie remembered to the minute the day she and Scott had arrived on Tybee Island. The day had promised storms off and on and now they threatened quite a brouhaha. The girls were expecting the couple for a long weekend providing an opportunity for them to get to know each other. Katie would stay with Dolly, and Scott would be next door at Catherine's. Everyone except Scott thought the idea to be perfect. He wanted to bring the charade out into the open, but he knew he and Katie could never sleep in the same room. Not without Dolly dying of a heart attack.

A quick freshening would be all the time they had before meeting Dolly and Catherine at the club for dinner. Katie was nervous and excited all rolled into one. She was presenting the man she loved to the two most important people in her world. Scott seemed cool and collected, not the least bit nervous. He insisted on taking a walk on the beach even though rain was threatening and they were running a bit late, something Katie despised. Though she protested, Scott won out, the two slipped off their shoes, and walked along the water's edge listening to the soft thunder of the approaching storm. The sky was a canvas of spilled oranges and pinks, dotted with purple and dark gray bubbling clouds. Suddenly, Scott grabbed Katie's hands and spun her towards him.

He put his hand behind her neck and pulled her towards him kissing her roughly and passionately. "Scott, what is the matter with you? You know we're late and you bring me out here to make-out. Plus it's getting ready to pour down rain," Katie sputtered as she pulled out of Scott's embrace.

"Katie, I can't wait a minute longer." Getting down on one knee, Scott proposed. Pulling out a Tiffany box that contained his promise of a lifetime of happiness, Scott popped open the top to unveil the most stunning ring Katie had ever seen. A very large, round center diamond stood guard over matching side stones. Katie was speechless. The diamond must have been close to three carats. It was truly spectacular.

"I know you love the beach more than any other place in the world, so I figured this would be the most perfect place to ask you to be my wife. With the girls inside waiting on us, I just wanted them to be a part of us from the beginning. I hope you'll say yes."

Scott's deep blue eyes searched hers seeking affirmation for the bearing of his soul. He loved her in a way that denied explanations. Sometimes he felt as if he would die without her. So much had changed in his life since the night they met. Their worlds seem to run parallel to the rest of the universe only touching the outside during the times they were not together.

Tears streamed down Katie's face as she slipped the ring onto her finger. The stone was huge and sparkled brilliantly as it perched atop her finger. "Yes, Scott, I will marry you. I will. I don't know what else to say."

"Kiss me and we won't have to say anything more."

With that, he picked her up and spun her around just like some commercial on TV. He was elated and relieved having overcome a deep-seated fear that Katie might reject him. Katie was aglow and hurrying in to meet her family and show off her ring. It was an amazing stone.

Katie and Scott entered the club and headed down the hall to the dining room. The lights were dinner-dimmed and most of the tables were full. Voices were hushed and candles flickered on all the linen covered tables. Dolly and Catherine sat out on the back porch that overlooked the tumultuous water. Ships passed behind them lit up like Christmas trees. It was truly a beautiful sight.

As Dolly watched the young couple hurry towards her, she felt a stab in her middle. It was a Holy Spirit stab that sent her quickly into prayer. It had been a warning she had learned about early in her Christian walk. Put on the full armor of God. Dolly felt total confusion, which was not a good sign. Here was the most precious thing in her life, her face glowing and her finger outstretched as if it were broken. So why did Dolly feel so anxious?

Scott was a charmer, handsome, well dressed, and well, slick as glass. It was too much for Dolly and Catherine. Expecting to meet Katie's boyfriend for the first time, they were stunned to find that Scott had now become her fiancé. Rarely lacking composure, Catherine was struggling for control. Dolly, on the other hand, made no bones about the hurried engagement. Sipping lightly on the Dom Perignon Scott so lavishly ordered, she eyed him carefully over her cocktail.

"Before I offer a toast to you both, it wouldn't be honest of me to keep my peace. To say it plainly and out right, it is just too soon, too quick, too hurried. Not enough time has passed to allow you to get to know one another. You act as though you have high school crushes."

The entire table sat silent as Dolly finished her words. Catherine tried desperately to withhold her "here, here," while Katie cringed at the sharpness of her grandmother's words. Scott fumed inwardly, but forced a warm and genteel smile. Inside he was practicing a technique he had perfected some time back, keeping the boiling rage just below the surface. No one at the table was the wiser.

As he started to speak, Katie squeezed his thigh under the table. It did not do the trick. Breathing deeply Scott began, "Dolly. Catherine. You do not know me well, and I hope to remedy that soon. You do not know much about me except what Katie has told you. And I give you that she sees me through tinted glasses. But I love her and do plan on marrying her."

Pulling her hand from under the table to his chest, he continued, "There is nothing more important on this planet than Katie's happiness, and that happiness is contingent on your acceptance of me and our marriage. As we are all adults here, can we put our discomfort aside and support our wedding plans?" What he said and what he meant was all too clear for the entire party to see.

Katie felt the slither of a snake cross over her belly. She instantly felt repulsed by the tone of Scott's voice and the placating way he talked to Catherine and Dolly. A level of panic rose in her so quickly she had no choice but to get up, excuse herself, and dash out of the club. She did so in record time. Down the corridors and through the French doors leading to the beach. All she could imagine was escape and a place to hide and figure out what had just happened. Scott had been a pompous ass and she did not know how to handle that. Running away, motored by the coursing adrenaline and panic, seemed like the best plan. At the very least, she would delay dealing with this mess until she could make some sense of Scott's behavior. It wasn't the mature thing to do or the right thing to do, but suddenly she was completely torn between protecting Scott, hating Scott, protecting Dolly and Catherine, being furious with them....so what else could she do but run away?

Heading towards the north end, Katie ran until she came to the sea walls and climbed up the boulders to reach the walkway. Then she ran looking towards the lighthouse, her mind a jumbled mess. All she wanted now was the lighthouse.

The rain came down again, but now it was a healing salve and not the pounding rain of rage and frustration. Katie lay up on the seawall wishing for a wave to wash her away. This was supposed to be so easy; you bring your fiancé home, everyone loves him, and you go off happily ever after. But nothing in her life was happily ever after.

The sky burped a low, long rumble as if sharing in her mood. She suddenly missed her parents so very much. *If only I could see you and talk to you. I don't know what to do, and I feel completely alone. Why does life have to be so damn hard?* Rolling to her side, Katie watched the wind whip the sea into white caps. She used to pretend that she could step on the white caps and go swim away with dolphins. Tonight she wanted to swim away and never come back.

"Pretty rough sea for anyone to take a swim." Katie smelled him before she heard him, Mr. Sarge smoking his pipe and ambling over to her.

"Mind if I join ya? You're looking mighty lonely out here tonight, and I'm not so sure this is the best place to be. How about a cup of coffee back at the house?"

"I knew you were there before you even spoke. It's funny, but sometimes I can smell you in the little store when you've been there before me. It's like a friendly reminder that you're always around. No thanks on the coffee. I've got some thinking to do."

"Can't think with a hot cup of coffee? There's a chill in the air and your clothes are soaked." Offering his hand, which she gratefully took, they headed back to the house. After brewing some coffee, half decaf and half regular per request, Mr. Sarge asked for the details. "I don't mean to get personal, but it's mighty late, and it's mighty stormy, so a guy has to figure something pretty rough happened tonight. Nothing wrong with Ms. Catherine or Ms. Dolly I hope?"

Pulling her dress down over her knees until it touched the top of her feet, Katie looked up at Old Sarge and smiled. He had the kindest eyes and the gentlest way about him. So unusual for a man this size. "I brought my fiancé home to meet the girls tonight, and it was a disaster. No, it was more than a disaster. They hated him and thought he was arrogant and conceited. I have never seen Scott act like this before, so it scared me. Then, Dolly and Cat acted as if he was some demon straight from hell, and the more irritated they got the more defensive Scott got –almost belligerent. So I did what I always do when I can't handle things, I ran away, I just left the yacht club and ran all the way to the lighthouse…just like I did when I was a kid. Maybe I'm not ready for marriage."

Katie laughed at how silly it all sounded and how she had really regressed in maturity. Maybe this was a sign that marriage wasn't such a great idea after all.

Puffing on that pipe, Sarge rocked back in the kitchen chair and searched Katie's face and his mind for a clue for what to say. Inside he whispered a prayer for guidance and asked the Holy Spirit to bring the truth.

Suddenly overhead, they heard creaking footsteps. Mrs. Hennessey called over the banister, "Is that you Howard? Who are you with?"

"Of course it's me, Lizzy. Who'd you think it would be sipping coffee in the kitchen in the middle of the night?" Howard chuckled and finished his last sip. "Baby, it's Katie Oliver down here, and we're just shooting the breeze."

"Katie Oliver! What in the world? How's Dolly? I saw her at church last Sunday, and she looked terrific. I've been meaning to go visit and sit a spell, but you know how time just runs away and hides."

"Ok, baby. That's enough. Are you joining us or just hollering down the steps?"

"I can't come down there in my night clothes. Katie, give Dolly my love, and I'll see you later. Howard, it's about time to come on up now. Who knew you were roaming out and about?"

Howard just smiled, a knowing smile, because sure enough Lizzy would crawl back in that bed and start praying for the two of them. Howard didn't make it a habit to fetch critters out from the rain, so if he brought Katie Oliver home, Lizzy knew she had some praying to do. So she began.

"Mr. Sarge. You seem to love your wife, and you have always seemed so happy. How did you know Mrs. Hennessey was the right woman?"

"Honey, I waited a long time for God to send me the right woman. I prayed and asked for the one he had picked for me. You know the Bible says that God knew me before I was born. So, I figured if he knew me way back then, he must've known who he wanted me to marry. I didn't want to get in the way and mess things up, like marrying the wrong girl and missing out on God's best for me. So one night I just said to God, if you want me to get married, you'll have to bring her to my front porch 'cause I ain't budging unless you do. It ain't laziness, Lord, it's just me trusting you. I knew that sometimes God just has to hit you with a brick to get your attention."

Katie started to laugh and then just couldn't help herself. She could just envision God dropping bricks on everyone to get their attention. "I suppose she just knocked on your front porch?"

"Pretty dang close to it. Lizzy and a group of friends had toured the lighthouse and climbed all three hundred and sixty stairs. It was hot as blue blazes outside and inside was a Dutch oven. I was walking in the door and she was walking out and just fainted dead away. I caught her just inches from the porch floor. I carried her to the swing, gave her some water, and married her four months later. I didn't need another brick to the head to see God's gift to me."

"I wish God would hit me with a brick, and then I'd be sure I'm doing the right thing. It seems like the right thing most of the times, but after tonight, I'm just not sure anymore."

Shaking her head, Katie finished her coffee and stretched. Putting the coffee mug in the sink, she turned back to Mr. Sarge. "Have any advice for me?"

"Sweetie, I thought you'd never ask. Go home and get before the Lord. Tell Him your dilemma, and ask Him what He wants you to do. Now remember, He doesn't talk back to us in a two-way conversation. He likes to mull things over a bit and then get back to you. So give Him some time. And if you don't hear back from Him soon enough there is only one possible answer."

"What's that?"

"Wait. Do nothing and just wait. I know it ain't the answer you want to hear, but it's the right one. Wait. God ain't never in a hurry." He lit up his pipe again and looked straight at Katie. "And Katie girl, sometimes God says 'no.' People don't like to hear that, but He doesn't always say yes, and you'll have to deal with that. I ain't saying this new man of yours is or isn't the one God has for you, but I can tell ya that you sure better know before you walk down that aisle. Even though you may not like it, listen to Ms. Dolly. Lord, everyone around here knows she's got a hot line to the Lord. Don't turn your back on that saint. Whoa, she's a powerful prayer warrior." Then, as if he'd run out of words, he stood up and headed to the door. "Let me drive you home."

"No thanks. I'll walk the seawall. I need to think over a few things. I don't like to wait, but it seems like the only thing to do."

"You take care and just let me know if you or Dolly need anything while you're home. Bring me your young man, and let me get a good look at him. I'll ask God to show you what to do."

Heading down the path to the beach, Katie turned around to the large man smoking his pipe. The moon had worked its way from behind the cloud cover and was taking its rightful place. That beautiful pathway to the moon appeared over the ocean and the white caps had gone someplace else to play. Suddenly Katie ran back up to her favorite savior and hugged him hard.

"Mr. Sarge? What happens if I don't care about God anymore? What happens to people like me?"

"Baby, you can run from God, but you can't hide. You can be so mad with Him you could spit. But he'll love you anyway. Try as you might, He isn't going anywhere. And remember, just 'cause someone denies His existence don't make Him disappear. You see, He don't depend on your belief to be real. Go on now, and maybe you could whisper a little something His way."

Katie hurried to the wall and jogged out of sight. She didn't really want Old Sarge to reply, she just felt she owed him something for tonight. No sense wasting his prayers and hers.

Dolly stayed at Catherine's for much of the night rocking on the screen porch and rehashing the details of Scott and Katie's behavior. They had left Scott to his own devices with a key to Dolly's where he could wait for Katie. Scott was stunned at the nonchalance of the girls' reaction to Katie. "She'll return when she's ready, Scott. That's all I have to say."

Dolly knew Katie would be at the old lighthouse should anyone need to find her. It had been her place of solitude since she was a small child and tonight she had seemed so very small. Scott, on the other hand, was bold and very large. His persona was grandiose and the more champagne he drank the more odious he became. The fool actually looked for her, continuously glanced at his watch, and checked the doors hoping to see her return. It spoke volumes to the girls of how little Scott really knew Katie.

The rest of the weekend went badly. Scott was defensive and abbreviated in his answers. He sulked and stayed out doors most of the time. Katie had hardly spoken to him while he remained furious that she had left him with the girls. It wasn't until late Saturday afternoon that they finally talked.

Scott watched Katie through the screened porch. She was lovely and so desirable. The wind blew her hair gently across her face, and she fussed with it while she tried to read. The book pages fluttered in the wind, and more than once Katie put down the book only to retrieve it just minutes later. She was a poster child for a restless creature. Scott desperately wanted to hold her and talk about the disaster of last night, but Katie was as distant as the moon. It would be on her terms and Scott resented that terribly.

In the meantime, Dolly and Catherine had been interceding for the young couple. Friday night the girls had decided to fast and pray for the three days Scott and Katie were here. Both knew the value of seeking divine intervention through fasting, and if they ever needed guidance this was the time. Dolly had a fear deep in the pit of her belly that stubbornly refused to leave.

Dolly's prayers continued in earnest. She prayed from deep in the hidden recesses of her heart pleading with God for wisdom, a greater measure of faith, and the ability to walk in the knowledge that she had to trust God, no matter what the outcome was to be. Dolly had suffered greatly through the unimaginable loss of her family and loved ones. Although Scott and Katie's relationship was not a death, she feared that Scott was an angel of darkness who would come in many forms. His defensiveness about the premature engagement seemed extreme and exaggerated. She could understand his disappointment and even how he could have taken it personally. However, his reaction bothered her on a deep level.

Her gift of discernment, that terrible, powerful gift of the Holy Spirit, drove her to her knees where she would spend many nights imploring the heavens to have mercy on Katie. If it were true that none are so blind as those who refuse to see, then a greater evil can befall those who can hear but are too deaf to listen. Dolly sensed a spirit of fear in Katie, lying just below the surface. Not the fear that had controlled her through panic, but a fear that drove her to Scott.

Yet, she knew God had a plan for Katie's life and loved her more than Dolly and Catherine ever could. She also knew God had given Katie a free will and that knowledge would test her faith and perseverance in prayer for months to come.

Dolly had held her tongue and offered Katie time and space to catalog her feelings. Never one to tread lightly, Dolly waited for the right time to say her piece. With the slamming of the screen door, she poured two cups of coffee and headed out to Katie who sat silently rocking in the chair, tears streaming down her face and watching Scott jog down to the beach.

"Katie, I brought you some coffee and thought we might talk. I know you'd rather we didn't have this conversation now, but putting it off won't change anything –not the way I feel, not the concerns I have, and not Scott."

Katie moved from the rocker to the love seat and curled her long legs up under her. She pulled the Scrunchi out of her pocket and pulled her hair back off her face into a pony tail that made her look even more youthful than she already was. Although she wore no makeup and her eyes were puffy from crying, she still looked beautiful.

"Dolly, I know what you're going to say, and I can explain everything. You just don't know Scott, and he never acts like this. I just don't know what got into him. Please give him another chance. I want you and Catherine to love him like I do."

Dolly took a deep, long drink of her coffee. It always amazed Katie that she could drink something that hot and not even respond to it. She looked into Dolly's face and was awash with love for this great woman. Nevertheless, she dreaded what she was about to hear.

"Listen carefully to what I am about to say. I do not want you getting defensive and shutting down. I've been in prayer for you and Scott, and this weekend only furthered my concern."

Katie visibly bristled and folded her arms across her chest. "Go on."

"You know I've been praying for God's best for you. A husband he picked who would be just the right match for you. I know you want that as well and think you have found it in Scott. Sweetie, I just do not believe Scott is the right man for you or the one God has chosen. You say you've been praying as well, but have you been listening or are you dumping your prayers and not waiting for an answer?"

Katie began to shiver as if it were cold on the porch. A beach breeze played through the screens, but at 75 degrees, it was hardly chilly weather. It was a reaction Katie often had when she was afraid. And she was afraid that Dolly would speak the truth, and she would want to hear it, but she wanted Scott more than anything in the world.

"Sometimes you are wrong, Dolly. You aren't an oracle or a prophet, and sometimes you don't get it right. How come you have a hotline to God and others don't? Why is your truth the best truth? Why does it supersede my truth? Suppose Scott is my best and I listen to you and you're wrong? What proof do you have? Show me!" Her words came out like a machine gun, never taking a breath between shots.

Dolly's white hair curled softly around her face. Years of pain had aged her heavily across the forehead and she suddenly seemed very old and very tired. It was if she were aging right before Katie's eyes. Her white brows had thinned and caused her face to fade. The once strong and lovely looks blended in a blur of paleness. Only those piercing blue eyes stood the test of time. Eyes that had seen too much death and sorrow. Eyes that had cried too many tears. Eyes that had danced over the joys of God's creations. Today, they penetrated Katie's very being and held her captive.

"God gave you and me free will, a will to choose or not to choose. To see or fail to see. To trust or fail to trust. To rely on your own feelings or listen for God's still voice. Scott is angry, Katie. Something in his past has hurt him and caused some deep suffering. Without Christ, he is unable to heal and I have seen the results of those wounds. He is controlling and self-centered and-"

Katie interrupted stammering out, "You are so wrong, Dolly. Dammit, you are so very wrong. You don't know him and how can you pretend to from one incident? One screw up and he is not the man for me? What about forgiveness? Isn't that what all of you preach? And Catherine? Doesn't she have that stupid forgiveness statue or whatever it is on her mantle? Forgive and don't go fishing? I am so sick of all of this I could scream. You are making up the rules as you go along. Ok. Scott was an ass Thursday night. He was so excited that he had asked me to marry him, and you and Catherine act as if he has the plague. A bunch of Christian snobs. I cannot believe we are really having this conversation. You are wrong, Dolly, and I don't want Scott to come between us."

Well, the threat was there. Katie could not stuff it back in anymore than she could stop a rocket headed into space. The force of her words could not have had a greater impact. Dolly sat stunned and fully aware of Katie's intent. Scott and me or nothing at all. Dolly took Katie's hands into her own and gently squeezed them. Katie had drawn a line in the sand and Dolly refused to cross it. There would be no stalemate here as Dolly had too much to lose. She would embrace Scott to the best of her ability and intensify her prayers. There was simply nothing else for her to do.

"Please trust that I know what I'm doing. Support me and be happy for me. I'm sorry we had this fight, but I love you and I love Scott as well. He is my future, and I can't wait to share it with him." Kissing her devoted grandmother, Katie slid on her sandals and headed towards the beach to find Scott. Dolly sat rigidly on the love seat and wondered if her heavy heart could withstand the pain she knew was sure to come.

Picking up the coffee mugs, Dolly wiped off the table, folded the throw, and wondered how this weekend could have gone so badly. Unfortunately, she had to admit that she felt cheated and disappointed. She had always imagined Katie's husband and what he would be like. She had known that they would instantly bond and be close forever. She would be proud to show him off and gladly give Katie to him. Could these feelings be interfering with how she felt about Scott? Could you be too close and actually be wrong about Scott? Were her personal feelings in the way so that she couldn't hear God? Suddenly she felt as if she had made a terrible mess of everything.

She knew God had a plan for Katie's life and loved her more than Dolly and Catherine ever could. She also knew God had given Katie a free will and that knowledge would test her faith and perseverance in prayer for months to come.

We sail within a vast sphere, ever drifting in uncertainty, driven from end to end.

– Blaise Pascal

CHAPTER 12

The prenuptial times had been filled with elaborate affairs with Cat and Dolly in the lead roles of dual wedding planners. Katie gladly gave them free reign to plan to their hearts' content. Who better to make the wedding of your dreams than the two women who loved her most in the world? Money was no object, as Cat insisted on paying for everything. "I didn't have any children of my own, and Katie is going to have the finest celebration money can buy. What good does it do to be this wealthy and not be able to spend it on the ones you love?" Cat had made a statement of fact rather than an actual question that required a response. Dolly gave in, and the next six months whirred by in a flurry of parties, showers, brunches and luncheons. All of Somerville society laid down the red carpet and feted the bride and groom in high style. Everyone loved Scott and Katie and they became the couple of the season.

And if all was bliss, someone forgot to tell Katie. Everything was as a young woman could imagine, the bell of the ball, the beautiful bride to be, the center of attention. What more could she want? There was a nagging, no, a tugging somewhere in her subconscious that said something was amiss. Her mind tried to wrap itself around the intruder, to qualify it as nerves or stress, but nothing lessoned the awareness of it. It was not potent like a headache, or persistent like cramps, but it was just there, brooding like a cloud on a summer day that would not release its rain.

Katie dismissed the thought but it always returned. One day she tried to discuss it with Scott after a meal drenched in rich food and flowing wines. She should have known better. "Scott, do you ever wonder if we are making a mistake, you know what I mean, about getting married and all?"

By now, she had inched her way up under Scott's arm and was tracing his buttons as she always did when she was nervous. Scott felt annoyed. He was full and sleepy and did not want to get into a serious talk tonight. "Honey, the wedding is six weeks away and you ask me now if we are making a mistake? Are you kidding me?"

His words had a sharp tone to them that set Katie on edge. A sliver of fear entered her heart and she scolded herself for being foolish, for putting words to a childish idea. "I'm sure it's just bride blues, don't you think? Maybe I am just overwhelmed right now."

Scott sighed and wrapped his arms around Katie. He always felt like he had to protect her; he was the knight she had dreamed of, the one that she had told him about so many times. *How does a guy live up to that?* "Katie, it is just nerves, and all the guys said they felt scared like they were making a mistake. It is normal, natural; we are taking a big step. Let's go home and sleep on it. You'll feel better in the morning."

They drove home in an uncomfortable silence, which sent Katie's mind whirling in a thousand directions. She felt like she did as a kid when she stepped on a small sliver of glass. She could feel it when she walked but when she showed it to her dad he couldn't find it. Nevertheless, it was there. Sometimes she felt it and other times, when cushioned with a sock, it disappeared. Katie needed a sock.

The sock came in a form she did not expect. Scott brought her home and helped her into bed. He knew she had had too much to drink and was getting a little weepy. He was used to this, her rush to tears loosened by stress and a bit too much of the god's nectar.

"I'll lock myself out tonight, honey so you get a good night sleep. I have to work tomorrow – I know it's Saturday so don't make a big deal about it. I'll call you when I get home from the office." He leaned down to kiss her goodnight and she grabbed him giggling and refused to let him go. "Wanna play rough?" he asked in a teasing voice.

"No," she whispered. "I just don't want you to go home yet. Will you stay and tickle my back?"

The familiar burning was back. It was about as dormant as a simmering volcano, one he watched constantly. Since the last and only night they made love, he had been beyond careful not to get into a situation where he could not or would not stop. Scott pulled up Katie's soft cotton tee shirt and began to rub her back, slowly enjoying the sensation of her soft skin under his fingertips. "Tickle it, please." Katie murmured into her pillow. Scott ran his fingers alongside her rib cage and then gently over her side dipping lower with each swoop. "Scott, don't do that. You promised nothing would happen until I was ready."

Flipping her over Scott pulled her up to him a little rougher than he had planned. "I'm tired of you toying with me, Katie, and I'm no automaton that can be keyed off and on again on some whim." It had been too long and there had been too many temptations. He had had enough of waiting and wanting her. Cupping her face, he whispered, "I love you, dammit, I love you. Hear it in the wind and the ocean you love so much. I cannot show you any harder how much I am eaten up with you." Scott's words penetrated Katie's inner core and she felt happy. *Just happy,* she thought, *I just feel happy?* The sliver was still there, and it still hurt just a little.

This time Katie did not cry and fuss at Scott. She was the enticer and she knew it. She'd set him up and had given him an inescapable situation. What was wrong with her? Oh, the sweet feelings of loving Scott would stay for a day or two, but the conscience of Katie was still moral and had a gauge for right and wrong. Plain and simple, no matter what the world said, Katie still believed in saving herself for marriage. However, there was a rift between her physical and emotional desires, and the remnant of her faith that kept her on edge. She could not make Scott understand something that she was unable to grasp. Why all the confusion? Why did she allow herself to get into these situations? She knew better and that was just the point. She knew better and did it anyway. So what did that say about her? Katie hated that thought and purposely banished it from her mind.

"Happiness is not in our circumstance but in ourselves. It is not something we see, like a rainbow, or feel, like the heat of a fire. Happiness is something we are"

– John B. Sheerin

CHAPTER 13

K atie and Elizabeth met around ten at Belle Vie bridal shop to begin the process to find the perfect dress. Her taste was simple and elegant and she wanted nothing of frills and yards of tulle or lace. Although the fashion in gowns showed bared shoulders, Katie knew that style was not for her. Yet someone forgot to tell her where to look. All the bridal books and displays showed blushing brides in tightly fitted bodices, which pushed up the breasts until some, resembled a poster for a brothel worker. Others were tasteful and beautiful and the brides looked stunning. However, for Katie, Dolly, Catherine and the church, a more demure gown would best serve her needs.

Belle Vie was a charming shop decorated in a style reminiscent of the French county chateau Malmaison, purchased by Josephine while her husband, Napoleon, conquered Europe. Located about fourteen kilometers from Paris, the country house was run down and outrageously overpriced. Yet that didn't stop Josephine from buying it and producing a magnificent chateau that would be the envy of most of Europe.

Katie and Elizabeth entered the splendor of the shop. To the left a richly colored wall mural of Malmaison set the scene as soon as one entered the store. It was a depiction of the grounds filled with plants, roses, swans, sheep, llamas, gazelles and zebras. To the far left, a replica of Empress Josephine's boudoir separated the bridal lingerie from the wedding gowns. A bed dressed in deep red and cream colored fabrics trimmed in gold served as a presentation for the most beautiful lingerie any bride could ever have imagined. Divine camisoles, teddies, and peignoirs created from the finest silk charmeuse and georgette tempted the eye as well as the purse. A deeply inlaid writing desk held tres chic bridal favors surrounded by a large screen of painted Souvenir de la Malmasion roses, the favorite of the Empress Josephine. The atmosphere was most perfect for the soon to be bride.

After a flurry of silks, taffetas, organza, and brocade Katie found the perfect dress.

The beauty of Bella Vie was not just the wedding finery, but also a service unique to any other bridal shop. A wedding planner. As part of a brilliant vision of the two owners of the shop, several quite reputable planners had contracted with Bella Vie to provide the perfect plan, with all the details for their brides. It had been a huge success as the business was thriving. However, the key focus remained on the blushing bride and her wants and needs. As a secondary note, the wishes of princesses did not come cheaply.

Elizabeth and Katie moved to their next appointment, which was meeting with the planner, the second most important person in the wedding party. Although Katie had given in to Dolly that the wedding would be in Somerville, she still wanted to go through all motions brides were awarded. She had dreamed of a large Atlanta wedding, but somehow the pull towards family and from birth friends won over. Down a short hallway, painted and carpeted in the same Malmasion colors, the girls entered the offices of the wedding planners. A lovely young receptionist, who obviously missed her high school cheerleading days, bubbled up until the girls had to hide their amusement. She was so gung ho that she was comical.

"Good morning, lovely ladies. Now, which one of you is the lucky bride?" That such a simple question could annoy Katie was surprising enough, but what came next floored her. "Today you have an appointment with Laura Anne Stapleton. I will buzz her and let her know the bride has arrived. May I serve you coffee or tea while you wait?" The girls shook their hands and murmured a conjoined, "no thank you." Katie smiled at the ironies in the world.

Her perfume Announced her coming, bearing a name that caused Katie to laugh inwardly. Pure Poison. A Christian Dior fragrance advertised for a new generation of seductresses in a woodsy-amber, musky smell –heady stuff. Katie had tried it several times but the chemistry was not right on her. The name was oh so devilish. As it should have been, for down the hall glides a long legged beauty, heavy blonde tresses and a kilowatt smile, Laure Anne Stapleton in person.

The greeting was warm and friendly just about as warm and friendly as the amazing office space belonging to Laura Anne. The focal point of the space was a solid mahogany traditional style, serpentine writing desk that stood proudly on ball and claw legs. Matching "hair on hide" leather lodge chairs fenced in a magnificent George II antique mahogany piecrust table. The Karistan rug dyed in a scrumptious dark green was bordered by a pale beige stripe surrounding tiny dots of white and maroon. It was stunning. Rich straw colored curtains pulled it all together and formed one of the best looking rooms Katie had ever seen.

Elizabeth had not missed a veneer, inlay, or designer pillow around the room. "I hope she isn't expecting you to pay for her décor. Although beautiful, it's hardly what an office should be," she whispered.

"Au contraire, it's exactly what an office should be, especially an office where very expensive events are planned for the most wonderful day of a beautiful bride's life," Laura Anne hummed.

Elizabeth wished she had learned finger talking like Annie Sullivan had taught Helen Keller. She desperately wanted to spell out, *But what if the bride is ugly? Does she have to go to the office decorated in early poverty?*

Sitting behind the great mahogany desk, Laura Anne started getting the details of the wedding, beginning with the lucky groom. Before she started, Katie just had to know. "Laura Anne. Do you remember me from Tybee Island?" Laura Anne squinted her eyes like seeing through binoculars might help her remember. "I'm sorry, Katie, but I really don't. Where did we meet? I hope I don't have anything to be ashamed of."

"Your uncle, Monsignor Stapleton, was a good friend of my parents and my grandmother Dolly. You-"

"Oh my gosh! You're little Katie? I went to your parents' funeral and I tried to call you when you moved back to Atlanta. My uncle Johnny kept the family posted on how ya'll were doing. Oh my gosh. I had no idea that was you, and I never put the name with Tybee Island."

Laura Anne gushed. It was almost believable that she cared one bit about Katie's life or where she had been all these years. Yes, Laura Anne was beautiful, but something about her brought back memories of Snow White's stepmother as she transformed from the elegant queen to the deadly spirit dragon from hell.

"Laura Anne, you used to come to our beach house and spend weeks at a time with us. Don't you remember how you liked to boss us around? All the kids looked up to you because you were so much older."

"Easy now, Katie," Laura Anne smiled a placid, sardonic smile. "I was only three years older than you if I remember correctly. Dolly was always afraid you were a little too immature to be unwatched at the beach, so she would pay me to babysit. I must confess I'd would rather have been playing with my own friends than watching over that group of beach urchins who tagged along everywhere I went."

Elizabeth and Katie sat there astonished. Had Laura Anne had a miraculous memory boost? For someone who had no memory of Katie as a child, she certainly seethed a rather old resentment for Katie and the beach kids.

"Well, I guess you do remember our summers together. I bet you came to Tybee at least two summers. And I guess with me being twelve and you a worldly almost fifteen, it must have been quite embarrassing to 'baby sit' me."

"Funny thing how a memory works. Just something out of the blue will trigger it. Of course, I remember now. You were darling then, just as you are darling now. How is Dolly?"

"She's fine and thanks for asking. She is just so excited about this wedding and making sure it is everything I want. I guess I really am the princess for now. By the way, are you married, Laura Anne?"

Katie had just unexpectedly iced the cake. Laura Anne's pupils just suddenly slit, just like cat's eyes when adjusting to light. Not a stretch to guess she was not married and was not happy about that either.

"No, I'm not married yet. I'm waiting on that special someone to come sweep me off my feet. Atlanta holds such promise for eligible young men."

Elizabeth smirked out, "Funny you should mention that. I just read the other day, that Atlanta was a terrible place to meet a husband. Katie, didn't we read that Atlanta was the old maid capital of the world?"

Laura Anne pushed back from her designer chair and excused herself. She promised to bring fresh tea and cake when she returned. Her face had appeared a bit red in the cheeks. Too young for a hot flash, but something touched a raw nerve.

Before she was out the door good, Elizabeth started to laugh, not even being careful that someone might hear. "Katie, she is dreadful and what a fraud. She remembered you right away. Oh, who am I fooling? Do you actually believe she didn't know who you were before you walked in here? What is she up to? Why did she act as if she didn't know you?"

"Beats me. But she has a hidden agenda. I wonder how she will act when she's had a chance to compose herself."

As if on cue, Laura Anne returned carrying the promised tea and cakes on a beautiful silver butler's tray. A Waterford sugar bowl was filled with Splenda while another, it's twin, held sugar. The matching creamer was filled with the real thing. "We only drink cream around here. You may be used to the powered stuff, which I find dreadful, so I hope this works ok for you."

The tension was begging to be cut. "Katie, who is the lucky man who won your hand?"

Unable to help herself, Katie smiled a ridiculously wide smile and said, "Scott Stewart from right here in Atlanta."

"Oh no! Scottie Stewart! Did he go to Georgia, let's see graduating two years ahead of me?"

Now Laura Anne was about three years older than Katie was so that would make Scott five years older and the man she was thinking about.

"Yes, that's my Scott. How in the world do you know him?"

"Scottie was the big man on a very large campus, probably I should say in the Greek sector of school. He was a KA and an all around great guy. The girls were wild over him, such a looker, but the guys all liked him as well. Scottie just seemed more mature than the other guys did, and it was appealing. He helped a lot of people with tutoring, and being a designated driver. He was always about helping the underdog."

"Thanks for the nice words. How well did you know Scott?" Katie emphasized the Scott without the "ie" on the end.

"Scott was engaged to my sorority sister and best friend Erika Couch. So we did everything together. He was such a catch that if she hadn't wanted him, I would have."

Katie could feel her palms sweating. She had not had a panic attack in quite some time, but suddenly all the old fears and emotions were bubbling to the surface. Brewing and threatening to force her to escape. "I don't remember how long they were together; how long was it?"

"Honey, it wasn't just together, they were engaged to be married just like you and he are now. Didn't Scott ever tell you about Erika?"

Laura Anne had a glimmer in her eye and a smirk on her face just like she'd eavesdropped on a dirty little secret. "Oh my! He didn't tell you, did he? Well, some men are just like that, wanting to keep secrets about their past love lives. It really doesn't matter because you have him, he has you, and you're going to be married. Now, let's look at some places to have the reception, and then we'll book the church."

Over the next two hours, the three girls dove headlong into the fantasy world of brides. That place where so many women from so many socio economic backgrounds, suddenly possessed a superior sense of entitlement and money was no object regardless of the state of the budget or the supporting bank accounts. It was the wedding planner's job, with her connections, to make the bride feel as special and as beautiful as possible. Katie found herself strangely affected by all of this. It was not the money or even the extravagances of the wedding, but somehow the spiritual side of marriage, the part that mattered most, was completely missing. Of course, the music in the church could be considered spiritual, in some strange stretch, but the focus for all of this was all wrong to Katie. Even though she was not going to church and was not exactly a practicing Catholic, she had the interior knowledge that if God was not the center of the marriage, and if He was not the head of the household, then there was no spiritual umbrella of protection. Katie fully understood that Laura Anne's job was not to convert people to Christianity, but something was just not right. She did not care a thing about the bride being the star, or the bridesmaids being beautifully dressed, but in no way upstaging the bride. She just wanted a lovely wedding where everyone came and had a great time. It was not the coronation of a queen.

Just as soon as Elizabeth and Katie jumped into the car, put on the seat belts and peeled away, Katie was digging in her purse for her cell phone. "Wait a minute, Katie. Take a deep breath and think about what you're going to say to Scott. Are you sure this is a cell phone conversation you want to have? Maybe this is a person to person, face to face kind of call."

Hitting seven, her speed dial to Scott, and speakerphone, Katie rapped her newly painted nails on the steering wheel. On the second ring, Scott picked up. "Hello, sweetheart, what a great surprise. What's up?"

"Do you remember a girl from school named Laura Anne Stapleton?" Katie waited for his response, which was entirely too long in coming.

"Yeah. We were in the same crowd of kids at school. Great girl. Why do you ask?"

"Great girl just informed me that you have been engaged before. I know that it's true because you were engaged to her best friend Erika Couch. Sound familiar?"

"Honey, now calm down. We weren't really engaged. We had been dating for several months and she was always talking about a promise ring, being pinned, and what type of ring she wanted. I swear I never asked her to marry me. We went home to go skiing at her family's lake house and when I got there, the whole damn family was there; cousins, you name it – all of her kin."

"So? Scott, this just sounds so rehearsed as if you're reading it from a book. How could everyone think you were getting engaged but YOU?"

"Listen to me, Katie. The family was creepy. They just kept grinning as if they knew something I didn't know. By late Sunday afternoon, I got the picture. Erika was graduating with a teaching degree for the youngest kids. She hated it and didn't want to teach, much less work. So she'd planned to hook a husband so she could hang with all her rich friends and be a woman of leisure. When we got back to school, she just started telling everyone we were engaged. There were two weeks of school left and I figured what the hell did it matter if she said that or not. I called her after school was out and I was back in Atlanta, and told her we were through."

"Scott, if you're lying to me I swear I'll never believe a word you say again."

Elizabeth slunk down in the chair and made a face at Katie that mocked Hattie McDowell in *Gone with the Wind* when she heard Miss Scarlett telling the biggest of lies. *How could she believe that trite answer? It is too perfect; too slick to be true. Just plain too rehearsed.*

"It's been a long day, Scott- oh I mean Scottie- and I'm tired. We'll talk about this later when you come for dinner. I've gotta go or we'll be stuck in horrendous traffic." And with that, she disconnected the phone and sat starring at Elizabeth. "You don't believe a word of his story, do you?"

"You know, I want to believe it, and it would make my life so much easier if the truth were that simple."

"Elizabeth, what reason does Scott have to lie about this? Yes, I am furious that he was supposedly engaged before, but that was a long time ago. I am not jealous of his old girlfriends. I just want to believe what he says. It does make sense because we've both known girls like that at school."

Elizabeth just took it all in and tried to figure out what Katie wanted her to say. "Look. I don't know if he was engaged or not. And, I know you're kidding about 'why would he lie to me?' I mean, if there's a chance to lie and get away with it, I think you've found the perfect opportunity. If he's being less than truthful, then he's a liar and you need to rethink this relationship. I told you when ya'll first met that he was a player."

"I knew you were going to throw that in my face. I never denied Scott was a player. But that doesn't mean he was engaged before. Let's just leave it alone now, Elizabeth."

"Gotta have the last word. I did nothing here. You asked me what I thought, and I told you I am suspicious, but I really have no idea. Let's see who's pressing the issue right now, and it sure isn't me. And I didn't throw anything! Done. Last word."

Elizabeth took a deep breath and started again. "And don't put that stupid hand up in my face like I'm going to shush. I'm not. Why are you sending me Scott's mail? If you're ticked off with him, then tell him. Don't take it out on me. If you think he's lying, then confront it. Good grief, call that girl he was engaged to."

"Supposed to have been engaged to. It was all in her mind, remember?"

"Ok, then she's going to tell you yes, they were engaged. So that was a crummy idea. Regardless, stop taking it out on me. It's not my fault you don't trust Scott."

"Who said I didn't trust Scott? I never said that. What are you implying?"

"Implying? Nothing. I'm coming out, and saying it. You are afraid that that Laurie girl was telling you the truth, and Scott twisted his version so you wouldn't get mad. That's what I'm saying, and I am not implying anything."

"Well, you're wrong. I'm just sure of it and..."

"If you are so sure he wasn't engaged, then what are so furious about? And put down that stupid hand of yours. Get it out of my face."

A dreadful silence then followed them towards Elizabeth's house. Every time Elizabeth tried to talk, Katie shushed her using her hand like a school crossing guard stopping traffic. She wouldn't let her say a word. Finally, they drove up Elizabeth's driveway and Katie mumbled something about a good day. Elizabeth just sat staring at Katie. "I did have a wonderful time today, and I'm sorry we ever saw Laura Anne Staple whatever her name is. Let's deal with all of this later. Now, if you don't mind, please take me back to Belle Vie 'cause my car's parked at the shop. Remember, we agreed to meet there today."

Both girls began to laugh hysterically. Tears rolled down their cheeks as they choked on their laughter. Katie popped in an oldies CD, and they sang at the top of their lungs to the Isley Brothers hit "This Old Heart of Mine." They didn't get all of the words right, but right enough to know that Katie's arms would always be open to taking the ol' boy back, no matter how bad he had been.

The next morning Katie left a message with the cheerleader at the wedding planners. "Please tell Laura Anne how much I enjoyed our time together. But Scott and I decided to have the wedding in Somerville. Tell Laura Anne thanks for the great ideas. Thanks so much. Good bye."

Katie was embarrassed at how good she felt inside. She told the truth, and she could close the door on all the foolishness about old girlfriends. Engaged? What a joke!

CHAPTER 14

T he morning of the wedding came plenty early that day. Katie woke with the reminder that she had slept for a mere three or four hours. The rehearsal dinner had run over and the party afterwards dragged on for an eternity. As odd as it seemed, Katie wanted some time alone with Dolly. She needed time to rest in her presence and hold her. She even longed for her prayers and blessings. She had not wanted to be out partying all night. Now the bride's brunch for all out of town guests was to start in just under two hours. So the rush was on again.

One hundred and fifty family members, friends and out of town guests filled Breckenridge House. It was a beautiful French colonial Creole plantation home sitting high on a bluff overlooking the Intracoastal Waterway. From the ground up brick pillars supported the wide galleries that wound around the home. French doors painted in a high gloss black beckoned guests inwards. The loggia surrounding the back of the home provided the most magnificent view. During the day or night, mighty ships and boats crisscrossed the waterways producing a show of their own. The setting for a party was just perfect.

Katie had recovered from her lack of sleep and was a breath of fresh air. She had chosen a sapphire sundress with a camisole bodice that made her look even smaller than she was. The dress was explosive in color and movement as only a fine silk can do. A pair of black strappy sandals made the perfect statement.

Standing next to Scott in his white linen blazer, pink pinstriped shirt and navy pants, Katie could hardly catch her breath at the excitement she was finally feeling. Scott pulled her close and kissed her passionately, a deep kiss that was more of promise of commitment than desire. If only girls could purr, Katie would have begun in earnest.

As they moved along their guests, Dolly and Catherine hurried up to them and embraced them both. "You two look like a couple waiting for their Town and Country shoot. How handsome you look, Scott. And Katie, you are beyond lovely."

The girls pulled them out onto the upstairs loggia and back to a table partitioned off just for them. Champagne cocktails were chilled and waiting for the family toast to come. Sitting down Scott and Katie found a package for each of them at their seats.

"Hey, what's this? I love a good surprise." Scott picked up his package and tried to shake it, but the insides did not move.

Katie reached for hers and found the same, soundless shake. What in the world was in there?

"Cat and I have spent a great deal of time figuring out a gift we could give the two of you. No one is starving or in need of anything financial, so we thought about what would be the perfect gift for a newlywed couple that has everything already. And so we decided on these. Go ahead. We don't have all day since you are getting married tonight. Open them."

Katie and Scott tore into their presents like little kids on Christmas morning. Scott opened his first and found a Bible. He was unsure how to respond, but knew he had to think carefully before he spoke.

"Open it up to the inside cover. Katie. Open to your inside as well." Dolly and Cat sat back in their chairs and waited. Katie continued to read the rest of the inscription, the same in both Bibles.

Our Dearest Scott and Katie,

There is little if anything that is more difficult or more rewarding than marriage. The storms that wash over you, and they will surely come, can never be used as an excuse for drawing apart; rather let them be the perfect reason for coming closer together.

We ask that you keep three very important things foremost in your marriage, which was blessed by God, promised before Jesus and man, and binds you eternally.

These three things are:

1. The book of Ruth, a story of loyalty, love, understanding, and kindness. Read it often and read it together. From this, you should find that understanding one another is a foundational strength for your marriage. And may you know, believe, and understand always this truth: "Where you go I will go, and where you stay I will stay. Your people will be my people and your God my God. Where you die I will die, and there I will be buried. May the Lord deal with me, be it ever so severely, if anything but death separates you and me" (Ruth 1:16-17).

2. Before God, you are no longer Katie and Scott. Memorize this scripture and brand it to your heart: "So they are no longer two, but one. Therefore what God has joined together, let man not separate." Matthew 19:6.

3. Finally, the message that JB brought to all of us, the promise of forgiveness, after true repentance, and the admonishment that what God has forgiven, no man can hold it against you. "He will cast all our sins into the depths of the sea." Micah 7:10.

When the arguments and squabbles come; when you wonder why you ever married in the first place; when you are tempted to bring old hurts and sins back from the past, that which has already been forgiven, don't. No fishing allowed.

We love you both so very much. Go forth and fill up the beach house with loads of babies. We are praying for twins to get us started.

Catherine and Dolly

Finally, Catherine pulled out a large box wrapped in gorgeous textured white on white paper with silver ribbons. Katie turned back the paper and sought the gift inside. With a gasp, she pulled out JB's Baccarat crystal vase engraved with "He will cast all our sins into the depths of the sea." Micah 7:10. "No fishing allowed." This had been in the family for years and Katie was stunned to hold it in her hands. This was not some talisman that promised good luck, or produced evil spells. This was the tangible proof that God forgives and man cannot undo what God has done.

"Catherine, we can't accept this. I know how much this means to you, and I just can't take this."

"JB would have wanted you to have it. Two young lovers, starting out in life as one, need a tangible reminder that forgiveness is the thread that binds them together. Please include the footnote, no fishing allowed, whenever you and Scott have a difference of opinion. It guided JB and me through many a disagreement over our time together."

Scott had no idea what Catherine was talking about or why Katie was so touched. The piece was a beautiful cut glass design, quite heavy, and quite impressive. But he didn't get the point of the gift. Noticing his confusion Katie whispered, "It's a long story, and I'll share it with you later. Trust me that this is the most precious thing Catherine owns."

CHAPTER 15

———————∼———————

K atie was beyond measure the most beautiful bride anyone had ever seen. Noting that most brides are lovely, dressed in all their finery, Katie had a magical air about her. Her gown was exquisite and fit her beautifully as it sat cinched at the waist. It was an ivory silk satin gown with slightly capped sleeves and a lovely shaped open neckline. Beads adorned the bodice, which hugged her body perfectly. A pleated satin skirt, classic ball gown silhouette, was embellished with rhinestones, crystals, and pearls. A cathedral train completed the look. The gown was simply elegant, and Katie was the consummate beautiful bride.

The church was packed with Scott's guests on the right and Katie's on the left. Scott had a nice crowd, but Katie's guests were slipping over to the other side in order to get a seat. The cathedral, one of the most beautiful in the southeast, was splendid enough without the addition of flowers and ribbons. It stood proud and dutifully honored the Lord inviting all inside to do the same in all its grandeur.

As Katie stood at the entrance to the church, she smiled at the crowd of family and friends who had come to watch her and Scott marry. It was so important to her that her loved ones were there with her. Somehow, it made it a little less painful that her parents wouldn't be there. Maybe in spirit, but not in person. Katie also felt a little sad for Scott. He never really mentioned his parents only that they had passed away several years ago. There were no relatives on his side, and she found that particularly disturbing. Poor Scott. She was all he had in the world.

Katie's dress behaved in the most appropriate fashion. It moved as if following the orders from the head dressmaker, which was to make Katie appear as a princess. Not a queen mind you, she was far too young for that, but there was something otherworldly about her that day, the beauty, the elegance, the simplicity of her love and devotion to Scott. She had not a care about any of the trappings, who was there and who couldn't attend; she cared not a bit about the reception or what people thought. She and the girls were planning a party to celebrate the life to come of Katie and Scott in the eyes of God. It was as it should be, as Katie knew enough to be afraid not to have God on her side.

Dolly had insisted on a nuptial mass and Katie had consented. For a brief moment she worried that it might be too long and that non-Catholics might feel uncomfortable or left out especially during the Eucharist. That thought passed as quickly as it came. For some reason, the mass had become important to Katie and that she did not understand. However, she did understand, on a secular level, that it was terribly foolish to have a twenty-minute ceremony while wearing an eight thousand dollar dress.

Ever so softly, the music began. Katie's wish for the church to be awash in soft lights was granted and the mood was set. A dear friend of Dolly's and Duncan's stood in the choir loft and began singing "Ave Maria" acappella in a clear and beautiful baritone. The guests grew still and quiet allowing the music to wash over them and penetrate their very being.

The bridesmaids processed down the aisle to a violin solo of Canon in D by Johannes Pachelbel. It was exquisitely beautiful and filled the air with excitement and anticipation. Elizabeth Hemming was lovely and glowed with the knowledge that her next trip down the aisle would be at her own wedding. She had been such a wonderful friend to Katie, remembering all the things Katie had so easily forgotten. She felt blessed to count her as her very best friend.

Finally, it was Katie's turn. The church lights were dimmed a bit more and all the candles flickered a holy looking light around the church. The trumpet duet began playing "Trumpet Voluntary" and the guests turned to watch the lovely bride slowly come down the aisle. Two handsome men, dressed in tails, held her on either arm and beamed as the three processed down towards Scott. Both men had a struggle blinking back their tears, not at just the honor and utter delight of walking Katie to her husband, but at the love in the church that night. Ed Burns looked around the congregation and counted himself as one of the luckiest men alive to live in Somerville and serve these fine people. Mr. Sarge indeed counted his blessings the day he first met his Katie. Today, he was honored with giving her away and cementing their lives together forever. It was an emotional experience that he was having a tough time handling.

As the three reached the altar, Scott stepped down to take his bride. He just could not believe how gorgeous she was, something magical out of a fairy tale book. He didn't care what anyone else thought, he knew in his heart that he alone was the most blessed man in this church, and probably anywhere else in the world. He was marrying the girl of his dreams, the girl who would forever change his life.

Katie and Scott had decided, as they were both pretty easy weepers, that they would follow the traditional wedding vows and not try to come up with their own. They both agreed that their personally written vows would be both sappy and melodramatic to the point of nausea. Staying clear-eyed during the standard vows would take super human strength from both of them. Once Scott passed the entrance test, watching his ethereally beautiful bride walking towards him, he found he could rest and start breathing again.

Katie, on the other hand, passed her test of kissing goodbye Dr. Burns and Mr. Sarge. She could not have asked for two better substitutes for her father. She felt he was most pleased. However, the true test, their Waterloo, would be the recessional. Mendelssohn's "Wedding March" played by cello, violin, and flute got them every time. They had practiced listening to it several times before the wedding, but Katie wasn't sure she'd survive it. The time came and the married coupled descended the altar steps, paused briefly and felt the chills brought on by the music. They were officially married, blessed by God, and loved by family and friends. They fairly bounced up the aisle smiling and waving to their guests. It was a fabulous sight and more than a few were dabbing at weepy eyes. Except the bride and groom. No tears and only intense and abiding love. What a joyous occasion.

Several days later while honeymooning in the Turks and Caicos Islands in the Caribbean, Katie found herself in the midst of paradise. Scott had planned the entire honeymoon and brought them to the Parrot Cay Hotel. It had taken Katie a while to come down out of the rat race of the wedding, gifts, and quests. Getting everything back to Atlanta and arguing with Scott over why she couldn't put away their gifts, had left Katie quite unsettled. But today, she appreciated the absolute beauty of this island.

The newlyweds spent their days scuba diving, snorkeling, and horseback riding. However, when it came to the more ambitious sports, Katie found herself on the beach with a good book while Scott tried kite surfing and some dangerous reef diving. Together they tried learning to maneuver a Caicos sloop. As with so many things, Scott easily mastered each new adventure he tried.

On the last day of their honeymoon, Katie suddenly remembered what she'd wanted to ask Scott. So over breakfast, and one last cup of coffee, Katie offered Scott her last bite of French toast while she ate the last paw paw. "You know who I was so surprised to see at the wedding?" Katie asked as she leaned over to kiss Scott.

"No, who would that be, other than the hundred plus people neither one of us knew?"

"Honey, I knew most of the people there. Many were old family friends of Dolly's and my parents. Did you feel like there were lots of people you didn't know?"

"Katie. Land the plane. Get to the point. I don't need a post-wedding pep talk. Who did you see for God's sake?"

"Sheesh. Aren't you a crab this morning? Anyway, I saw Laura Anne Stapleton, and I'm positive her name wasn't on the guest list. She had some friend with her, but I can't remember her name. Did you see her?"

"I did and her friend's name was Erika Couch, the girl who said she was engaged to me. I talked to them for a while."

"What were they doing there? Did they just crash our wedding party? Oh, that's so annoying."

"Katie, it's not annoying one bit. What difference does it make anyway? If you remember, Laura Anne's uncle is Monsignor Stapleton and he is best friends with Dolly. He probably just asked her to go with him. Not that it matters one bit."

Katie pondered, truly pondered over what Scott said. It was so evident in her next question. "Did you think Erika Couch is as pretty as she was in college when you weren't engaged to her? Did she flirt with you?"

Scott pushed up from the table, stretched, and arched his back. "I'm going for one last swim before we have to check out. Wanna come with me? We can do a little skinny dippin'."

Katie pulled her hair up into a ponytail and cinched her belt around her terry robe. "No. I believe I will take a luxurious bath and then work on packing. It takes me so much longer than it takes you."

Scott came over and slipped his arms under her neatly tied bow. He started to kiss her neck and then take little nibbles on her ears. "I can come take a bath with you and then get in the way while you try to pack. Sound interesting? Any takers?"

Katie laughed and threw her arms around this handsome, tan man, who just happened to be her husband and her one true love. "No, you go on and play or we'll never check out of here. I'll see you later. Love you."

"Love you, too. "

Halfway back to the room located on the bottom floor, right at beach level, Katie shouted. "Hey, Slick. You didn't answer my question. Is she prettier or uglier?"

Scott was no fool and he knew of only one way to answer that question. "Honey, she hasn't aged well and is not nearly as pretty as she used to be. But either way, she'll never be as pretty as you are." Scott increased his pace and started scampering as if he was on hot coals.

"You won't get off that easy. Go swim, but the Inquisition has just begun." Katie laughed at her wise man and shuttled off to the overwhelming task of getting them packed, checked out, and on time for the flight home. Home. Mr. and Mrs. Scott Stewart. It sounded so wonderful. She walked by the desk and saw the hotel stationary sitting to the right. She plopped down and wrote Mr. and Mrs. Scott Stewart over and over and over again. She loved the way it looked holding a sort of importance in the name. She believed she would never grow tired of writing it. That is until she realized she had over two hundred thank you notes to write when she returned home. Ah, so much for the little joys of life.

The plan had been to stay in Scott's house for several months until the newlyweds could pick out a new home. The lease was up on Katie's house and boxes were now stacked sky high in Scott's house. The term he referred to constantly. My house. Let's go back to my house. Katie couldn't wait to find a new home that was theirs.

Two days after flying in from their honeymoon, Scott made a big deal about missing Mass that morning. It seems something very important had come up, and he had to leave on a quick errand. "I'll just take my car and meet you at church," Katie offered.

"No, that won't work. Just wait here for me, and I'll be back in about fifteen minutes." Scott noticed the frown on her face and begged, "Please don't ruin the surprise. Can you just trust me on this one? Baby, it's going to be the surprise of a life time."

Driving into a tony neighborhood always thrilled Katie. She had been raised quite comfortably, and was often lavished like royalty by Catherine, but she loved looking at the fine architecture and the gardens of these beautiful homes. As usual Scott was instructed to drive very slowly, turtle speed, so Katie wouldn't miss a thing. She often pulled on Scott's sleeve to get him to roll to a stop so she could wave to strangers and comment on their lovely homes. It tickled Scott to see her like that, and he couldn't wait to share his surprise with her.

Turning into the long, winding, climbing driveway, Katie whistled at the beauty of the home perched atop this grand hill. The house sat on a one-acre lot offering loads of space between neighbors. It was a hard coat stucco two-story abode painted in the warmest mocha. Stacked stone offered a pleasant textured contrast to the small white columns that held up the front porch. The yard was professionally landscaped and not a blade of grass dared to step out of line.

Inside was even more breathtaking. Five bedrooms, three fireplaces, and five full baths made this home a true showcase. However, the backyard cinched the deal. A finished terrace, complete with outdoor kitchen and bar, over looked a large lake complete with honking geese. Katie fell in love with the entire home immediately.

"Honey, this is the greatest house I've ever seen. When we can afford it, I'd like to use these plans and build a smaller version of this for us. I just love this house. I'm curious. How much is it?"

"The new owner doesn't want the plans sold to anyone else. And the cost is affordable, around 800,000. But, the house has already been bought and the people move in next week."

Katie reached up and hugged the man she adored. He was so patient to drive around and look at homes with her. She doubted most men would give up a Sunday to spend it climbing in and out of homes, especially these pricey ones that were way out of their league. Turning to leave, Scott called to her.

"Katie, wait a minute. I forgot to look in the garage and I'm curious about their tank-less water heater. Be right back."

"Tank-less water heater? Are you kidding me? Can you see a tank-less water heater?"

Scott walked back in to the kitchen carrying a box with the top half off. He put the box down and out popped the most adorable yellow lab Katie had ever seen. The puppy came right into her arms, licked her face, and fell fast asleep.

"Where did you find this puppy? Oh Scott, he is adorable. Whose is it?"

"It's yours, goofy. I bought him as our first house warming present."

"What are you talking about…oh no you didn't. Scott, you bought this house? This is our house? This giant thing is ours? When did you do this? Oh, we can't afford this. Scott you are crazy." Katie was off and bubbling. When she got excited or even very angry she sounded like a champagne bottle spewing its treasure. No one could ask as many questions as Katie Stewart and Scott felt consumed by his love for her. He would literally devour her if it would not mean the loss of her forever. A thought he could not bear.

He picked her up, puppy and all and swung her gently around her new house. She had reacted just as he had envisioned, and he was completely satisfied. Katie was at a loss for words, which was a unique situation in and of itself.

"Scott, five bedrooms? Can we fill them all with little Scott's and Katie's?"

"We can talk later about making babies and filling bedrooms. Right now, we've got a puppy to raise. By the way, his name is Beauregard and we can call him Beau."

"It's a perfect name, and a perfect puppy, and a perfect house, and a perfect husband. I love you so much and thanks for making me so terribly happy."

Feat accomplished. Scott puffed up like an air balloon. He would give her the moon if he could. Happiness felt great and he planned to keep these feelings for a very long time.

Soaking in the tub that night gave Katie a chance to think about all that had transpired that day. Yes, she loved the house and could decorate each and every room. And if she was stuck, she knew two really talented girls living on Tybee Island who had exquisite taste. She didn't care about the house being a showcase; she just wanted it to be warm and inviting. A place to raise lots of babies, where friends and family would always be welcome. And dogs as well.

However, a small warning flag was blowing in the wind, right beside logic and reason. It didn't demand much attention, but it wanted to be noticed. A thread of thought moved through Katie's mind as she soaked, just little things, really: *Scott bought the house without me; Scott bought the dog without me; I didn't even get to choose the name. Scott wouldn't let me keep working.* Little things.

Suddenly the door pushed open and a fat, wobbly puppy nosed up on the side of the tub whimpering his way into her arms. Katie knew then he was destined as a Hollywood heartthrob for no living thing could possibly worm its way into your heart this quickly. Nothing seemed to matter anymore. Not when you were holding this little thing.

As time passed, little things accumulate in the large piles of things. A duster can scatter little things for only so long. A little thing can hide behind a bigger thing, only so long as it stays smaller. Little things have a penchant for growing into very large and unmanageable things; things that refused to remain little things gather all the other little things and make something big and onerous.

Scott was an old school husband and had determined early on that he would be in charge of the finances. He had so many investments in and out of his CPA practice that he knew Katie would not be able to follow or understand. A checking account with a standard monthly balance would keep Katie happy and occupied. She would have plenty to spend.

However, one thing bothered Katie: how did they afford a house at just under a million dollars? Scott was doing very well and his practice was growing exponentially. He had just added a few more accountants and had promoted several more. A new man came in as a managing partner. Yet, that didn't explain the new club membership, with initiation fees of 75,000, the new cars they had looked at, or the vacations he had talked about for Christmas. The house though, that's what bothered her the most. The other big tickets could somehow be written off as business practices, Scott was a genius at anything tax related, but the house was just too much too soon. Now, sounding way too much like Scarlett O'Hara, she decided to think about that later and enjoy her new everything that had just come her way. She turned on the hot water, refilled the tub, put Beau on the floor, and luxuriated in mounds and piles of bubbles.

Yet, if Scott was busier and busier, always at a meeting, out with new clients, playing golf, an endlessly full calendar, Katie was growing restless after six months in the house. She was quite busy with all the household duties and interior designing, but she was getting bored with all of that. Katie loved being with people, and with her anxiety under control, she felt more confident than ever before. She had lost some contact with her teacher friends, as their worlds were completely different now. Although they got together occasionally, Katie missed the rigors of teaching, the relationship with colleagues and of course the kids. There was always tennis, as Scott so frequently suggested, but she wasn't so sure that held her interest anymore. Katie had played on her high school tennis team, but she seemed to have lost that competitive spirit.

Right now Katie needed something to do, something that made her feel as if she had some value. She had a very spoiled husband who expected things to be a certain way and she was willing to make it just right for him. But really, he could hire someone to meet all of those needs, except for those wonderful intimate needs that still rocked Katie and Scott's world. They had the perfect chemistry, a blend by the master alchemist, and they felt most blessed. And it wasn't a one-way street. Both of them loved their times together, skinny dippin' in the lake late at night, watching old movies with a bowl of popcorn until the wee hours of the morning, long sessions in the steam shower, and marathon rounds of back tickling. Each touch from the other was so deeply personal, Scott's morning exit was often quite difficult and time delayed. That part of their marriage was something you write about in a book.

From all outward appearances, Katie and Scott had it all. Yet, there were things that caused Katie to chafe around the edges. Scott possessed some obscure notion of women and the work force. He had made it perfectly clear that no wife of his worked outside of the home. To Scott, that directive meant he was to leave each morning after a warming breakfast and return home each day to a house prepared for an *Architectural Digest* cover. Dinner would be nearly ready on a dining table dressed and waiting for something gourmet and as far from gourmand as possible. This all established in an atmosphere befitting a king, with a beautifully groomed wife eager to receive her husband. It was a childish thought symbolic of fairy tales.

To Katie, the directive meant control. Complete and utter control. Katie wanted to work and she had loved her teaching job. She had completed her master's degree in middle school education and was enjoying bringing home a nice paycheck. Compared to Scott's it was not significant, but it was Katie's and she was proud of what she did and what she earned. Scott called it chump change. He hadn't meant to be cruel, Scott would never hurt Katie that way, and he just didn't realize that his words and actions could have devastating effects. It would be a lesson he would have to learn the hard way, 'cause if Scott had a real fault, he had this one in magnified proportions.

Each morning took on a familiar pattern; waiting on Scott's every beck and call. It ranged from the sublime to the ridiculous. The ritual was mechanical and sequential. Alarms rang at 5:30 each morning insisting Scott wake and greet the world, which he did loudly and with no regard to others who might prefer sleeping a bit later than Scott might. As soon as Scott's feet hit the ground, the preprogrammed coffee maker began its task, the steam shower's temperature rose to a comfortable 123 degrees, and the mirrors all fogged nicely. And as if in some slapstick comedy, Scott dropped his boxers to the floor, stepped out of them, flexed a few times in front of the ceiling to floor mirror, and finally entered the steam. His morning music filled the bathroom and he smiled as he entered paradise. He knew when he was finished

Katie would have warmed towels and breakfast waiting for him. He had a beautiful wife who adored him, a great house, successful business that grew daily, a cool dog, and, well, life was just grand. A man could not ask for more.

"The most authentic thing about us is our capacity to create, to overcome, to endure, to transform, to love and to be greater than our suffering."

– Ben Okri

CHAPTER 16

———————⌇———————

I t had now been about five weeks since Katie missed her period. She had imagined all kinds of symptoms to confirm her pregnancy. Her breasts were sore and she felt more fatigue than normal. Maybe even a little more emotional, teary eyed over inconsequential things, nothing new there, but a little bit of excitement had begun to whirl up inside her. Could this be what pregnant women feel? She put her flat palm across her belly, right where she thought the baby would be, and whispered a welcome to him. "Hello, sweet baby. I'm so glad you are here. Your daddy is going to be awfully surprised and just as excited as I am. Soon we will share our little secret."

Tonight's dinner would be something extra special. Katie was delighted to be pregnant without any morning sickness, finicky cravings, or changes in the foods she loved. So tonight would be shrimp Newberg, one of Scott's favorite meals. He liked a load of shrimp and baby green peas, sweet like LeSeurs, with a nice salad and a pile of rice. He always ate the meal as if he had been starving. The pies de résistance would be the small present wrapped in angel paper that would help Katie tell Scott that a baby was on the way. She hadn't told Dolly or Cat, but had wanted to tonight right after she told the daddy to be. A three-way call would put them all on the phone together so no one missed any of the details. Katie was beside herself with joy. Scott had been working so late into the night and keeping long weekends at the office that Katie hoped the baby would bring him home more often. Certainly, Beau had failed in that regard.

The table was set, the candles were lit, Beau was in his crate, and Scott sat down to dinner. He gushed in all the right places and they both enjoyed this fantastic meal. Although Katie ate far less than usual, she managed to eat a ridge around her plate. She refused the wine that Scott offered. "What's the matter with you? Aren't you having wine with dinner? Come on, have a glass."

Putting her hand over the goblet, Katie smiled "Scott, I have a little present for you."

"A present for me? What's the occasion? It's not my birthday, and I can't think of another reason I'd get a gift…unless you just love me that much." Then he smiled his most adorable smile and offered Katie a place on his lap. "Now, tell me what I've done to get a gift."

"It's really from two people." Katie watched him as he opened the gift looking for any clue that he might have suspected already. Scott tore open the box and found a sterling silver baby rattle with a blue and pink ribbon tied around the middle.

"What is this?"

"It's a rattle from me and the baby. Scott, we're pregnant." Katie was aglow with eager anticipation. She had rehearsed this scene a hundred times that day. She and Scott were going to have a baby, and she had a hard time containing herself.

Scott look positively stunned, not at all the reaction that Katie had expected. His face grew cloudy and looked like he was about to blow.

"You're pregnant? You're sure? Cause if you're pregnant then you've been having an affair with someone, cause it sure as hell ain't mine."

Katie didn't know if Scott was kidding, in some sort of sick way, but his response stunned her. "Scott, what are you talking about? Of course, this baby's yours. What is the matter with you? Why are you acting this way?"

Draining another full glass of wine, Scott stared at Katie with an evil glare that smacked of a Charles Manson look alike. He very matter of factly put the glass down and pushed back away from the table. For a moment more, he just stared at her. Putting his hands on his knees, he leaned forward in a most threatening manner. "There's no way that baby is mine. So who have you been sleeping with? When is the baby due? What's the man's name, Katie?" Then shouting until the veins in his neck turned purple with rage he spit out, "You tramp! Who the hell have you been sleeping with? I can't believe I'm married to an adulterer."

Katie felt as if a train had run over her, dragged her down the track, reversed and smashed her one more time. The room began to feel surreal and she found it hard to breathe. Sitting back down in the chair, she grabbed the rattle and held it to her chest. Raising her voice, Katie screamed back, "I don't know what's the matter with you, but this is insane. Who would I be sleeping with? I just don't understand your reaction. I thought you'd be happy not call me an adulterer. Scott, it's our baby!"

Scott poured another glass of wine and swigged it down in two gulps. He leaned over the table and said with a snarl, "Read my lips, liar. It ain't my baby. It ain't our baby. It might be yours, but it's yours and someone else's."

If he had spit in her face, Katie could not have felt more repulsed. She wanted to slap his face, make him reasonable again, and bring back her Scott. She had no idea who this man was sitting in front of her. "Scott, stop doing this! I feel like I'm losing my mind!" Katie picked up the wine glass and threw it at Scott hitting him on his shoulder. He spun around in furry and raised a clinched fist to her face. Something invisible pulled it back, and he fell into his chair.

At this point Katie began to cry. Beau was quite nervous about the raised voices and anger in the room. Nudging the unlocked door of his crate, he crawled commando style and landed between Katie's feet. She reached down to reassure him while Scott dropped the last bomb.

"I know it's not my baby, Katie, 'cause I can't have kids. So, obviously you have been fooling around while I've been working. I've been killing myself staying on top of this house payment and trying to grow my business, while you've been off doing God knows what with God knows who!"

"You can't have children? What are you talking about? I'm pregnant so you're wrong. There must have been some mistake. The doctors were wrong. Scott, I'm about five weeks pregnant."

"Doesn't matter how long you've been pregnant Katie. Five years, five months, five days. It's still not my baby." He walked out of the dining room and into their bedroom. He fell heavily onto the bed and pulled his arms crossed over his eyes and forehead. He felt like he had been kicked by a horse right in the middle of his chest. His sweet Katie, the love of his life, the woman he had never even dreamed of having was the same as all the rest of them. He watched his world melt in a molten lava drip into oblivion. In one sweet moment, the nightmare of all nightmares spilled into his life and destroyed everything he had loved. Sweet Katie, who didn't even want to sleep together before they were married, was having an affair just months into their marriage.

Katie was too stunned to move. She didn't know where to go or what to say. How can you iron out madness? How can you take total unreality and fix it so it becomes real again? Now what? And after an eternity, she felt the strength slowly fill her again. She headed to their bedroom and sat beside Scott. She tried to lie down beside him, but he brutally shoved her away. "Get away from me. I hate you so much right now."

"You hate me? Oh my God, how do you think I feel about you? I tell you I'm pregnant, and you tell me I'm a tramp! And what do you mean that you can't have children?'

From behind his arms, still crossed over his eyes, Scott spat out, "Listen to me very carefully, Katie girl. I can't have kids. Period. I had an undescended testicle as a kid and my psycho parents didn't do anything about it. Later, when I was in college, I went to donate sperm at a center to get some extra cash. And guess what? Blanks. All blanks. Not a single swimmer in the bunch. Not a one. No little Scottie. No little Katie. No doubts. No maybes. Never gonna have kids, Katie. Do you get that? So you're pregnant and my sperm is paralyzed, so you do the math."

Katie just started to laugh. She rolled back onto their bed and held her sides until her laughter turned to hysterical cries. Where had all of this come from? What about the baby?

Scott rolled up onto his side and whispered rather loudly and in a very threatening tone, in Katie's ear, "Now, sweet cheeks, you can keep the baby and go find your lover. On the other hand, you can have an abortion and still get your butt out of my house. I just can't and won't raise a kid that's not mine."

Scott grabbed his keys and left the house. He slammed the front door on his way out and peeled the car down the street and out of the subdivision. You could hear him for miles. Katie simply did not know what to do. At first, she thought she would call Dolly, but she was too stunned and horrified to tell her. Catherine would be no better. Elizabeth was out of the question. She wanted a glass of wine, but it wouldn't be good for the baby. Katie just couldn't sit still. She paced around the room and then moved to the den. Lying on the sofa, propped up with pillows, she tossed and turned. Going out to the porch, she still moved feeling restless as a cat. Her stomach hurt, and she felt suddenly so tired, like someone had sucked out all of her wind.

That old tingly sensation was back. That one that promised panic was on its way. Katie knew instantly that all the stress and all the pressure that had been building up for so long, was forcing the issue and demanding attention. Anxiety was marching home and reclaiming Katie. Without a second thought, Katie went to the bathroom and filled the tub with hot water and her favorite bubble bath. She turned out all the lights and lit candles all around the tub. And just before she slid into the tub, she turned back and grabbed the pregnancy test she and Scott were supposed to share together. Her plan had been to bring him into the bathroom and run that test as new parents. She wanted him to read the blue PREGNANT sign and be as excited as she was. She had the camera ready to take a picture, which she would send in a card to friends and family announcing their pregnancy. Now, she ran it through the urine stream and waited. And waited and stared in utter disbelief. She was not pregnant. Katie threw it in the waste paper basket and watched it slide to the bottom. So, she wasn't pregnant, just late. Too late.

"The deepest hunger in life is a secret that is revealed only when a person is willing to unlock a hidden part of the self."

– Depok Chopra

CHAPTER 17

S cott didn't come home that night, but just in case Katie had slept in one of the other four bedrooms, none of which would ever be a nursery or a kid's room. Ironically, she had slept in the mother –in-law suite, of which neither of them had. Irony was not one of Katie's favorite things, and she found that ironical things often turned out to be cruel and hurtful as well. And so all this followed suit.

When Scott presented the mini mansion to Katie, his sacrificial gift to the love of his life, he had failed to mention that Dolly and Catherine had both invested heavily into the new home. How Scott had the audacity to ask them for the money was something Katie would one-day question. However, the girls were delighted, indeed grateful, at the opportunity to give something to the young couple. By going to the girls, Scott had scored quite a coup. He showed that he was interested in involving them in the marriage; he showed he wanted a beautiful home for the most important person in their collective lives; and now he offered them a voice, an opinion, a say so, because they were now money partners. It was the perfect solution and kept everyone happy, except Katie who had no idea the house was an extended family financial affair.

Katie didn't know how she slept the night of the baby disaster. She had chosen her favorite bedroom, the Dolly room, and the closest she could get to her, as a place to hide away. The room was beautifully decorated in shades of red, beige, mocha, and warm green. It was inviting and alluring all at the same time. The queen size bed was covered by a tapestry style fabric made of birds with plumes of red streaked with beige and green. A large footstool stood on the ready dressed in a deep red with marching elephants splayed across it.

Beau on the other hand was delighted. As a crate sleeper, he was always tucked away in the kitchen when everyone else went to bed. He'd longed to be with them and often whined when they left him. This night he was freed from his confinement and offered the best of all worlds, sleeping with Katie. Scott would have been furious as he was totally against the dog sleeping in the bed with them. He was so concerned about Beau thinking he was the alpha dog, but he wasn't that stupid. Only one alpha in this family, and it was hands down Scott. But it didn't matter anymore. Beau would have a new place of honor for as long as they both shall live.

Red Queen Anne matching chairs covered in a rich, textured fabric interwoven with diamonds of beige and green, sat on either side of the fireplace. A room sized Karistan rug, navy, red, green, and beige covered the royal mahogany hardwood floors, and a white on white textured love seat finished out the room. It was beautiful and peaceful and a place where Katie had envisioned long conversations by the fire. She could never have imagined that she would be the only attendant at her baby's funeral and the funerals for all the ones who could have been, but now no longer had any possibility of sharing a life with her.

Katie did not call Dolly or Cat, and she didn't hear from Scott for two more days. At first, the silence of the house and the smothering disappointment threatened to send her careening downhill. Her nerves were shot and everything, every movement, even the sound of the air kicking on, made her jump. She drank wine by the plenty and wandered around the yard and lake like a homeless person searching for a place to lay a weary head. A weedy garden gave her a distraction; the house was spotlessly clean. Only the place in the dining room, where the crystal wine goblet had shattered, showed any hint of disturbance. She had worked meticulously on that so Beau wouldn't get glass in his paws.

Late on the third day, Scott came home laden with gifts and apologies. Beau ran to the door wagging the tail until it shook his body, and Scott responded with a grandiose display of love and affection. Beau was delighted with the attention, while Katie felt sick to her stomach. She didn't know what she was most angry about; not telling her he was sterile, accusing her of being a tramp, or leaving her alone for three days without a word or concern.

Katie sat in the den on the cranberry striped sofa nearest the fireplace. The view overlooked the lake and the moon lit up the back yard making all the edges look clean and sharp. A gentle wind blew through the trees and made shadows on the French doors. Katie had a bottle of wine opened on the coffee table and sipped slowly on a wine spritzer. Too festive a drink for such a somber occasion.

It was of no surprise that Scott came bearing gifts. His arms were full of treasures that he hoped would win favor with Katie once more. He should not have bothered. Her heart had been shredded by the razor sharp accusations hurled at her, and her mind had shut down all but the simplest emotions. Only Beau could feel the love. Katie had avoided Dolly's phone calls and knew that if she didn't return one soon, the other owners of the house would arrive on her doorstep. Right now, she was hardly able to deal with the current situation, much less project into the future to see what it held for her. There was certainly no promise of happiness.

Putting down his peace offerings, which Katie ignored, Scott bent on one knee, tried to lay his head on her lap but she pushed it gently away. He tried to take her hand, but she crossed her arms instead. He got down on both knees and asked for a hug, and she got up and went into the kitchen. This was not some simple, "I'm sorry we had a fight." This was a serious situation where all of her dreams and hopes, her babies, had been destroyed and left unburied. There had been no ceremony, no sympathy, just a tough luck, you slut, goodbye. How was she to handle Scott now?

"Katie. I know you hate me right now and dear God, I hate myself more than you ever could."

Katie interrupted, "Not possible."

"Please let me finish. What I did was so wrong, so terrible, that I can't believe I did it."

"But you did do it, and these stupid gifts won't come close to making up for all the terrible things you did that night."

"Katie. Be fair and please let me finish what I have to say. Then you can berate me and tell me how much you despise me and anything else you want to say. I deserve them."

Katie started to laugh. "Be fair? Are you kidding me? Why should I be fair to you? Since we were engaged, you had one mission in mind and that was to control me. You didn't want me to work, so I didn't sign a new contract. You wanted a stay at home wife and the perfect house as well. Check that off your list. You wanted to entertain and make everyone so envious of your situation. Well, buddy, you got that as well. I gave it all, every part of my being. And when I'm so excited, no, blissfully happy, that we, not just me, but we are going to have a baby, you verbally beat me within an inch of my life! Why didn't you tell me you were sterile?"

By this time, Katie was shouting and Beau had snuggled onto the sofa next to her. Scott tried to move Beau so he could sit there, but Katie moved his hand and pulled big ol Beau onto her lap.

"He stays. He will no longer be something you play with and put away when you're done. He no longer will be seen and not heard. He's my dog, given to me by you, and he'll have all the rights and privileges due a dog of mine."

Scott got up and sat on the coffee table facing Katie. "Where do I begin? I've been wild, crazy with grief over what I've done to you, no, done to us. I don't expect you to forgive me; I know that will take time. But you have to hear me out, please. Just give me a few minutes and hear me out. If you still want me to leave, then I will. What do you say?"

"Have your peace, Scott. Not that I think anything could help you or us now."

"Mind if I fix myself a drink?"

"I do. Do you need a drink to tell the truth?"

Hanging his head down, Katie could now look at this man she loved so much without their eyes meeting. Those eyes always saw through her and could find any source of weakness that may be lurking there. For some strange reason she wanted to touch the back of his hair, the place just where the hair stopped on his neck, and stroke it like she always did. She wanted to bury herself in his arms and feel his strength around her. She wanted to listen to his heartbeat, that heart that had loved her unto death. But the thoughts conflicted with the repulsion she felt. Opposite feelings running parallel to each other, going on into infinity. She was so confused, and she withdrew her hand that had been subconsciously moving towards him.

"Go ahead, Scott." Her voice was flat and emotionless.

"When I was a little boy, things were crazy at my house. I knew that my house was different from other kids just from the way kids talked at school. My dad was never home very often and when he was, he did not have much to do with me. He had nothing to do with my mother. It was many years later before I understood why our house was dead."

Scott picked up Katie's wine and finished it. Walking into the kitchen, he grabbed a chilled bottle of wine, corked it, and came back to the table. Changing his mind, he pulled over one of the matching captain's chairs and continued, sitting up towards the edge of the chair and gulping down the wine.

"Have you ever heard of the term "no affect"? It means having little or no feeling or emotion especially shown by a lack of facial expressions or body language. That was what the doctors said about my mother. She had no affect. She wasn't showing anything because she wasn't feeling anything. She was shriveled up and dead inside. Something had killed her and she never came back to life again.

"She was officially diagnosed with a psychotic disorder that was poorly treated early on in her disease. Something misfired and broke in her brain chemistry making her unable to show love or even feel it. Her meds were killers as well. I would come home from school, and I'd never know what to expect. Dad had hired nurses to be with her for fear she would harm herself. Mom had been in facilities before, but dad always brought her home when too many people stopped believing she was on a trip or the doctor had said there was no hope. Even dad needed to have a bit of hope."

Scott stopped to catch his breath hoping beyond hope that Katie might reach out and offer comfort, some type of emotion, some love that might still live inside. No such luck as Katie had "no affect" down to a science.

"Mom stopped caring about the way she looked or even if she took a bath or not. She had once been so beautiful and full of life. She'd had a reputation for being the town's catch and everyone loved her. The nurses had a struggle even getting her into the tub. The doctors increased her meds, and then all hell broke loose. Her speech was confused and incoherent. She started to act even more strangely than she previously had. Katie, she was so detached. She was so cold to me. I don't believe she really even knew who I was."

Scott opened his arms and reached towards Katie. "Katie, please, this is so damn hard."

For once, Katie's innards were titanium. No sad teary tale this day could erase the severe storm that had still held her under water, daring her to gasp for breath.

With Katie's steely gaze boring through him, Scott struggled to maintain his composure.

"One day I came home from school and no nurses were there. The house was still. I ran into dad's room and a suitcase was packed on the bed. Then I ran into mom's room and dad was on the phone calling an ambulance. Mom was in a catatonic state, a far cry from the wild leg and arm movements she often displayed. She just sat there staring into space as dad folded the commitment papers and slipped them into his vest pocket. I ran out of the room and hid until dad returned later that night. It was the last time I ever saw my mother. She died at the institution ten days later. They said her heart gave out. Who knows what really happened. My dad returned home, and other than the fact that mom was gone, things returned to abnormal."

Taking another sip of wine and catching Katie's eyes, Scott finished. "For a long time I knew that something was wrong with one of my testicles. It didn't hang all the way down, and it scared me to death. Who was I going to tell? I didn't see a regular pediatrician and I sure as hell wasn't going to tell my father. When I started playing sports, I knew something serious was wrong with me. Years later, I had it fixed with an implant. So now, I look normal, but it's not normal. If it had been taken care of sooner, I probably wouldn't be sterile."

Katie laid her head back on the sofa and stroked Beau who was not riveted by Scott's story. He stretched out and was soon chasing squirrels in his dreams. High drama was not of any great interest unless it involved him. Scott leaned over to rub Beau and continued.

"Psychotic disorders can be inherited. The disorders tend to run in families but they haven't isolated a gene for it. Mom had the worst of it with her hallucinations and delusions. Today's drugs are so far superior to the one's Mom took. Very few side effects in these new ones and the psychotherapy is much better. Bottom line, dad was furious mom got sick, but if he'd paid any attention to her really, he would have seen that she was getting sick when he married her. He felt cheated that he had a wife that was so sick, and he allowed it to ruin all of our lives. If he had only gotten involved personally, not through the nurses, if he had only put as much time into her getting well as he did making money, Mom would still be alive today. But the most fearful thing to him was that I might have inherited her psychosis and he would be stuck with another living nightmare."

Scott's voice began to crack, "My dad died without even talking to me. When I finished high school and went off to college, he paid all the bills and kept money in my account. I wanted for nothing except him. Only, he wanted nothing to remind him of my once beautiful mother and the tragedy of their lives. It could have been so different. If only..." Scott dropped his hands into his face and cried as if finally bringing up the tears of that little boy who had suffered neglect and a terrible, terrible loss.

Katie moved Beau and put her hand on Scott's shoulder. "I'm so sorry, Scott. I'm so very sorry." She stood up then and looked down at Scott for a minute as if deciding what to do next. She looked slowly to the right and then the left as if picking which way she should go. She picked up the novel she had been trying to read earlier, walked out the French doors calling Beau to come. After a bathroom break, they came back in, so matter of factly, and went to Dolly's room. Scott called to her, "Katie, wait a minute. We're not finished talking. Come here, please. We need to talk about the baby."

Katie officially understood what it meant to be turned to stone. It wasn't so bad, really. Her blood had stopped flowing and she felt very cold. Her body felt stiff as if cramped from a long plane trip. But her heart. It seemed to beat irregularly as if it couldn't catch its breath. As if it was afraid to beat less, someone noticed it was barely alive. However, fragile and on the precipice of despair, Katie was alive, and although barely beating and breathing, she swirled to face Scott.

"I'm not pregnant. It was all a silly mistake. I spoke too soon. It was all a big mistake."

Scott jumped from the sofa and ran towards Katie. "Oh, I'm so relieved. Katie, that's wonderful, just wonderful. Now we can put all of this behind us. Oh, I'm so happy, aren't you?"

In a voice that mirrored the status of her heart, Katie eyed Scott. "I imagined you would say many things to make me happy. But in my wildest dreams, I never imagined you would say anything as asinine as what you just said. Start over? Put it all behind us? How out of touch with reality are you?"

She ran to Dolly's room, slammed the door, and locked it. She could hear him crying in the den, but she didn't care. *Let him cry and suffer like I have.* Katie cried herself to sleep while Beau slept on her pillow, blissfully unaware of what had just transpired.

The next morning Katie left Scott a note. Her mind was so scrambled emotionally that Katie wasn't sure what she wanted to say. She had to leave for a while and get her thoughts aligned. Everything was foggy and out of focus. Heading to the beach was a safe place to go figure it all out.

Packing the car and getting Beau ready for the trip, Katie hesitated over the note she'd left. Should she have said more? Should she have even left a note? So unsure. But she was sure of one thing; she had to get out of town. And that was no easy task. She was feeling high levels of anxiety and dreaded the ride to the beach. She double checked to make sure she had her meds; planned out her trip down to the stops she would make with Beau, and timed her travel to the last minute. A book on tape would help her focus while she drove, and a sleeping Beau would add comfort. That's the strange thing about anxiety disorder; none of those things can do anything to help avoid a panic attack. Truth was all the therapists said you have to accept them and they will pass, let them float over you, and you'll survive. However, floating denotes some type of peaceful existence and nothing about panic was peaceful, rather the complete antithesis, the total absence of peace. Katie was driven now to leave. Stay with Scott and suffer or drive to the beach and suffer. Of the two places of hell, the beach was the better choice.

Her iPhone started ringing about an hour outside of Atlanta. It was Scott, and Katie had nothing to say to him. After several unanswered calls, Scott began texting, which she completely ignored. Finally, he began paging her, that dreaded old timey pager he insisted she keep. Knowing his persistence, she took a deep breath and answered.

"What do you need, Scott?" Her voice was still flat and emotionless and the only way she could stand to interact with him right now.

"Where are you? I've been calling home and you didn't answer. Katie, we need to talk. We can't keep going on this way. Please talk to me."

"I'm sorry Scott, but right now I'm headed to the beach, and I'm staying until this gets all sorted out. There just isn't anything to say right now."

"Can I come down there and see you?"

"Please don't do that. Please stay in Atlanta. I need to get away."

"How are you driving down there? Are you having any panic attacks? Honey, I'm worried about you driving down there alone."

"I'm not alone, Beau's with me, and we'll make it down there okay. Scott, I need to hang up now. The traffic's slowing and I need to watch the road. I promise to call you when I'm ready." And with that, she disconnected him.

I wish I'd never gotten her that dog, Scott fumed. In reality, he knew the problem wasn't Beau, and it wasn't Katie. It was him and it had all landed squarely in his lap. He loved her, and that's what drove him. He needed her and couldn't imagine his life without her. He had royally screwed up everything, and he didn't know how to get out of this mess. He couldn't decide how much time to give her before he followed her to Tybee. He didn't know how Dolly and Cat would counsel her, but deep down, he knew to get down there as fast as he could.

The traffic had been terrible causing the speed limit to hover around twenty miles per hour. The rain made the roads slippery and steamy. The weatherman Announced warnings of hail embedded thunderstorms followed by record high winds. It all promised to be a hell of a mess.

The trip had gotten the best of her, and utterly defeated, Katie turned around and headed home. Her anxiety levels stayed too high, and her focus remained on her panic and nothing else. All she had learned and read went right out the window. She couldn't think clearly, and the whole world seemed surreal. The rhythm of the windshield wipers made her want to scream, and the constant lane changing of the drivers on I-75 reminded her of racecar drivers jockeying for position. It was utter chaos.

The only thing that calmed her somewhat was Beau, who was in the back seat, behind the grate separating him from the front for the safety of all. All Katie could do was coo to him and explain what was happening. Something impossible to do, as she had no understanding of what was happening. The last thing she wanted to do was come home to Scott and deal with all the elephants that now marched around them both. Trumpeting, Snorting. Demanding attention and refusing to be ignored. Some people were great at ignoring the elephants in the room, but when a herd invades your life, somebody has to pay attention before someone gets trampled. Oh, wait, someone already was.

Katie picked up her phone from the seat and scrolled over to Dr. Martin's number. She needed to see him and get some help dealing with this new disaster in her life. She felt he was her only lifeline in this insane world she had entered.

Dr. Martin's secretary had penciled in an emergency visit for Mrs. Stewart. Chris was surprised when he felt a little trickle of excitement when he read her name. "Call her back, and tell her I'll make time to see her."

"By the way, Mr. Flemings cancelled his four o'clock and he was your last appointment of the day. That leaves you with an extended visit time for Mrs. Stewart if you want to block out two hours. She sounded so very upset."

Normally Dr. Martin was annoyed when patients cancelled. He was a very busy man and found that an unexpected free hour wedged in between patients was a colossal waste of time. Today, rather than being irritated, he was eager to see Katie and find out how she was doing. Obviously, not much had changed in her life.

CHAPTER 18

⎯⎯⎯⎯⎯∿⎯⎯⎯⎯⎯

T he days had dragged on endlessly as Scott and Katie managed to coexist. They continued to sleep in separate bedrooms and maintain a killing silence when in each other's presence. Katie followed her schedule, made meals, and kept the house clean, but she provided no other services including a conversation. It was like living with a robotic mute.

As with all straws, one will eventually break a camel's back, and this one was no different. The camel hungered for touch and laughter, for a life that had once been lived to the fullest, for peace in his heart and soul. He understood in every fiber of his being why God said it was not good for man to live alone.

After another stone silent dinner, Scott felt the straw weigh him down so heavily that an upward movement was impossible. As Katie came to clear off his plate, he grabbed her arms and pulled her down into the chair closest to him. Strangely, she resisted not at all and looked into his eyes like a wounded animal begging to be put out of its misery. "Katie, we can't go on like this. We are both miserable, and I cannot stand it a minute more."

Holding her hands tightly in his, he pleaded with her for something, anything, some emotion, some connection. "I know you don't care how I feel, but I want you to know that I take all the responsibility for the state of our marriage. I know I screwed up everything. You see, I love you so much, and I can't stand seeing you this way. I hate the way I feel. I can't sleep, I can't work. I can hardly eat. Katie, please, please can we try to work this thing out?" He pulled her cold, damp hands to his face and kissed them gently. He trembled as he touched her as it had been weeks since they had any type of contact.

Katie did not pull away which gave Scott the first glimmer of hope since that dreadful night. She didn't smile or open up to him, but the fact that she didn't pull away provided enough encouragement for him to continue. Walking over to the mantel, Scott picked up JB's forgiveness statue and brought it over to Katie.

"I never thought we'd need this, or that I'd ever understand the story behind this."

Katie sucked in a breath and turned away from Scott's eyes.

"I do need you to forgive me. Jesus said we have to forgive others or he will not forgive us. Tanta Corrie forgave that guard who killed her sister. Have I done something so utterly unforgivable that you are willing to bind yourself in unforgiveness?"

Scott's voice was earnest and strong. He was pleading but not begging. He was a man prepared, and it sure sounded like he had done his research. Scott watched for some reaction on her face, but she was still and emotionless like the guards at Buckingham Palace. It was time to play the trump card.

"Look, I'm not sure how you're going to take this, but I called Dolly. I told her what I'd done, and what I'd failed to tell you. She was quiet for a long time, and I didn't know what she was thinking. She told me to come to the beach and meet with Father Dowling, and he'd help me work things out. She said she and her prayer group would be in prayer for us. "

Katie showed no reaction and sat there, still as a dead cat, watching, waiting, listening.

"So, I went to see Father John, and he was terrific. Since I'm not a Catholic, I didn't go to confession, but I got a lot off of my chest, and I told him everything, Katie, I told him everything I'd ever done wrong. I blubbered like a baby, but he told me God could heal this marriage if we were willing to do our part. I'm just asking for another chance, so can you forgive me? I'm not asking you to forget what I've done. I'm just asking for us to work through this and move on."

Katie put the forgiveness statue on the end table and looked into Scott's incredibly blue eyes. She realized now that she had missed him and had to admit that she was touched that he went to a priest. She took that as a sign that he was sincere in his desire to work on this marriage.

Taking a deep breath, Katie tried to lay it out for Scott. "You touched all the bases and did everything right, even bringing the statue into play. I can tell you've had this planned for some time. At least this has been destroying you as much as it's been destroying me. I have missed you, and I know that I still love you, I may not like you, but I still love you."

Scott reached out to grab her and shout hallelujah while doing so.

"Wait. Please let me finish. What you need to realize is that forgiveness is not the only issue. It's about lying and broken promises and cruelty. But most important of all, it's the children we will never have. Scott, forgiveness is the easy part."

"Look. I've done nothing but think about this since the night I nearly destroyed our marriage. I said some terrible things, and I regret each and everyone one of them. I was a fool and acted like some mad man. I've also talked to people who've adopted kids, and I've changed my mind about that as well. Aw, Katie, I was just running off at the mouth. I didn't mean any of those things I said to you. We can have kids that we'll love just as much as if we'd made them ourselves. Father John even suggested adoption."

Adoption was something Katie had not allowed into her realm of reality. She'd love to adopt; she'd go half way around the world to adopt. She needed to open her life for a baby. Now that Scott was open to adoption, Katie could begin to hope again. It wouldn't change what he had done, and she would forgive him, but something was broken and she doubted that it could ever be fixed.

Katie suddenly realized that Scott truly believed everything he was saying to her. With no true malice towards his parents, he saw himself a victim of an unhappy marriage. He had been ignored while the damage was done, and then like a scorched cake, it was iced over to camouflage the taste. There was no hiding what had happened, real or imagined, in Scott's mind. He stood before her now with emotions as raw as a wounded child. He acted like a child, explosive and angry, unreasonable, rambling. She actually thought he might stamp his feet but he did not. Katie was oddly stirred by the intensity of his belief that he had been treated unjustly and as a result, he was somehow not as responsible for his actions. He was mindful that what he had done to

Katie was terribly wrong, but in his desire to make things right between them, he took responsibility for only so much.

For now, Katie didn't care whose fault it was. Seeing Scott tonight had softened her heart just a bit; she was not ready to receive him again, but at least she felt a stirring of compassion. She imagined him as that little boy he still was and wished desperately that someone had loved him. Maybe none of this would ever have happened if his mother had lived and his father had cared. Now fearing the loss of control, Katie zipped up her heart tightly, cocooned against Scott and the turmoil he brought. He had cost her greatly, more than just the loss of children, but a break down with the girls. Katie couldn't tell Dolly all the details, and she let Cat's phone calls go to voice mail. She felt dreadful about pulling away from them, and she missed them terribly. She had no problem with pride and admitting that Dolly was right all along about rushing into marriage and that Scott might not be what he presented to the world. It was more than that. To admit this would send a tremor throughout her very existence. If she could have been so wrong about Scott, how would she ever trust herself again?

Fatigue won, and Katie gave up. She took one last look at the handsome man now standing before her. She could smell his cologne and almost ached to touch his face and feel his arms around her. Yet, she did not, nor would she be persuaded. She would turn to Beau instead. Faithful, trustworthy Beau. For the time being, Scott would have to wait until Katie could steady her world.

CHAPTER 19

---~~/---

I t was another therapy session with Dr. Martin, and Katie was looking forward to seeing him again. After the terrible incident with Scott, when he confessed to his sterility, Katie's anxiety had become full blown once more. Always just under the surface, tucked away but always in reach, the anxiety drove her life, controlled her and her thoughts. Everything she did was planned around her levels, how she felt today, who she could call if her levels became unmanageable, always planning, touching base along the way.

Sometimes Dr. Martin saw Katie once a week while on other weeks, she came in twice. The anxiety had been the major focus, but now it included walking Katie through her marriage. Katie needed to learn how to let go and accept what she couldn't change. If she was committed to this marriage, then she needed coping skills and some support in order to get Scott into much needed therapy. Chris Martin doubted very seriously that this marriage would last much longer. He also doubted that Katie was as committed to the marriage as she professed.

Katie and Dr. Martin had some contentious discussions regarding forgiveness. It was not a simple thing like when little kids forgive each other. Adult forgiveness, when the wound is this deep, takes a great deal of faith and reliance on Jesus. Chris Martin had that; Katie Stewart did not.

Each time Katie left a therapy session, Chris struggled with his emotions. For the past ten years, he had prayed diligently for a woman who would be his soul mate. A woman who would know him intimately, love him intimately, and posses him with a God given love. God had promised him a mate, for Chris was a man made to be married.

It was true that Katie was getting better and was getting a grasp on how to breathe through her panic attacks. With the proper support, Katie had made huge progress and could now recognize that what she feared was a hormone, adrenaline, which gave her that fight or flight response. She learned she could control or at least manage that surge by breathing. She faithfully practiced her breathing exercises and could often be seen with her hand on her belly making sure her breathing was abdominal rather than thoracic. Katie was a smart woman and was determined that her life go on in spite of the anxiety and in spite of her collapsing marriage.

But if all was working for the better with Katie, Chris was struggling with her as a patient. At night, he had prayed about his feelings for her, those that surpassed the normal doctor patient ones. On Sunday's he'd offer up his mass for her and beg God to heal her. He'd beg God to show him what to do about her. On Mondays, her standard appointment days, he felt foolish at how happy he was to see her. When she walked into his office, everything seemed to come alive. Surely, it must have been like dolls and toys that wake up and energize after midnight. He had never met a more intriguing and enchanting woman. Although he had dated others who were more beautiful, he had yet to meet one who so suddenly and so easily had stolen his heart.

Today they would finish their session early, and then Chris would have the talk with Katie, the one he had rehearsed repeatedly. He knew it was time, and he knew it would be difficult for both of them. He had sensed, no, not really sensed, but hoped that she might be feeling some of the same feelings for him as he felt for her.

Chris thought again about his conversation with Kevin Brennan. Chris had met him while playing in a charity fundraising golf tournament and liked him instantly. Everyone around them seemed to like and respect him. While out on the course, Father Brennan had noticed the torment surrounding Chris. Choosing a three wood, Chris set up the ball and backed up to take a swing. Suddenly his eyes met Father Brennan and something exchanged between them. In a split second it was gone, but it left Chris rather unnerved. The rest of the round was uneventful and the moment was forgotten. Until the foursome finished up at the clubhouse. Father Brennan shook Chris's hand and exchanged the manly pleasantries of a good round of golf. It's a special gene that men possess that most women seemed to have been passed over; but a man can remember all eighteen holes, what shot was made and with which club, how far each went, and numerous other details that will be remembered for hundreds of years.

"Great golf, Chris, I enjoyed it tremendously. I'm a little rusty, but today has reawakened that old desire to play again. Hope we can do it again some time."

"My pleasure, Father. Any time."

"By the way, Chris. If you ever needed anyone to talk to, under the seal of the confessional, I'm here if you need me. Just call the parish office, and leave a message. I'll get back to you as soon as I can."

"Thanks. Is that a perk you offer all your golf buddies or is it something you picked up on playing with me? If so, I need to be more careful next time." Chris said it with a laugh, but in reality, he was bothered by Father Brennan's discernment.

Putting his hand on Chris' shoulder, Father Brennan made eye contact and said, "Sometimes you get a knowing that everything is not as it seems. All I'm doing is responding to that prodding of the Holy Spirit. The rest is up to you."

Chris chuckled. "You know I'm a psychiatrist and pretty much have a stable full of therapists available if I need one." It sounded a little more arrogant than Chris could ever imagine him sounding. Father shrugged it off and continued, "There's a major divide between what the world offers in counseling and what God offers. So, consider the door always open."

After a sleepless night, which was quite unusual for Chris, he put in a call to Father Brennan and received a call right back. An appointment was set for five.

Five o'clock came and the parish receptionist showed Chris to Father's office. "He's just walking an irate parishioner to her car. It seems Mrs. O'Malley didn't like the altar flowers last Sunday. She donates the money each month in her husband's name, God rest his soul, so she's finicky about the florist's taste." She smiled a knowing smile and closed the door leaving Chris alone with his thoughts.

He looked around the office and was impressed with its pure comfort. The walls of the study were lined with books that would make any small library envious. The paneling was light, unlike the smoldering darker studies of so many others Chris had seen. The mahogany walls so characteristic of a man's study often smothered and overwhelmed with a depression era feel. Chris preferred the lighter more welcoming feel of Kevin's study. Sturdy but comfortable overstuffed leather chairs and ottomans in a rich cocoa, invited a burdened soul to take off a load. A bisque throw, made of bamboo and cotton, hung over the armrest of a long sofa that sat tucked under a large bay window.

It was a perfect place to visit, unload, or set the mind at peace. It seems Chris would need all three.

The two men sat down to some serious business. Two men who knew their business and knew why they were together. There was no small talk, as they had spent most of yesterday together. Both men knew that this was an ordained meeting and things needed to be discussed.

"Father Brennan."

"Chris. I'm not going to sit here and call you Dr. Martin all day. So let's dispense with the titles and get a bit more familiar. Please, call me Kevin."

"Ok, Kevin. Here's my problem. I have a patient, a beautiful, wonderful, unhealthy patient who is in a very bad marriage. She is a Catholic and married in the church, but she found out several months ago that her husband was sterile. He knew it before they married and chose not to tell her. I don't believe she is in love with him anymore, and frankly, I'm finding myself drawn to her in a way I cannot explain. So, therein lies my dilemma."

Father Brennan sat back in his lounge chair and eyed Chris carefully. Most men he counseled didn't come in his office and unload so quickly. Chris was driven and needed help to sort out the quagmire he was in.

"Beautiful? Wonderful? I don't often hear doctors discussing their patients using such adjectives. Chris, is there something else going on here?"

"I'm afraid so. I'd like to deny it and claim that she's just another patient, but she's not. I am so torn by doing the right thing by removing myself from a potentially disastrous situation, and helping her in therapy. The guy she's married to is such a jerk, and he doesn't deserve her. Her anxiety attacks are rough, and she has no support at home. I guess I'm afraid to cut her loose to fend for herself."

"Chris, we've been very honest and straightforward here. We both know what's at stake, so do you want it sugar coated or straight?

"Straight."

Father Brennan took a deep breath and cracked his knuckles. It sounded obscenely loud in the midst of the deathly still study. Chris sat back in his chair and then edged towards the front again. He was clearly uncomfortable over what was to come.

"Here it is straight. I believe you know exactly what you need to do, and you just want someone else to put words to it. Here's the directive: send her to another therapist. Stop coveting another man's wife, regardless of how entitled you feel to her. Go to confession. Then spend time with the Lord before you talk to her about this. She can't be made to feel penalized or rejected because her doctor crossed the line, and her husband doesn't deserve her regardless. This is not an easy move, but it is the only right and responsible move to make. Straight enough for you?" Father Brennan said with a smile as he watched Chris for signs of something, anger, frustration, relief, some emotion. However, he didn't get what he expected.

"Pray with me, please. I know what's right, but I know how hard this is going to be. I know how wrong I've been, in my thoughts and in my mind, and it scares me that I could slip over the line so easily. I guess 'remove me from the near occasion of sin' has more meaning to me than it ever has before."

And then they prayed. It was a powerful prayer imploring Jesus to send help for Chris, Katie, and Scott. A prayer that called for honesty and the responsibility to follow God's law. There would be no compromise. No one would turn a blind eye. They knew God's truth.

Chris Martin knew what he had to do. He had known it all along, but it was too painful and too final. He wanted to help Katie, and he knew he could. But he also wanted her to be his, and he had relished the thought too many times over too many nights and too many days. Never had he looked forward to a patient coming to see him. Never had he dreamed of her perfume and the way it made him smile. Never had he wondered what life would be with her. He was headed for trouble, and he knew it. This loss of Katie would be so painful, for she had become what he had always dreamed of having. God had said no, and yes, one can argue with God, but He has the final word.

But after a brutally honest discussion with Father Brennan, Chris walked away knowing that he was coveting another man's wife, regardless of how worthless that man could be, and he was on the verge of crossing the ethical line between therapist and patient. For everyone's benefit, today would be the day to break all ties between them.

In all of his years of practice, Chris Martin had never served his clients coffee. Yet, he and Katie had a standard closing procedure that included decaf, real cream, and a brief rehash of their session. Chris loved her intelligence and lack of a victim attitude. Katie loved his intelligence and wisdom about everything. She considered him to be the only one capable of bringing her back from the brink of utter despair.

Today would be no different. Thirty minutes into the session, the preprogrammed coffee maker burst in full steam and began to brew coffee. They had previously agreed that they were coffee purists and didn't care for added flavorings like mint or hazelnut. "I think it's almost criminal to make a mocha coffee. It's right up there with dipping perfectly formed and fabulously tasting strawberries into chocolate. They're already just right –why does everyone need to try to improve on perfection?' Katie had a straightforward opinion about many things, and if Chris had been getting ready to eat a chocolate strawberry, he would have immediately gone to rinse if off. She may not have the most advanced pallet, but she knew what she liked and what she didn't. She liked things simple and uncomplicated and felt the whole world was spinning its wheels instead of resting in the ease of living. *How much harder do we make our own lives?* she pondered frequently.

The discussion that followed was deep and thought provoking. The core of the discussion was finding God's will for your life. If anyone really had the answer to that, then guess who would be an instant millionaire. Katie saw it differently. "When I was growing up, I read lots of books on men and women dedicated to God. I guess some people loved all that suffering and sacrifice, but I wouldn't ever start believing in Jesus after reading those biographies. Later on, I realized that they were different and called to a different life, one I am so happy I wasn't called to follow. They were so happy in the midst of all the terrible stuff they lived through and longed to continue suffering for Jesus. I just don't get it. But, I did learn that even when you're doing God's will, things aren't going to be so great all the time. Sometimes you've got to experience that alienation that separates you from all you love so that you'll choose God. I feel like I'm going through that now, not totally alienated 'cause of the girls, but the difference is, I don't see myself running to God. Some people run towards Him when they are in pain because they trust Him. I don't know Him enough to risk trusting. God never said we'd like everything that happened to us on earth or that we'd always be happy. It really isn't very appealing, is it?"

Her words rang in his head: "He never said we'd like it." *And I don't!* he shouted in his inner thoughts. He wanted to play the "what if" game: *what if I had met her before Scott did? What if I hadn't fallen for her? What if I'd gone into surgery rather than psychiatry?* They were stupid and unanswerable questions, and what difference would it make if they did have an answer. Not one bit. If he weren't a Catholic, he wouldn't care if she got a divorce. If he weren't a practicing Christian, he wouldn't care if he had an affair with a married woman. That lack of conscience thing might just have something to it.

Chris was eager to walk down that path thinking of ways to twist scripture, things that the Church had taught. Good Lord, it was tempting. For a while. But he knew. The sweetness would last but a moment in time, and the rotting, stinking smell of adultery and lies would stay on them both forever. Oh, people may not be able to smell them, but they would know that something was amiss. They would find them odious and whisper gossipy tales about them. Should one think that all that ended when Anna Karenina took a dive into that moving train, or when Rhett had had enough of Scarlett's imaginary love affair with Ashley; or for modern day just ask Ms. Lewinsky if she had to do it all over again...how sweet was the smell now?

So, the times change and morality is stretched to the limits. It becomes thin and fine like pizza, and can be molded in much the same way. But a funny thing about the truth, when it comes to light, it sets people afire with wonderment. And not like a wonderment at the beauty of Christmas lights or Santa's trip down the chimney, but a questioning of why'd you do it? Was it worth it and the answer can only be "yes", IF it comes with "and they lived happily ever after". But no one gets that true fairy tale ending, 'cause life's tough enough when God's the head of the household, but when that foundation is built on sand, and those walls are papered with the rejection, tears, shame, and hurt of loved ones plowed under by your selfish desire to throw fate to the wind and have it your way, then the devil gets to write the ending.

He was facing her now, sipping his coffee and begging God for the right words. She was still fragile, and he worried about that. She was falling for him, and he was scared about that. And unless he was the biggest fool and the stupidest therapist alive, he knew Katie would walk out with him if he ever offered her the chance. Did she know it in her head? He didn't think so, but he knew she felt it in the small part of her heart that still believed in love. She had already paid a huge price for love; could it have cost her anything more?

He was anxious and it was a feeling he did not like and had experienced very infrequently in his lifetime. "Katie, we need to talk."

"Haven't we just done that for nearly an hour?" She smiled her warm and inviting smile. Box it and sell and she'd be wealthy for eternity. It wasn't a sultry, come on and get it smile. It was one of those true smiles that meant 'I find pleasure in you.' It was disarming and shined a light on how sweet and vulnerable she was in this great time of need.

His mind was racing and his thoughts were scattered like debris after a tornado. Katie wasn't some heroine who could be rescued and hidden in that tower. She would have to live in the midst of the world in spite of what it had to offer. Her prince had turned into a cancerous toad that had threatened the very lifeblood of her. *Dear Lord. How can I not rescue her?* The slope was so slippery. Chris knew every time he came near it, it threatened to grab him by the ankles and pull him down, down into the deepest recess of sin, the worst of sin, the justifiable sin. But isn't that what temptation is? A struggle and then a release. A giving in to a time on the edge. Yet, what a strange magnetism it had. A pull like looking at a car wreck on the highway. Repulsed. Horrified. Yet, somehow just having to have one last look. But if you aren't looking ahead, the road you're traveling just became more dangerous. *Look ahead Chris.*

"Hey, are you still here? What are you thinking about, Dr. Martin? Want to share it with me?" Katie's voice was so upbeat and playful. She was getting so much better, and Chris was delighted with that. Yet the interior struggle to change directions was killing him. *Katie, if you only knew how much I dread sharing any of this with you.* "I'm sorry; I guess my mind is a million miles away today. So, let's get back to discussing some things that have come up recently."

"Wait." Katie sat up straight on the sofa and put her feet on the floor. She leaned in a bit as if Chris had been hard to hear. "That sounds serious like you just found some suspicious lump. What do you want to tell me? Ok. Now I get it. I'm crazy. I've finally crossed that invisible line that only therapists can see, and now I'm one of the crazies." She was nervous and starting to feel anxious. But a different anxious. Yes, foreboding, but not about losing her mind. This time it was unfamiliar, and she didn't know how to categorize it. Looking into his eyes, she became afraid. He had masked his thoughts and emotions, and he scared her. What was going on? She wanted to get up and leave, but she found she had no power to move.

Clearing his throat unnecessarily, Chris began. "As you know I'm Catholic."

"Yes, I do know that, and I promised not to hold that against you." Smiling cautiously, she asked, "So what?"

"Katie. Please don't interrupt me. This is serious."

"Serious? Hasn't all of this been serious?"

"Katie, wait. Stop. Damn. Just sit and listen to what I have to say. You're not crazy and this doesn't have anything to do with being crazy. But it has everything to do with your therapy."

Holding up his hand, he motioned for her to stop. "Not a word until I'm finished, and then you can have all the time you need." *Forever if that's what it takes.* He watched the anxiety crawling all over her, and he felt terrible about what he was going to put her through. Trying to soften the blow, he smiled at her and made his voice a deep baritone. "Want it straight or gussied up?"

"Straight."

That's my girl, he thought proudly followed by, *what a colossal fool you are, Chris.*

"Straight it is. I can do straight quite well. Father Brennan offered it to me straight, and I thought it was a great technique. Straight is the best. Don't drag it out, just get to the point."

"Dr. Martin. I said I'll take it straight. Stop playing around and follow your own advice. I can handle it at least temporarily. And if not,

I'll take an Ativan and then go home and cry. I've got the routine down pat."

"I can't be your therapist anymore. But you will or can see either of my partners who are excellent therapists. I mean, they are available and will gladly take your case." He just blurted it out like reading words off the typed page. Emotionless. Rapid fire. Wrong.

"I'm a case to you? I'm a CASE?"

"Please wait for God's sake. Hold your questions, would ya?"

She nodded a quite forlorn and punished nod. The breakup was upon her, and she never saw it coming.

"Look. Straight. OK? Straight. I'm having trouble keeping my feelings for you separate from our therapy. You're no longer just a patient that I care about as a patient; you've become important to me in a way that has the potential to cross ethical boundaries. I guess you could say that I've fallen in love with you." Foolish man, after getting it all out, he grinned at her like a preadolescent waiting for his first kiss. Did he want to be praised? Or was he dangerously close to the slippery slope?

She said nothing. She just sat there chalking up points against all those who had left her, abandoned her, and disappointed her. But this was so different. He didn't leave her for any reason other than he loved her, or at least he thought he did. Maybe this one didn't count as a full strike.

"I have no idea how you are feeling right now, and I'm not going to ask. So, I've got to finish before I can't say anymore. The next part-" Katie interrupted him again. "There's more? What the hell else could it possibly be?"

"Katie, just bear with me. I'm leaving my practice for a year and will be on sabbatical. I've been involved with a research study on a new anti-anxiety drug, and we're ready to start the trials. I had planned on this for some time now, but it just seems to have come up at an inopportune time."

"Inopportune is not exactly the word that comes to mind. I'm being dumped as a patient. Does it get much worse than that? When I see you on the street, can I wave to you or can I call you if I'm really stressed?" *Like right now, I'm feeling a large level of anxiety, and I'm all muddled up inside.*

"Oh, God, Katie. Are you getting any of the big picture of all of this? I'm leaving because I'm in love with you and sitting here with you now only hammers the point home. I want to put my arms around you and make it all better. But, it can't be all better between us, and you know it. And whether or not you're mad with God, His truth is still His truth. You're married, and I want you for my own. Coveting and adultery are two pretty high up there transgressions."

"Oh grow up! I don't care about your imagined transgressions. We haven't done anything to be ashamed of, and I can't help the way you feel about me. So, because you love me, I get to suffer. The only therapist in my life that has ever helped me make sense of the dragon is abandoning me because he's crossed some fictional ethical line. What line and where was I when you crossed it? What'd I miss, huh?"

She was getting furious. While she continued to steam and blow, Chris prayed. He'd handled this like a freight train sliding into first. He should have known better than to try STRAIGHT. What was he thinking? And, that's just the point. He wasn't thinking straight. He couldn't think straight. He only wanted her.

She was standing now and pacing. No more eye-to-eye contact. She was ticked. Every fiber in her being shouted it. Her body was rigid, and her arms were crossed tightly across her chest. She would fume for a nice long time, and then emotionally crash. But, the damage wasn't done.

"I'll say this as fast as I can. My sabbatical will take me out of town for one year. I will come to Atlanta periodically for meetings and such, but the rest of the time I'll be doing research and speaking in Europe and other places on anxiety and new treatments."

It was silent for a moment. Silence that takes a while to notice. Silence like when the birds stop singing or the bombs finally stop falling. The bombs had stopped, but both of them knew the fall out could be deadly.

Not letting time pass too quickly, Chris handed Katie her appointment reminder for next Monday. Same time. Same place. New therapist. A Dr. Schladenhoffer. She took the card and read it. She looked straight into his face and laughed. "Schladenhoffer? Are you kidding me?" She didn't care how childish she sounded judging a doctor by his name. Why, he may be the one who rescues her from the dragon forever. But she just couldn't help herself. She wanted to be childish. She wanted to start throwing things. She even wanted to kick the doctor. Damn, she just needed to do something. Yet, nothing real came to mind.

"Trust me. He's a better therapist than me."

"Well, after today, I wouldn't be surprised if they were all better than you." Instantly Katie regretted her words. Why doesn't the sword meet its mark every time? Why does it miss so often when you are aiming for a direct hit? Why did this make it home when it was a sissy swing and not meant to do anything but break up the stagnant air that was no longer filled with their laughter and their kudos to a therapy session well done.

"Katie, please don't leave this way. We have more to talk about."

"Sorry. I can't take another one of your emotional bombs. I'm done, and you're done. So let's be straight. God, I hate that 'let's be straight.' I'll come see your partner, and when I'm all done and cured maybe you can start seeing him. Looks like I'm not the only crazy in this room."

She grabbed her purse and slipped on her shoes. She had announced one day that shoeless therapy was a lot more successful, and he had loved her all the more for it. She ran her fingers through her hair and straightened her belt. She turned towards the door and then pivoted a bit. Turning back she looked down at him. Chris was paralyzed. This had not gone well at all, not at all. Her face looked so sad, but her tongue was sure to be sharp. "Look. I've got a treatment plan for you. Travel all over the word and tell everyone what NOT to do to their patients. Then, because you're so damn good at it, go pray and ask for forgiveness!"

She made it to the door and then she just couldn't help herself. "Where will you live while you're on sabbatical?" Her voice had lost its edge and was now soft and afraid. *Please don't let it be so terribly far away, Lord. Please let him be close by.*

"Here and there, and nowhere for very long." His answer was so cold and detached. She smiled at him as she walked to the door resisting the urge to resist the urge to slam it as hard as she could. So she did. And it left the intended impact.

Left behind, Chris was amazed at how royally he had screwed it all up. Had he ever been a successful therapist? This was terrible, and he knew the only place to go was to Jesus. He could unburden and start afresh. Yes, that's where he'd go. Adoration, to see Jesus. He went to close the blinds and just happened to see her pull away. *Bye, Katie. And that sabbatical? You'll find me in Tybee Island.*

Katie couldn't even think, and she wasn't sure how she even made it home. Had she stopped at the light on Spalding and King? She couldn't remember. One thing was certain though, and he'd be waiting for her at the front door. He'd heard her car and was pacing and whining like a mad dog. "Beau, my sweet baby boy. Come here, boy. Oh, I love you so much. Good boy." And she meant every word.

Grabbing a glass of wine, Katie kicked off her shoes and opened the back door leading to the lake. A nice walk and a chilled glass of wine would either numb her or help her think. Beau ran forward and turned back as if to hurry her along. "Not today, boy. My hurrying days are done. Bring me your toy and we'll play. Go get your toy, Beau. Go get it. Oh! What a good boy!"

After a hard play, dog and master lay on the grass and watched the sun set. Katie was calmer than she expected, but it was more than just the wine. She didn't want to rehash the day, it felt like a day to the dentist when last words are, "I've given you plenty of Novocain, and you won't even feel this." Garbled words drool out of the side of your mouth "I feeeel that, stop!" "Oh, no," said the jolly dentist from another planet. "I gave you three good sticks, you can't feel this." *Oh, yes I can, Chris Martin. There was no Novocain, and I can feel every single move you made. Oh, yes I can feel every single jab of pain.*

Katie called to Beau after one last good chase of the ducks. She could feel the fatigue now, deep into her bones. Surely, this must be the onset of posttraumatic stress syndrome, and maybe she would be hospitalized for the rest of her life. The only case of PTS outside of a war or a very serious trauma. Oh, well, it would probably be the first of her many firsts.

Beau fell asleep after inhaling his dinner. Katie soaked in the tub and then turned on an old Bette Davis movie *The Little Foxes*. It was one of her favorites as she despised the character Bette played, Regina Giddons, the wife of poor ol' dying Mr. Hubbard. She let him die over money, a perfectly wretched woman who would kill for money or just maybe because she wanted her way. She wanted to control. A perfectly wretched mother who did not love her daughter. There would be a perfectly horrible place for her when all this came to an end someday. But there was something brave about Regina. Not something to emulate, but nevertheless, she was brutally brave. *I need to be braver. I must learn how to care less and be braver. People will see me and think I'm the bravest woman in the world. One day I'll be very, very brave.*

It was late and Scott was out of town, again. More meetings. More dinner dates. She had a sneaky suspicion that all was not as it seemed, but she couldn't deal with that now. Turning out the light and pulling Beau next to her, she started to drift off. Her thoughts meandered in and out of her memory looking for a safe place to rest their weary heads. They had worked overtime today, and they were crawling all over each other, making a jumbled mess. Suddenly, Katie sat straight up in bed, startling Beau out of a deep sleep. She remembered the words she had uttered this afternoon *Lord. Please let him be close by.* Katie was stunned. She had actually prayed. When she was the lowest, she looked up and prayed. Deep down, did she still really believe?

CHAPTER 20

The weeks were rolling by and things had reached a low simmer with Katie and Scott. They were cordial but not too friendly, but at times, they did lapse into some semblance of a marriage. Scott was so desperately in love with Katie that he moped around like a sick puppy. He thought about her day and night and any time in between if possible. It was unimaginable that his life had gone from a lover's high to this wretched depth of despair. How did it all happen so quickly?

Katie on the other hand was existing but beginning to see a glimmer of hope. She was stepping out boldly and planning a life for herself within her life with Scott. Dr. Schladenhoffer had promised her that it was possible and indeed doable. Katie could be at peace in the midst of her circumstances. He had even suggested on numerous occasions that Katie could turn to God for help. But she couldn't help that she was still mad with God. She felt like He always came out on top, as if she was sort of stuck with Him. He always won. If life was awful, then you prayed, and He made it better. But, if He didn't make it better, then you offered up your suffering to Him. Offer it up for the poor souls in purgatory. They really needed your prayers, especially those who had no one to pray for them. But, what about the poor souls walking on this earth who are suffering and don't know what to do? How do you ask God for help when you don't trust He will do it? Can he? Sure, but Katie had decided a long time ago that God was on assignment elsewhere when she needed Him.

It was Wednesday night and the girl's weekly dinner date. It was Katie's turn to choose the place, and she had picked one of her favorite Atlanta restaurants, Pappadeaux Seafood Kitchen. An adorable young man was their server, and he entertained them with his personality and charm. The restaurant would be wise to hire hundreds of uber enthusiastic, but very cool people for their wait staff, for this one was a real delight.

Deciding on a meal was easy as Pappadeaux had fantastic food. Katie ordered the almond crusted Idaho River trout with lump crabmeat and tomato in a light brown butter sauce. Elizabeth wanted to try the cornbread stuffed salmon fillet with a shrimp. Both dinners sounded divine and would follow in suite with everything else they had ever eaten here.

Dinner came quickly, and the girls dug in tasting each other's food and insisting they would trade meals the next time they visited. Things were lovely until Katie brought up *The Game*. At first, Elizabeth couldn't remember the movie, but after a brief synopsis, she blanched at the memory. "Ugh. I hated that movie. Can't we talk about something else? How about *Pride and Prejudice*? A fantastic love story."

Katie shook her heard. "Silly, it isn't about the movie per se, it's about me."

"You? What do you have to do with that scary movie?"

"Lizbeth, it wasn't scary, but it was a psychological thriller. And that's what I feel like I'm going through now."

"Wait, you feel like you're in a game? Sorry, I don't get it."

"Look, remember when Michael Douglas and Sean Penn got involved in the game and Sean Penn says that his brother failed the test so he couldn't play the game? We'll that was part of the game. Remember? Do you?"

Elizabeth rolled her eyes in response. "Of course I remember, and it gave me the creeps. You know, we watched it together and had a hard time shaking it."

Taking her last bite of dinner, Katie chewed quickly, swallowed and continued. "What I'm trying to say here is that all the creepy stuff in the movie made Michael Douglas wonder if what was happening was real or some nightmare. What appeared to be real actually was real, or was it not? It was this hideous attack on Douglas's mental and physical being, attacks that might have driven a weaker person off the ledge. And, I agree that it was a most disturbing film. But that's not the point."

160

"Katie, would you mind getting to the point? I want to order desert. Do we share one or get two and share?"

"Let's get two and share. I'm gonna have the turtle fudge brownie, heavy on the pecans and chocolate sauce over my ice cream. What are you going to have?"

"Maybe the Crème Brule with fresh fruit."

"Lizbeth. This is decadent night so no fresh fruit. We eat that every day. Go for something swimming in carbs."

"Ok. Ok. How about cheesecake? Praline or plain with strawberries?"

"Go with plain and you can have your fresh fruit. Now, can I get back to my story?"

"Si. Continue."

"As I was saying, Michael Douglas has this super organized life where he controls everything. He has a bad marriage and suddenly he starts doubting everything about himself. Finally, he's about to lose it, as he cannot tell what is real and what is not. That's exactly how I feel. With everything that has happened between Scott and me, finding out he can't have kids, seeing how controlling he is, I don't know, I sorta felt like I was kind of similar to Douglas. Does that make sense?"

Elizabeth had two more bites of the Turtle Pecan Brownie and ignored the fresh strawberries around her cheesecake. "This is fabulous. Why'd you order the cheesecake?" Both girls hooted over Elizabeth's admission that the chocolate feast met their needs far better tonight than divine cheesecake. Chocolate is a tried, trusted, and tested cure for what ails you.

"Do you get what I'm saying? Sometimes I want to wake up and find out that this is all just some crazy dream, but I know that it isn't. But suppose it was a game? Suppose Scott is psycho and is trying to drive me mad? I swear I'd rather that be true instead of his sterility."

Elizabeth patted her hand and then scooped the last bite of ice cream. "That was just fabulous. Let's have coffee and mull over *The Game*."

"Good idea. Please order decaf for me while I run to the ladies room. Be right back."

Katie scooted out to the little girls' room weaving in and out of the tables in the packed restaurant. It was such a great place to eat that she wasn't surprised it looked full to capacity. A large party who was spilling out of their tables made travel difficult so Katie detoured and ended up in the farthest part of the restaurant. As she looked around to find the bathroom, a familiar face caught her attention. It was Laura Anne Stapleton sitting across from a broad shouldered man in a dark suit. Katie hesitated for a second trying to decide whether or not to stop by. Laura Anne saw her and quickly lifted her menu in an effort to hide her face. That was the red flag that Katie needed to egg her on. If she didn't want to see Katie, then Katie would make sure she didn't get what she wanted.

Taking a deep breath and putting on her best smile, Katie walked up to the table. "Hello, Laura Anne. Gosh, I haven't seen you in ages. How are you?"

From the look on her face, Laura Anne had been sick. She had no color to her face, which was quite unusual in that she played in the makeup heavily. "Katie Stewart. How nice to see you."

Katie turned to the man sitting at the table and waited for an introduction. Suddenly it seemed as if the whole restaurant stopped. Katie made eye contact with the man who happened to be her husband, Scott Stewart.

"Scott. What are you doing here? I thought you had a meeting in Savannah tonight, some business meeting with a new client. What's going on here?"

Scott pushed away from the table and stood up. He went over, kissed Katie lovingly on her cheek, and gave her a sweet hug. Pulling out a chair, he asked her to sit down. Stupidly, as if in a daze, she did.

"Laura Anne is my new client and she came home early from a trip to Savannah, so we decided to meet here. Laura Anne's expanding her wedding planner business to include catering on a much larger scale. It's a fantastic plan, really."

Laura Anne just smiled this thin-lipped sickly smile like the boa that'd just eaten the baby rabbit. She gave Katie the creeps.

"Scott, you never mentioned your new client was our dear Laura Anne. With our family connections, it would be natural for you to share that. You know small world and all. So, why didn't you?"

"You two talk while I go powder my nose. Will you excuse me?" Not waiting for an answer, Laura Anne left the table sashaying like a model on a runway. More than one male head was turned which was exactly her intent. Katie hated her.

"If I find out you are having an affair with Laura Anne Stapleton, I will have you assassinated by a member of the mafia. You will be strung up and tortured, castrated, and lose the use of your tongue. Are we quite clear on how I feel about this right now?"

Katie stood up prompting Scott to as well. "I am not having an affair, and I don't appreciate the accusations. I am having dinner with a client who just happens to be someone you can't stand. Please remember that I knew her long before I met you, and I wasn't attracted to her then, and I'm not attracted to her now. End of conversation. I'll see you when I get home."

Katie turned around, started to walk away, and just as suddenly turned back. "Scott, when were you going to tell me you didn't go to Savannah? This morning it was, 'I'll miss you.' You even said you were playing golf before you left Savannah. Laura Anne any good on the course?" By now, Katie was beyond furious. If she had any doubts about being in *The Game*, they had passed. Whether Scott was gas lighting her or not, someone was doing an excellent job of stripping her to her last, long-suffering nerve.

"Look Katie, you're making a scene. Laura Anne's partner is whom I was playing golf with, a man named Ryan Seamans. Try as hard as you can to make something out of this, but this is what it is, a client dinner."

"Ok, Scott, you win as usual. I hope poor Ryan isn't waiting to tee off in the morning."

She took a breath and spat out, "This is the last thing our marriage needs right now. Darling, there is that trust issue that just continues to rear its ugly head." That was it. As Katie headed back to the table, she met Elizabeth half way. "Don't say a word and we'll discuss it in the car. I feel a fight welling up in me. So all I want to say is, 'let the game begin.'"

Elizabeth was appropriately scandalized. Even if she suspected Scott was having an affair with Laura Anne, a thousand Arabian horses couldn't have dragged that out of her. "Katie, things are not always as they seem so keep that in mind before you go off on Scott. Give him the benefit of the doubt. If you two are going to work on your marriage, then you have to be patient and fair."

"I agree that I need to be patient and fair, because I haven't done anything wrong. I'm the one who has to get over anxiety attacks. I'm the one who has to be the perfect wife, cook the perfect meals, and I'm the long suffering one who always has to forgive and be patient. Well, dammit, I don't want to be that person. Lizbeth, I'll just murder him if I find out he's doing it with her. Ooh, I'm just furious."

"One day at a time is all I can say. By the way, does this cancel dinner on Saturday with Evan and me? His parents will be so disappointed you didn't come to their party."

"We'll be there, don't worry."

They arrived at Katie's where Elizabeth had left her car. After a quick hug, the girls went their separate ways.

CHAPTER 21

———————∽———————

Katie couldn't help herself. She didn't know if Scott was coming home or not, but she bet he would just to prove he wasn't having an affair. Which proved nothing of course. But she was learning how Scott's mind worked. Make everything seem as normal as possible, keep the routine, and stay structured. One day follows the next. However, that wasn't how Katie lived.

Katie piled up pillows on Dolly's bed and settled in with the remote, a book, and Beau. She uprooted the sheets tucked so tightly under the mattress and fluffed the down comforter until it was cloud like. She was so keyed up that it was too farfetched that she might actually sleep tonight. She was itching to get into a fight with Scott, but she knew he wouldn't fall into that trap either. Beau on the other hand was a clean easy read. A dog biscuit and a belly rub had him eating out of her hands literally and figuratively. Ever faithful Beau. He found his place in the small of her back and began to snore slightly, the good kind of snore that belongs to dogs who run with the angels at night.

Katie heard Scott come in and suddenly lost all desire for a confrontation. He'd caught her with the lights on so it was ridiculous to pretend she was sleeping. But he surprised her and didn't come in. Straining to hear what he was doing, Katie went to her closed door and tried to listen. He'd been in the kitchen and Katie suspected he was fixing a drink, but she was wrong. After what seemed an eternity, Scott moved into the den and started rummaging through drawers as if searching for something. The commotion briefly woke the little prince whose eyes fluttered back in his head as he rolled back over. Such an amazing watchdog.

Suddenly Katie heard the sound of music and was startled as Scott caught her listening at the door. He was standing there with his hand held out to her and seeing the pleading look on his face, she accepted. Pulling her to him, he led her to the den and enveloped her tightly in his arms. Then she heard the Righteous Brothers singing one of her many most favorite songs. She ran the words repeatedly, agreeing with the boys that she was no good without him.

And they danced and danced. Scott had programmed the music to restart each time the song ended so they moved across the den floor like the young lovers they had forgotten they were. Scott held Katie's hand in his, holding it tightly to his chest. With her free arm around his neck, he wrapped his arm around her waist defying anyone to remove it. He was where he was supposed to be and had longed to be for so long.

And all the walls came tumbling down. Releasing his catch, he looked down into Katie's beautiful eyes and saw hope for the first time in many, many months. She no longer held revulsion in her eyes; she no longer looked like she would rather swim with sharks than be with him; she looked as if she had found buried treasure and that treasure was once more, him.

Something had happened inside of Katie. Scott had caught her off guard, as he was so adept at doing. Seeing him with Laura Anne was a devastating blow igniting a wallop of jealousy she would have gone to her grave denying. When she least expected it, he found a way into her heart, a hidden opening she swore wasn't there, and like an arrow seeking its mark, he found a way in. Oh, how wonderful it felt to be in his arms again; she breathed him and released all the love she had banished to the dankest dungeon, chained and manacled to a prison wall. She had wanted no more of the pain that came with loving Scott. Now, all she wanted was Scott.

Nothing was said, not promises of repentance, not plans for the future, not hope of reconciliation. The now had no words written for it, nothing could be spoken, and words could not birth what they felt. This coming together was intense and thorough all the way to their marrow, it was love ignited once more. Then they slept, a night of togetherness and peace, a peace that was deep and healing, and filled with fantasies of new hopes and love fulfilled. The morning brought smiles and laughter that last night did happen, and they were not awaking to another dawn of darkness. For now, it was just Katie, Scott, and Beau, the three of them nestled in the bed, jockeying for the covers and enough room to stretch out. It was not perfect, not perfect by a long shot, but for now it would have to do and would do rather nicely, it seemed.

I love those who can smile in trouble, who can gather strength from distress, and grow brave by reflection. 'Tis the business of little minds to shrink, but they whose heart is firm, and whose conscience approves their conduct, will pursue their principles unto death.

– Leonardo da Vinci

CHAPTER 22

———————$\sim$———————

The months had passed and things had gotten better between them. Certainly not perfect, but filled with the hope that life would go on and they could be happy together. Katie had come to terms with the idiosyncrasies that made up her husband. She had accepted that in all things she was committed to this marriage. She no longer loved Scott with an adolescent intensity, but had matured into acceptance of the very human man she had married. At times, she was saddened by all the things that would never come to pass, but she found that if she didn't focus on her disappointments and looked to be content, if not happy, then she would survive.

The trials they had been through actually made Katie stronger, less dependent. She no longer wanted to please Scott for the sake of his pleasure. Rather she expected a mutually respectful relationship where both partners gave equally, knowing full well that at times the giving would see saw unequally, but would even itself out in the end. She had come to the conclusion that she couldn't stay home anymore, and she needed to go back to teaching. She loved it and knew she was well trained and successful at what she did. It didn't matter if Scott protested; he was simply no longer the center of her universe. It was good to get off the thin ice. She knew she would survive if their marriage ended. She was realistic about the emotional cost, but it no longer frightened her as it used to. Her old spirit was returning and she welcomed it like a long lost friend. Dr. Schladenhoffer had reminded her, "Baby steps. One step at a time. One day at a time. Keep your eyes forward and never look back." She took it to heart and it became her mantra.

There were other changes as well. Katie had started to pray a little. They weren't very powerful prayers, and they didn't ask much. It was more of just "getting to know you and testing the waters a bit." Katie had no idea what to expect from her prayers, but she liked talking to him again. Sometimes at night, with Scott and Beau trading snores, she'd imagine Jesus holding out his hand to her the way you might to a frightened kitten who desperately wants to come to you but is simply too afraid. Afraid that you might capture her and never let her go. Afraid of the unknown and the strangeness of your hand and your voice. Wanting the comfort you offer and the safety from the world, but needing more proof that what you offer is just that, an offer for you to come. She was afraid and excited all at the same time. Much like that little kitten who purred while she was scampering away, turning back at the corner and longing desperately for you to come get her. So Katie had whispered softly, ever so softly, "Come get me, Lord." She reminded him that she wasn't sure she'd mean it in the morning, but for tonight, she longed for his touch.

Katie had sent out numerous resumes and followed up with phone calls and emails. She had been realistic in this tight job market, but she felt part of the world again. She knew when the time was right, she'd find employment. She just wanted the time to be now.

The mailman had finally arrived and Katie hurried to grab the mail. She was waiting on the all-important letter from her previous school telling her she had gotten the position. All Katie had thought about was that letter and the joy of teaching once more. Grabbing her letter opener and kicking off her sandals, she plopped down onto the sofa and read. The news was not good as a hiring freeze was on due to the economy, and school systems everywhere were cutting back on personnel. They expressed a desire to have her return as soon as the recession ended. Attached was a lovely, hand written note from her principal that softened the blow of the standard rejection letter.

Dolly would say that God's timing is perfect, and if you operate within His perfect will, you will see that the wait time was part of God's great plan. So far, God's great plan for her had been anything but great. Katie thought God was a little early on testing her hesitant invitation to be on speaking terms again. However, she refused to let it get her down.

Baby steps, and at least she lacked the financial anguish of being unemployed. Things could be a lot worse.

Katie knew that Dolly's response to that would be "sometimes life's consequences were caused by you, the collective you that is, when you operate in and out of God's will." It was all so confusing, and all Katie knew was that she didn't have a job and wasn't going to get one anytime soon. She tried not to think about it, rather she deliberately set out to find something to do while she waited. She knew she could only clean the house, weed the yard, swim in the lake, play tennis and play with Beau for so long until her mind begged for stimulation. Part of the problem was that she was in a neighborhood filled with young, upwardly mobile families crawling with children. She thought she'd scream if she were invited to another baby shower, where everyone was a mother, pregnant, or nursing. She felt like an outsider and people acted so strangely when they asked her the inevitable question. "Do you and Scott have kids?" No. "Well, are you guys planning for any?" No. What else could she say? Each time the question was asked Katie was tempted to swim in despair. However, she had grown up enough to know that despair was like a monster that multiplies the longer you feed it. Recognize it, but send it on its way. Yes, there was a world without children, and she could try to live with that. But, the world she was trying to enter again was closed. What was she to do? Her choices were few and simple. Don't deal with it. Avoid thinking about it. Living a life of solitude, pain and anxiety were things of the past for Katie no matter how hard they tried to come home and roost. It was tempting she must admit, to go down those roads again, and sometimes, late at night, she'd venture out and travel that path again. Yet, the light and promise of new things so over shadowed the dark pull that it was beginning to get easier and easier to tear up the ticket to the dark side.

The doorbell rang delivering her from planning a pity party that had been attended far too many times. Today had been a rough day, and she was frustrated that she wasn't breathing rainbows. She couldn't imagine who would be coming over, but she would be grateful for a visit. Opening the door, she was surprised to see an older man, in his early sixties maybe, handsome, and looking remarkably like her husband Scott.

"Good morning." Katie offered while bending out from behind the door. "Can I help you?"

"Good morning. Are you Katie Stewart?"

"Yes, I am. What can I do for you?

"Katie, I'm Brandon Stewart, Scott's father."

"I'm sorry; there must be some mistake because Scott's father has been dead for several years. Maybe you are confusing me with someone else." Not for a minute did it register as truth.

Reaching for his wallet, Mr. Stewart took out a picture of Scott and offered it to Katie. There he was sitting at a party toasting his father, arms around each others' shoulders, and smiling that million-dollar smile. "This is my son. Do you recognize him or do I really have the wrong Katie Stewart?" He smiled a warm and inviting smile, nothing sinister or frightening.

"Please come in Mr. Stewart. I'm afraid I'm at a loss for words just now." Katie led him into the kitchen and offered him a seat at the table. She offered him coffee, which he gladly accepted, and waited for it to brew. Suddenly Katie turned around as if it had finally sunk in. Her hands started to tremble and she felt that old familiar bolt of electricity surge through her body. If this was truly Scott's dad, then the implications were more than her mind could fathom.

"Your home is lovely and the view back here is just beautiful. I'm sure you must enjoy it tremendously." Right off the bat Katie could tell that Scott's father was a well-educated man. His suit was impressive, he held himself with great bearing, and he was articulate in his speech. She was trying to imagine the previously dead man's profession when he interrupted her train of thought.

"This is not an easy thing for me to do. But there is so much I need to discuss with you."

"I assure you that sitting with you, the only resurrected soul I've ever met, is a little daunting. Would you mind waiting for a minute while I call Scott? I need to ask him what's going on here."

"Katie, please don't call Scott. It will serve no purpose now and may only further jeopardize things. You'll just have to trust me on that. Please, come sit here, and I'll explain it all to you."

Trust. There was that word again. They just didn't get along. Katie heard warning sirens going off all around her. *Be wary of the man who talks about trust.*

He was kind and seemingly sincere. He had a gentle but strong voice, which offered something to hold onto. It was as if Scott were sitting in front of her twenty years from now.

Katie's mind was running wild with imaginations. Every day of her life with Scott had been filled with extremes, extremes of love, hate, happiness, despair, excitement and disappointment. It had been a life filled with promises that soon burst, spewing acid on everyone around. No, Katie just wasn't sure at all what Mr. Stewart came a callin' for.

"Mr. Stewart."

"Katie, please call me Brandon. After all you are my daughter-in-law."

"I might need a while to get that connection since I have cried with Scott over your death several times. You see, Scott told me you died when he graduated from college."

It was odd. Brandon Stewart didn't act startled or surprised. He wasn't shocked that Scott had buried him years ago. He took it in stride as if he had always known that.

"Did he also tell you about his mother's death?" Katie was still back on the funeral of Scott's father. But, Mr. Stewart was continuing as if he was going line by line on a checklist. Next. She didn't even have time to process the fact that he was even sitting there in front of her much less that it had implications that were light years away from her reality.

"Yes, he did. Frankly, Mr. Stewart, Scott blames you for his mother's death. I don't mean to appear cruel, but having a mentally ill mother, especially one as sick as Mrs. Stewart, was a devastating environment in which to grow up. I'm so sorry for your loss and the sad state of Scott's upbringing. I can only imagine how difficult it was to be married to someone with a psychotic personality disorder."

Brandon had a queer smile on his face. Not a sneer or anything that frightened Katie. Maybe it was more of "here we go again."

"If you can give me some time I can explain all about Scott's upbringing and the reason that I'm here. It's a long story, so I'd be delighted to have that coffee."

Brandon Stewart watched Katie as she moved around the well-appointed kitchen. He was not surprised that she was lovely; on the contrary, Scott had a magnetism that confounded the wise and the beautiful. Yet, there was something much deeper about this woman, in the graceful way she moved, in the warmth of her invitation into the home, in her sincerity that shone right through her eyes. As he so frequently thought, *my son is a damned fool.*

Katie poured the steaming coffee and dressed it. She cut two slices of her divine coffee cake, loaded with pecans, and popped them in the toaster oven. In just a few seconds cinnamon wafted across the kitchen making their mouths water. Katie added a dollop of butter and gently spread it over the heated cake. Lastly, she moved them outside to the back porch and nestled in on the sofa. Now facing each other and Beau under her feet, Katie anxiously waited for Brandon to start.

Brandon cleared his throat. "Some of this may not make sense at first, but give me some time and I think it will all play out. The details are important, so forgive me if I sound long winded." "Long winded is not such a bad thing if you're trying to get to the root of the matter. Have at it because none of this makes sense to me, and I'm frankly a little afraid of what you're going to say."

"Katie, I started to date my ex wife, Anne, when we were in high school. I'm ashamed to say that Anne got pregnant, and we were forced to marry. Anne's father was an attorney and did not want his daughter to have a stained reputation. My father was the CEO of a large corporation in a small town in South Carolina, and he aligned with Anne's parents to force the wedding. It was a mistake from the very beginning. Anne came from a great deal of wealth and although my family was quite comfortable, we were not on the same social register or if we were she held first position while we barely hung on to last. Her family hailed from pre - Civil War royalty while mine had actually migrated as carpetbaggers. It made no difference to anyone, but the old money in our town held a far higher prestige than the nouveau riche. Nevertheless, Anne expected to live and spend as she had while living under her father's roof. I, on the other hand, wanted to make it on my own without anyone's help. Anne did not approve nor did she wish to struggle. The word appeared obscene to her."

Brandon reached down to sip his coffee but passed on the cake. "We were married for three years when Anne ran off with another man. This man was quite wealthy and able to give her all that her heart desired. She took as much from me as she could possibly get, but mercifully, she left Scott to me."

"She didn't want her only child?" That was unfathomable to a woman still in mourning over the loss of her children never to be born.

"I'm afraid not. When she left us, she was only 21 and she hated our life together. Her friends were off at college or doing the traditional summers in Europe. I know that it sounds terrible to you, but Anne was thoroughly spoiled by her parents, her father particularly, and that was all she knew. She didn't want a family dragging her down, so she left both of us."

"But I don't understand why Scott lied to me about his mom. I don't care if you guys got a divorce. No wait, I didn't mean it like that. Of course I care, but it wouldn't have made any difference in how I felt about Scott. I just don't understand."

Brandon asked for another cup of coffee and had a bite of his coffee cake. "This is delicious. I drove in from Spartanburg this afternoon and haven't stopped for breakfast or lunch." He washed his bite down with a large swallow of coffee.

"When Scott was in the fifth grade, I got a call from his teacher. She was very worried about him and asked that I come in for a conference. His grades were good and he had many friends, so I had no idea what she was talking about. When I get there, she starts to tell me how sorry she was about the death of my wife and how Scott was having trouble dealing with it. She suggested that we go see someone to help us through the grieving process. It seems that Scott was getting upset at school and failing to turn in homework and other assignments. He told the teacher just about the same type of story he told you. Only, his mom was alive and living in Columbia, South Carolina. It was all very perplexing."

"Mr. Stewart, please stop for a minute. I'm lost. Is Scott's mother alive or not?"

"She's alive, lives in a nursing home. She was diagnosed with dementia ten years ago and has progressively gotten worse. She stayed married to the same man, who unceremoniously dumped her in the nursing home as soon as he possibly could. None of her family is left to help her."

"Then shouldn't you tell Scott that his mother isn't dead? Doesn't he deserve to know that?"

"Katie, Scott knows his mother isn't dead. When she first got sick, she called me to see Scott. She wanted to make amends before it was too late. The sad thing was she remembered Scott as a small child. When she walked out on us, we remained the same, stuck in some time warp where we would never age. When I went to visit her in the nursing home, she had only one picture by her bed, and it was of Scott on his third birthday. It was so terribly sad."

"Mr. Stewart. Would you mind if we walked a bit down by the lake? I really need to clear my head. I'm so confused and I'm surprised at my reaction. I guess that's it. I'm not reacting at all."

They walked down the path towards the lake while a nice breeze blew around them. Katie's gardens were magnificent and Brandon seemed quite familiar with gardening. "Your flowers and shrubs are beautiful. Do you spend a lot of time out here?"

"Actually, I do. I find that it's good therapy and it gives me something to do while Scott travels or works late, which he seems to be doing more and more frequently now. Do you have gardens at home?"

"It's my therapy as well. I enjoy golf and tennis, but when I really need to do some deep thinking, I head out to the garden and weed or plant. It is most satisfying."

Katie smiled at his choice of words. He sounded a bit British.

Katie's garden was filled with Pink Charm daffodils, white and red lantana, dwarf crape myrtle, dragon wing begonias with vibrant hues of pink and red, and a magnificent row of rose creek abelia to attract humming birds and butterflies. It was a gardener's paradise and Katie possessed the necessary green thumb.

They sat down in the white latticed gazebo and looked out over the lake. Katie needed a reprieve from her trip down to Dante's inferno. At this time, she would suggest that he add a new level of hell and suffering for Scott Stewart. None of this made sense. All of this defied logic. It had to be a lie, but deep inside, Katie knew it to be true.

From out of the doggie door, Beau bounded down the hill and slid into Katie's lap as if he were a mere puppy. At ninety pounds, he was anything but. Beau possessed a great love of people and was supremely happy when plopped down in dead center of any activity surrounding him. Now the mallards on the lake taunted him with their calls, and he sped off to direct them. Katie loved their colors, the green and walnut blend of their feathers, but most of all she adored their red shoes that complimented their look so nicely. Why couldn't the world always be this serene?

"Do you have to bathe him frequently?"

Katie turned and looked at Brandon. "I'm sorry, what were you saying?"

"Oh, just that Beau must stay in the lake a good bit, being a Labrador and chasing ducks, it must make for a great deal of work. Lakes and dogs make a pretty smelly combination."

Katie opened her arms to welcome the returning master of her home. He bathed under her chin and checked for crumbs around her cheeks and mouth. Content that she had appreciated his kisses, he laid his heavy head on her lap. Without thinking, Katie began to stroke the velvet softness of his ears and smile at the beauty of this wonderful dog.

"Beau is afraid of the water. He was with Scott early one morning and fell into the lake. He was just two months old, and I guess he never recovered. He's had an aversion for water ever since. Funny, now that we are talking about Scott and his life of lies, I've always suspected that Scott threw Beau into the lake to make him swim. It's terrible I know, but how many Labs do you know who avoid water like the plague?"

It was the first time Katie had ever verbalized her accusations about Scott and Beau. The story just didn't make sense when he told her, but ever-smooth Scott had such a way of making her feel so stupid if she questioned the logic of anything he said. Suddenly she knew Scott had been impatient and wanted Beau to swim early. It was all so silly, but it was the way Scott wanted it to be. On his terms and on his time schedule. Sadly, it backfired on him as so many of his lies have done.

Brandon reached over, stroked the underbelly of the dog, and admired his fitness and strength. "I guess Beau makes you feel pretty safe, as he looks like he'd make an excellent guard dog."

Katie started to laugh. Not a hearty belly laugh, but a chuckle at something humorous he'd said. "Although we have a high tech alarm system, you're right, Beau's who makes me feel safe. He's great company when Scott travels or works late, which is all the time now."

Brandon rolled and unrolled his napkin. He was obviously uncomfortable as he thought about what he was about to say. He knew this was the make it or break it question so he plowed ahead. "Katie. This may sound like an odd question, but do you love Scott? I mean really love him. And are you committed to this marriage no matter the troubles that may come your way?"

Katie rubbed Beau's ears and stroked his chest. He had planted himself between her knees in an ever-protective position. She thought for a few moments and responded. "Do I love Scott? I honestly don't know any more. Can we get past all that you've just shared with me? Mr. Stewart, nothing you've told me has sunk in. I feel like you're pouring water over oil. It just seems unable to connect with me. I keep waiting for you to scream April fool's or something. Candid Camera maybe or how about the Twilight Zone? I'm sorry about the futile attempt at humor, but I honestly don't know what else to say. Why do you ask if I love Scott?"

"Because what I have to tell you is quite difficult. It will take deep love and an even deeper commitment to walk Scott through this. I'll get to the point. Scottie's partner, Jim Burns, called late yesterday afternoon very concerned about Scott and some trouble he had gotten himself into. It seems that Jim believes Scott has embezzled company funds. Jim says it looks like he has pulled 200,000 out of the company over the last two years. He has hired a forensic auditor to come in and comb the books, but the evidence is pretty clear. He has asked Scott to return the money or face prosecution. Jim doesn't want an ugly scene, so bad for an accounting firm, so if Scott returns the money and resigns, then Jim will be satisfied. Scott will receive no compensation or earnings from the company, as he will have to forfeit any rights to the company. Frankly, Jim is afraid that as the auditor digs into past years, they will find that Scott has been doing many shady things, things that Jim has long suspected but did not have the proof. Through a series of errors, Jim stumbled upon Scott's dirty dealings. He suspects that Scott has a gambling problem. It's a damn good offer and an overly generous one as well. But I know my son, and he won't be able to handle this without you."

"Mr. Stewart, Brandon, this is really too much for me today. Frankly, I'm scaring myself at my lack of response. I feel as if someone has vacuumed out all of my emotions and left me completely empty. Right now, I have to decide what to do when Scott comes home. The embezzlement. The lies. God only knows what else he's lied about, or what other trouble he's gotten into. If he is gambling, then I think things are going to get much worse before they get better."

Katie shifted uneasily under the weight of her now snoring Beau. Clouds were rolling in ready to bring a nice chilling rain. "Brandon. There's so much I want to ask, but for now, I just need to know one thing. Why, when Scott had the physical problems, didn't you take him to get help before it was too late? Because of that, you know Scott's sterile."

Brandon shook his head slowly as he gathered his thoughts. He was starting to get concerned about Katie. She was beyond pale, now the color of grey. Her hands were beginning to tremble and she had a wide-eyed fright to her face. He knew he'd have to be very careful in what he said next.

"Scott has had some serious issues with lying his whole life. When he was growing up, he would lie just to have something different to say. I worried that he would rather lie than tell the truth. He has always lied to get out of trouble. We went into therapy together after Scott started telling wild tales about his mother and her death. I don't mind admitting that it scared me to death. All the therapists said the same thing, that Scott was responding to his mother's rejection by creating a world he could control, and he controlled it with lying. It isn't much of a stretch to see how many people responded to a little boy whose mother had died when he was only three. Scott has always gotten away with it. He has always been so handsome and charming. People wanted to believe him."

"But what about you? Why didn't you try and stop it?"

"Look, I've made so many mistakes over the years raising Scott that I do assume much of the responsibility for how he's turned out. I blame myself for so many things I have done poorly. Over the years, we've seen some of the best therapists in the southeast and tried many different drugs. However, it was more of a spiritual thing. No drugs helped. Church didn't help. Nothing helped. It seems I made it worse by not knowing what to do. I spoiled Scott and spent a great deal of time talking to him, trying to explain everything to him. Now I know that there needed to be consequences for his actions, and I just didn't do that. Maybe a good paddling now and again and a few restrictions might have made a difference. I guess I failed my son completely."

Katie thought for a minute about Scott's life and the suffering that made him so miserable. She suddenly felt so terribly sorry for him, and her anger began to abate. She of all people knew how hard it was to live without parents, but at least she had hers until she was twelve. Scott lost his mom when he was just three. That must have awful for him. Part of her heart wanted to retreat and start building the wall again as quickly as she could. The other part, the damnable part she fought so hard against, wanted to rescue Scott and offer him a way out. She wanted, no needed to feel angry, but the nothingness she felt frightened her more than any panic attack she'd ever had. Was all this, all that she had worked so very hard for, all for nothing? Had she opened her heart to Scott once more only to give him more room to crush her? She had no idea where time was as her thoughts ran like scattered blind mice.

Brandon waited for a few moments before he continued. Katie had nodded along as Brandon shared about Scott's lying. She had caught Scott in some suspicious stories, but he was such a convincing liar. He always asked, "Why would I lie about a thing like that?" Katie waited for Brandon to continue.

"Katie. I know all of this is coming as quite a shock to you and to me as well. I had no idea Scott has kept you in the dark over so many things. So I might as well tell you everything so we can plan on what to do next."

"I'm not sure I can handle anything else. But I do believe in getting it all out in the open." Katie looked down at her watch and saw that they had talked for hours, which meant Scott should be coming home soon.

"Scott's sterile because he had a vasectomy. When he married his first wife, she wanted to get pregnant right away. Scott knew he'd make a huge mistake rushing into a marriage with a woman he hardly knew. The more she pressed for kids, the more detached he became. He was afraid she'd lie to him about birth control just so she could conceive. So, in typical Scott fashion, he went off and had a vasectomy. You know how he hates to be controlled, so he always makes things happen the way he wants them to. I don't know what he told you about a physical problem, but he never had one."

Suddenly it all came crashing in. The emotions, held together like a jigsaw puzzle, crumbled and fell around her feet. They threatened to overtake her as they screamed to be heard. Her head was swimming and she felt the urge to scream and scream until the world ended. Another wife? Maybe she could find a way to deal with that. The lies? Wasn't he the master liar of all times? But, as odd as it seems it was neither of them. Oh, it was terrible that he had been married before and didn't tell her, and it was terrible that he was such a compulsive liar. But, to deliberately close the door on children over a control issue and then blame it on your parents was obscene. Now it was Scott's fault that she wouldn't have babies. Their babies that she longed for so much. And, that was the match that lit the tinderbox, the fuel that set it all ablaze, and the sword that pierced her heart.

Her mind was racing as if playing tag with a room full of children. What of last week when they had danced their sorrows away? When the Righteous Brothers gave a voice to the urgency in their hearts? Katie and Scott had decided then that life was not so great when they were not together and had recommitted themselves to a marriage forever and ever, amen. Now everything seemed surreal and absurd. Who was the man she married whose words oozed out of his mouth sounding like pearls and diamonds but turned into lizards and vipers in the real light of truth?

Katie stood up dumping Beau on the floor of the gazebo. She slid her hands into her pockets and then just as quickly, crossed them over her chest. Tears of rage and frustration streamed down her face, and she stood totally beaten, down cast, destroyed. It was if the world she knew no longer had a floor, no earth under her, no foundation, and below that was the darkest abyss, one that people would be too afraid to imagine. Katie knew she would have to make some painful choices, or she would be a permanent resident in the land of total misery, a place she had been visiting for far too long.

CHAPTER 23

It took Dolly and Cat just under four hours to get to Katie. It was so very disconcerting to get the phone call from Scott's father, the man whose soul rested in purgatory and was the recipient of so many nightly prayers. Suddenly he was alive, and Katie was teetering on the edge of something sinister and dark.

His call shocked and upset them both very much. He seemed like a nice man and genuinely concerned over Katie. He explained that he'd had no idea that Scott had hidden his first marriage from Katie, and he felt terrible that he had been the one to bring her so much bad news. He was used to Scott and his lies, but Katie had been kept in the dark over so many things. Brandon loved his son, but he knew he needed professional help. Now he feared for Katie, as Scott had swung way out in his sanity and reasoning.

They would take her home and let her heal. The beach with all its sounds and smells would reach deep into places that voices could not. The roots of home would keep her safe and locked onto this earth.

The trip home was a fog. Katie had doubled up on her Ativan and slept most of the way home. When she finally did wake up, her mouth was dry and dusty much as her heart was. Her bodied ached as if she had been in a war zone and just maybe she had. She'd never liked the saying "get my mind around" something, but today she understood it better than before. How could she catalog all that had just happened? For now, she would tuck it away on a top shelf and leave it alone for a very long while.

Katie set up her room and unpacked her bags. Her true feelings had been docked at the front door and she carefully avoided losing control.

She so desperately feared that facing the reality of her situation would be more than her fragile mind could handle. Dr. Schladenhoffer had warned her quite sternly of stuffing her emotions and putting them aside to deal with when she felt like it. However, for now, she could only move one foot in front of the other if she didn't think and didn't project into the future. It would all come oozing out like the head of a boil, and she knew it. She just couldn't bring herself to lance it today or anytime in the near future. Let it take care of itself.

Today Katie smiled at some of the things she'd packed, none of which would do her much good at the beach. However, a few things were quite important: a framed picture of her parents, a puppy pic of Beau, and Dr. Chris Martin's business card with his personal cell phone number on the back. She slid it into her bedside table just after she saved it in her iPad. Finally, she opened her laptop and posted a Tweet. *At the beach. All hell broke loose, and I've left Scott. Give me some time and I'll reenter the world. Right now I need some time alone. Hugs.* She closed the computer and slid it under the bed. She knew Scott would go to her Facebook and Twitter pages and then respond. She could turn off her phone, ignore his calls to the beach house, and unplug him from her life. At least temporarily. Right now Katie had to focus on herself and getting spiritually and physically well again. She couldn't have been in better or happier hands.

Katie grabbed a pen and a notebook sitting under the bedside table. After a week of shock, despair, and tremendous anxiety, she knew today would be step number one. All she had to do was decide which way to go and how to get started. So, she began with a list of books she wanted to download to her Kindle. This would be a perfect time to try to sit still and read. She had scoffed at the new Kindle that Scott had given her. Why in the world would someone prefer a wireless reading device to a book? With a book you can dog ear the pages, bend the spine for an easier read, write in the margins, and underline parts of important text. Yet, being on the beach, with the wind blowing, it was awfully difficult to manage a book. Scott first bought the Kindle 2, but returned it for the Kindle DX. Katie hated to admit how delighted she was with her new reader. She could now go to the beach with a hundred books and not carry a single one. Chalk it up to one thing Scott did extremely well.

Katie then added a visit to Old Sarge and Mrs. Hennessey. He was still in the nursing home but was making some progress with his speech. Katie had been delighted when she heard the good news and was anxious to go see him. Finally, she would go see Father John. There was much she needed to discuss with him and for the first time in many years she was ready to listen to something about God.

The mind is its own place and in itself, can make a Heaven of Hell, a Hell of Heaven.

– John Milton

CHAPTER 24

S cott was pacing the den floor. At times, he had to step over books and bric -a -brac that he had tossed in a fit of anger. Bottles of empty wine were on the coffee table and littered across the back deck. His hand, especially across the knuckles, was bruised and cut where it had made contact with his father's jaw. Scott choked once and then spit a wad of blood that appeared to contain a tooth or two. It had been an ugly scene ending only in the final break of their relationship. Each had banished the other from their lives permanently.

That afternoon, the day that Brandon Stewart came to Scott's home, was one of the worst Scott had ever lived. After a rough day at work, with his partner screaming like a banshee, Scott had headed home to his Katie. Things were not great, but they were getting better. A night of dancing, holding each other tightly, seemed to scrape off some of the old scabs that were stopping their healing. Hope had entered then, and Scott was ecstatic to have a chance with Katie once more. He swore he would make it all up to her. He would give her the world, anything, if she would only love him like she had before. No, not like she had before, not controls or expectations, dear God, just love me anyway you can.

Yet, the earth pulled out from beneath him as Scott came face to face with his dad sitting in the kitchen. Katie was gone along with Beau, and Brandon Stewart was to blame. The ensuing arguments were heated and ugly with Scott taking no responsibility for them. "Why'd you have to come here? Why didn't you just meet me some place or call me, Dad? Damn, why'd you come see Katie?"

Scott was so mad he was sputtering and his face was turning a deep, dark maroon. When his dad told him Katie had gone to the beach, Scott

186

was so angry, he wanted to kill his dad. The feelings were so intense it scared him to death. He no longer saw his dad standing there in front of him, but instead he saw someone who had gotten in the way and had caused Katie to leave him.

Brandon looked at his son and felt all the life drain from him. He had had no idea Scott would react the way he did. He suddenly realized that Katie wasn't just Scott's wife, the woman he adored, but she was something that belonged solely to him, and he couldn't bear the thought of losing that. Brandon knew that his son was on the edge of the life he had been living, the lies that had blurred into reality, were now taking over his mind. He was truly afraid for his son, this young man who stood before him now, anxious, depressed, desperate, and afraid. Much afraid. It was a dangerous combination.

"Couldn't you just leave us alone? She's gone now, Dad, and it's all your fault. Dammit, stay out of my business." Scott was mumbling and whining like a child. His brows were knitted together in a deep scowl, and he appeared to be pouting.

"What did you tell her anyway? Something terrible or she wouldn't have left me. Tell me now, Dad. Tell me." Scott began to pound the table in perfect sync with every word he formed.

Brandon knew he would need to proceed with caution. Reasoning was out, and Brandon felt emotionally trapped. He didn't want to set him off anymore, but he had to do something.

"Son, I'm here to help you, and you do need help. Your partner called me about the embezzlement and the other issues you are having. Scott, you're in a great deal of trouble, and I don't think you realize it. You have to pay that money back. Jim called me and told me how serious the situation had gotten and that he would press charges if you didn't pay it back. We need to deal with this now. Scott. Do you hear me?"

Suddenly, Scott pushed back out of his chair and lunged at his father. He was screaming, "Oh, hell yea I hear you. I hate your damn guts. I hate you!" Over and over, he repeated those words until spittle was coming out of his mouth. Suddenly, he reared back and hit him squarely in the jaw. The shock pushed Brandon over another chair and down onto the floor where Scott jumped on him and started to pound his face. It was unbelievable to see father and son going at it like that. Brandon pushed Scott off him and got up trying to reach his phone. He didn't want to hurt him or to get hurt anymore himself, but Scott needed to be stopped. It felt like a million years before his fist made contact with Scott's face. That handsome face that snowed the women and drew people to him. The face of his boy, the hope that sustained him when Anne left. That winning, charming smile was now covered in blood that oozed from the once patrician nose that was most certainly broken. Scott fell back and was out.

Brandon called his best friend Sam Banneker and told him what had happened. In less than a half hour, he was at the house and taking care of both patients. Scott indeed had a broken nose, some missing teeth, and a mild concussion. Brandon would be fine once the bruises and cuts healed. However, the memory of his son's assault would stay with him forever. It wasn't that he couldn't forgive Scott; it was now a part of Scott's personality that he had never seen. A frightening, violent one that had never reared its ugly head, and one he hoped he'd never see again. Scott needed help desperately, and regardless of his refusal to seek help, Brandon was sure to force the issue.

After Dr. Banneker patched them both up, Scott began to clear his head. He was in a good bit of pain, but he didn't care. All he wanted was Katie. "Dad, will you try to get Katie on the phone, please? I really need to talk to her." Scott sounded like a kid again. He voice was pleading, hoarse, a desperate tone to it, urging his dad to call Katie.

"I don't think she'll talk to you or that her grandmother will let her talk to you. Katie was devastated by your past. I was worried about her as well. I just don't think calling her is a good idea."

Scott started to shake and his nose started to bleed again. The doctor was pressing gauze over the top of his nose, but Scott had pulled away and was cursing like a sailor. He began to threaten his father and spit out profanities in a way they had never heard before. He sounded like a crazy man. "Call her now!" he screamed balling his fist and posturing towards his dad.

Dr. Banneker grabbed Scott by the shoulders and pushed him back down. He took out a syringe and filled it with Valium. Rolling up Scott's sleeve, he jabbed him in his shoulder and talked to him in a stern but controlled voice. Brandon stood there staring at his son and felt totally useless. His son's emotional pain was destroying both of them, yet this was not the end, rather the beginning of health or death for Scott. "What's next, Sam?" Brandon was pleading with his eyes hoping that Sam had some answer and could offer some hope.

"Scott needs some professional help, and he needs it right away. He's on the verge of a nervous breakdown and this will get a lot worse before it gets better. There's a great treatment center run by a buddy of mine. Let me call him and see if we can bring Scott over there now."

"Call him."

Sam made the call and the arrangements. He understood that Scott would have to agree to go and would need to sign the treatment papers himself. He didn't think it would be easy. If he refused, there was always an involuntary commitment for a brief period of time.

"I'm not going anywhere until you get Katie on the phone." With each word Scott's voice got louder and louder, but the effect of the Valium was already starting to be noticed. Brandon went to the phone and called Dolly Prescott. He knew Katie wouldn't talk to him, but he had to do something. Dolly answered the phone on the second ring, recognizing the caller ID on her phone.

She said hello and prepared to disconnect when Brandon begged her to listen to him. He explained in the simplest, calmest way he could about the trouble Scott was in tonight. Tears streamed down her face as she anguished over poor Scott. Nevertheless, she would not put Katie on the phone.

"Please let me talk to Scott. I can't let Katie on the phone, but maybe I can convince him to go with you. Please let me try."

Dolly could hear Brandon in the background asking Scott to talk to Dolly. While Dolly waited, she prayed. Scott was losing ground and was giving up the fight to talk with Katie. He finally agreed that Dolly was better than nothing.

"Dolly, is that you? Are you there? It's me, Scott."

Dolly's heart broke into a million pieces. Scott was suffering the curse of the damned, and it hurt her to hear him. She was instantly relieved that she had not put Katie on the phone.

"Hey, Scott, sweetie, I'm here. Now, I want you to go with your father and that nice doctor to a place where you can rest. You and Katie both need some help and while we're getting Katie some help here, why don't you get help up there? That way, when you are both better, you can sit down and work out your problems. How does that sound, Scott?" Her voice had been even, soft, and soothing.

"Dolly, I love Katie so much, and I want her to come home." He was whispering and begging and it produced the most heartbreaking sound. Dolly was steadfast and would not be moved by Scott's emotions and demands.

Dolly interrupted him. "Scott, listen to me. Katie cannot come home until you get well. I'm getting off the phone right now and you go with your dad. I'll call you later and let you talk to Katie. Hang up now, Scott."

"I'm hanging up now if you swear Katie will call me." Scott was slurring his words, and his tongue was getting thicker. "I promise, son, Katie will talk to you once you get better." Dolly hung up the phone and called Cat. The two began interceding for Scott for peace, for a willingness to get help, and for reconciliation with his father. What happened tonight was a relationship breaker if ever there was one.

Several hours later, the phone rang again, and it was a grateful Brandon Stewart. "Dolly, we got him to the facility although he pitched a fit when it was all said and done. He'll be in for at least two weeks. I guess I'll call his partner in the morning and let him know what's happened. Maybe that will buy Scott some time."

Brandon's voice began to crack. "Dolly, thank you so much. I'm so sorry things are such a mess. Please let me know about Katie, and what you've decided to tell her. I won't try to call her and neither will Scott. At least I hope he can't find a way to do so. Please keep me posted. And, Dolly, will you add me to your prayers? Dear God, please pray for us. Goodnight."

Dolly hung up the phone and walked out onto the screened porch. She looked out over the ocean and watched the sun begin to rise. The birth of a morning sun had always thrilled her. Nothing was purer or more brilliant to behold. It often came with the promise of a fresh start, a slate wiped clean. Yet, she didn't feel that way today. This morning she felt like she was stuck in the spin cycle with no hope of getting out unscathed. She had no idea how she would tell Katie, and suddenly she knew. She wouldn't tell Katie a thing. Katie didn't need to know, and she could do absolutely nothing about it. So the matter was settled. Only

Dolly and Cat would know of what had transpired. No sense heaping more heartache on a such a wounded heart.

CHAPTER 25

Today's weather offering was hot and then hot some more, and then brutally humid. This was the type of day that tempers flared. Skin fried regardless of the sunscreen, and the wind hid all day. A blistery hot day where no one could get comfortable. This day called for heavy air conditioning and powerful fans. Not a day for beach combing.

Katie woke up to damp hair and that icky, sticky feeling of humidity that had attached itself to you like gum on your shoe. There simply was no shaking it. It downed the moods and led melancholy minds towards despair. Katie had read, long ago, about the weather and what it could do to the mind and the mood. There was little one could do to escape it, especially when the ocean water was tepid.

Dolly had fixed her famous breakfast. By all means eat away the humidity and heat. You have nothing else to do. Dolly placed a steaming plate of cheese grits before Katie. A large pad of butter, sweet cream as a matter of fact, sat melting across the mound of grits. A perfect square of corned beef hash sat over to one side, while a very obese biscuit balanced on the rim of the plate. It was a carboholic's delight. A glass of iced coffee stood sweating on the table. Katie dug in. Her appetite had finally returned, and it seemed that Dolly wanted her to make up for lost time. Today would be no challenge.

But, halfway through her feast, Katie put down her fork and felt an overwhelming sadness covering her. A gray cloud had temporarily covered the sun and the world lost all color. As silly as it sounded, her breakfast was also Scott's favorite, a treat she had made for him on numerous Saturday mornings. It just happened that the arrow of despair met its mark this morning, and Katie was surprised.

Dolly noticed that Katie had stopped eating and stopped jabbering about this and that, her favorite morning activity. Katie never woke up sad and rarely needed a few minutes to wake up. She was a happy morning person who seemed to be coming around more frequently.

"What's the matter? Grits need salt? More butter? Ice coffee refill?"

"Oh, I don't know. Sometimes I feel like I'm on a swing. When I pump up high I'm ok, but when I swing down low, I'm sad. Am I always going to be this moody and emotional?"

"Sorry, but yes. Forget all that you've gone through with Scott, but remember that you're a female, and most of this stuff we're just stuck with. You don't have to end your life over it, but we do have more than our fair share of fluctuating emotions."

"I know that, and I can deal with it. Dolly, it's just that I feel the despair. The broken dreams of what will never be. I'm scared to ever dream again."

"I don't want this to sound harsh, dear, but the death of a dream does not automatically start the funeral march for all other dreams to come. Push the dead dream over to the side, move it out of the way, toss a little sand on it, and move on. You can't carry a dead dream. It's too heavy, has no value, and honey, after a while, it starts to stink. A decomposing dream is ugly and bears no resemblance to what it once was. It is a wasted exercise."

Katie listened intently wanting desperately to have it all make sense. Dolly pulled out a kitchen chair and leaned into Katie. "You must not mourn for what might have been. If you could go to the land of What Might Have Been, you wouldn't recognize it. None of it is in reality land. You could drown in the pieces of broken dreams and slivers of dashed hopes. No one has any idea of what truly might have been, so why waste your time wishing and hoping and missing and longing for what you think you might have missed."

"But I don't want to give up my dreams. I feel like I have to have something to hold onto."

Resisting the urge to wrap Katie in her arms, Dolly sighed and pushed the plate out of the way. She grabbed Katie's hands and held on tight. "Look, I'm a little long winded this morning, but I just have to have my say. Don't waste your sorrows, and stop inviting yourself to the pity parties. By the way, if you haven't noticed, you're the only guest.

However, you are not the only one to have found themselves in this situation. Your situation is not a death sentence. Starve the despair. Pay it no head, and you will see the sunrise again. In color this time. So be it."

Katie got up and hugged Dolly. She was such a wise and wonderful woman who had the power to verbally pop her upside the head and get away with it. Her truth was painful, but as contrary to reality as it sounds, her truth healed. It made sense, parted the cobwebs, and shook her out of her self-centered, woe is me attitude. Dolly was indeed quite effective at the hard line pep talk.

"Thank you. I suppose I'm a bit of a melodramatic princess. I actually knew I was always destined for the stage." The girls laughed and stayed embraced for just a few more seconds. "I love you, baby girl."

"Ditto."

After clearing the dishes and working up a nice sweat, Katie and Beau headed down to the beach. The loggerheads had hatched all over the island. The end of July brought the last clutches of the eggs laid two months before. Hundreds and hundreds of the baby turtles were navigating their way to the ocean, the call so strong they could in no way ignore it. Katie sat on the end of the boardwalk and watched them scurry frantically, little wild frenetic movements pushing towards the water. Other watchers were all over the beach herding the little fellows to the sea and keeping them from the gulls who had hoped for a breakfast buffet.

The turtles were adorable. Each hatchling was light to dark brown with a white-gray border to their flippers. Their little underbellies were covered with a shell painted ochre, a tint of fading yellows. She laughed at the antics of the turtles as they got their bearings straight and headed into the water. The easy waves cradled them and carried them into the surf zone. It may take up to a day or so before they would be able to swim out to the sea. They were so innocent not having a single thought of the dangers they would face in order to stay alive.

Katie hated that predator prey relationships existed in the world. It was bad enough in the wild where animals were innately driven to do what had to be done. Survival at all costs. There was no mercy in that world, and it was harsh and cruel. However, it was a survival of the fittest, and she understood that. However, it didn't mean she had to like

194

it. She hated that cruel part of life where mercy should have reigned supreme, but on the contrary, there were predators everywhere especially in her world. Bullies of all shapes and sizes were found in every nook and cranny, wherever humans lived. Bullies waiting and watching for the meek and the mild, the ones who would become easy prey, the ones who had little "fight back" in their makeup. Those most easily clipped from behind.

As a child, Katie had always hated the bullies; she used to think that they were always the fat, freckled-face kid with the red hair. Yes, a terrible stereotype, but at least she felt safe in categorizing him that way. It was not until she got older that she found that girls made magnificent bullies, and they didn't always have markings for identification.

A bully is a sick person who wants desperately to control his life. Katie didn't care one bit about a bully's background or the suffering he had undergone. She didn't care about the political correctness of saying he or she. All she cared about was the tremendous amount of torment one person could cause another. It was painful to admit, but Scott had been an adult bully. But, oh, a very sly bully who used his master manipulation skills to control and be cruel. Scott was the most dangerous kind of bully. Because he could make you love him, and he could love you in return. His inner bully stayed hidden for much of the time, but unlike a vampire that comes out at night, Scott's bully showed up when no one expected it catching its prey off guard. Yep, that was Scott. Always catching Katie off guard.

A bully is self-centered, ego centric, and maybe even narcissistic, call it what you like. Surely, it would take those traits in order to ruin the lives of the people around him. And, that was Scott. Bullies were always first and there was no second, third, or fourth. Just last. Scott was first and Katie was last. She had learned that being last didn't mean that you lost. And being first certainly didn't mean that you won.

Bullies usually get theirs in the end. It was a terrible thought and one Katie was none too proud to think about. Scott wasn't ended. He wasn't over. His time wasn't up. He was forever out of her life and on his way to another. She wanted his life to run parallel to hers with no possibility of intersection. He was now a cipher, a giant zero, who needed to be erased. Yet, she would try. The divorce had come through and legally freed her from that marriage. She had met with the Catholic tribunal and because Scott had been married before, and was purposely sterile, the Church granted Katie a quick annulment. Either lie would have freed her. Scott had entered into a binding relationship of which he was not free to do. Now Katie was free to marry again or to try finding love once more. It was a hideous thought and one that she couldn't bear to entertain. Marriage again? She doubted she had the stomach to go through the mating, dating dance again. No, she'd rather not just now, thank you very much.

Katie knew she had to be so careful and not dwell on what had happened keeping her eyes on today. So, for this day, she would find joy in the hatchlings, and with Beau straining at her side to go play with them and all the people on the beach. She wouldn't look back no matter how tempting it may be. She had learned how dangerous it could be to look back. Just ask Lot's wife, spending eternity as a pillar of salt.

Gathering Beau, Katie headed back up to the beach house. She began to hum an old familiar song, one she used to sing in happier days. It was perfect for this morning when life seemed a little cleaner and the sea offered a mist of hope to her otherwise dry life. Unable to carry a tune in a bucket, Katie offered a mea culpa to the Five Stairsteps, and belted it out anyway. The harder she sang the more she deviated from the lyrics, but it was a soul freeing song that lifted her spirits and welcomed back the sun. Even Beau could tell that some of the old spark was back as he danced around his silly master trying to do cartwheels in the sand.

"So do not fear, for I am with you;
do not be dismayed, for I am your God.
I will strengthen you and help you; I will uphold you
with my righteous right hand." (NIV)

– Isaiah 41:10

CHAPTER 26

S t. Benedict's was the only Catholic Church on the island. It was a small, but lovely church constructed in red brick surrounded by bits of grass interspersed in sand. The steps leading up into the church were marble, and the two entrance doors had been imported from Italy. A small alcove surrounded a statue of the Virgin Mary followed by a series of small crosses to commemorate the holy innocents.

Inside the old church, probably built in the early thirties, small rows of pews showed years and years of wear and tear. Small black ceiling fans, the color of a witch's cauldron, lined up parallel to the pews. A generous benefactor who could not suffer through another summer Sunday mass without air conditioning had long ago put them out of commission. The parishioners protested against the removal of the old fans, and so they stayed.

The altar was plain and adorned with the simplest linens. However, they were quite special, as a rather gifted Italian immigrant had sewn these cloths so very many years ago. The altar boys were either locals or summer people who diligently served mass each Sunday. Their tanned faces and often bleached out hair testified to how they spent their summer. Usually the entire congregation went to communion, which was still served from an imported French communion rail. Indeed, the church held great meaning for the worshipers, many of whom had been coming to Tybee Island since before the church was built. The oldest parishioner was ninety–two and still made it to daily mass. He was almost loved as much as the parish priest, Father John.

St Benedict's saved a good forty-minute drive into town to attend mass. They had a seven thirty morning mass each day. The pews were not but a third full, but in those seats were the faithful, those who were drawn to mass regardless of time or weather. Father was committed to saying daily mass. If storms were threatening, he encouraged his parishioners to come against the weather; if a hot spell was threatening to melt Tybee Island, they'd pray a rosary invoking Mary's intercession. They prayed for one another and their families, the intentions of the Holy Father, and those unspoken in the recesses of your heart. He was a good and wise priest.

A small school was attached to St. Benedict's, an elementary and middle school for island children. These of course were not to be confused with the beach kids who summered at Tybee Island each year. Those kids went to private schools in Somerville or attended well-respected public schools. However, for the island kids, who lived on Tybee year round, St. Benedict's was a perfect place for them. There were no school buses or carpool lines, only bikes, skateboards, and weary feet. It was a great community, a wonderful environment, and a school who needed quite a lift towards academic excellence. Father John was in prayer over what to do for his failing school. The diocese paid teacher's salaries at roughly forty percent of what they would make in the public sector, not a very inviting beginning. The school was not high tech, and most of the kids were not computer savvy. Yet, Father knew that kids could learn the old-fashioned way with the right teacher.

Katie came back from the beach still singing her new favorite happy song: "ooh ooh child, la-la-la-la-". Allowing the screened porch door to slam behind her, a habit most screened porch doors insist on doing, Beau, always in the lead started his spiral spin as he coyly approached Father John. In a second, Father was on the floor and wrestling with Beau. From the spectacle before them, Dolly and Katie couldn't tell who was enjoying the romp more, Beau or Father John. After a while, Beau had had enough and retreated to his place on the sofa to begin his morning nap. He was such a creature of habit.

"How about another cup of coffee, anyone? Anyone?" Dolly asked as she poured herself a final morning cup. No takers.

Father John brushed off his black jacket and looked at Dolly as if waiting for directions.

"Why don't we go join Beau on the porch? It's going to be a scorcher so we best enjoy this morning. I'll have to darken the whole house if it gets as hot as the weather man predicts."

Katie sat down next to Beau and began to stroke his belly. Magically he stretched his body and grew several inches. She just laughed at her prince who truly thought he was the center of the universe. "That's one special dog. How'd you get so lucky? I mean labs have a great reputation for being a real people dog, but Beau's just great. I wish I had room to have a dog." The conversation was a bit stilted, and it sounded more like people getting acquainted for the first time rather than family friends sharing chatter on the porch. Katie wondered if something was up. Her inner warning signals were going off, and she figured Dolly was up to something.

"Ok, I'm not stupid, you two. What's up?"

"I'll jump right in since I'm in a pinch and up against a deadline. Katie, I need a middle school language arts teacher. Mrs. Dowerly called yesterday and has resigned. Her husband is sick and she needs to stay home and nurse him back to health. It's a blessing in disguise as she's old as dirt and has the engaging powers of a dead person."

Katie and Dolly both started to giggle over Father's unkind description of Mrs. Dowerly.

"Oh, I know it sounds terrible, but I've watched the kids' academic performance slide for years. She's just does the same ol' thing every year. The kids read the same old books. They write on the same old topics. We need some new life breathed into our school." Father John reached over and scratched the prince's belly. He looked up into Katie's face and asked. "Katie, Dolly says you're certified to teach middle school. She also told me that you'd planned to stay at the beach at least for a year. I'm in desperate need of a good teacher and I've heard that you're it. Now, before you get mad, I've already called your old principal and asked for a recommendation. The women crowed over your skills and told me she would have hired you back if they weren't in a hiring freeze. So, would you come to work at the school? And, I have to tell you that the pay is terrible compared to what you used to make, and yes, I checked on that as well. But you aren't paying rent and-"

"Enough already! It seems that you and Dolly have worked this thing all out for me. Have you gotten my back to school clothes yet?" She laughed in spite of herself.

"Look, all I'm asking is that you think about it before you say no. I have no carrot to dangle, except the new air conditioner works great in the school. But I can say this; the kids deserve a great teacher, and I've heard you're just that. Would you just consider it, please?"

Katie looked over at Dolly who was unusually silent. Why of course, she was praying. Dolly has something to say about everything, so Katie should have known that the great intercessor had other worldly business. "How long have you known Father John was going to ask me about this?" Katie looked straight at Dolly and felt a smile coming to her lips. "'fess up. How long? And why didn't you say something to me?"

Dolly started to laugh. "I talked to Father John about two weeks ago after morning mass. He asked me to pray about a new teacher to replace Mrs. Dowerly, as he'd heard rumblings about her retirement. It was so close to school starting that he was afraid the kids would end up with the bottom of the barrel. So, I told him about you. It's not unusual that the school needs a teacher, and you need a job. I'd say that's a perfect match."

Without further contemplation, Katie simply said "Okay. Yes. I'll do. I'll need the curriculum standards and textbooks and my class lists. If I can get those things right away, I can start planning. You know... I'm kind of excited about this."

"Thank you, Jesus. And, thank you, Katie. There is nothing worse in the world than interviewing teachers! I'll get everything ready so you can come by any time after noon today and get your materials." Father John hopped up and hugged Katie, spun around and hugged Dolly, and bent over Beau to ruffle his head feathers. "Blessed be God. This is a great day."

He went out the front door praising the name of Jesus, while Katie and Dolly sat on the sofa and just hooted.

CHAPTER 27

T he school year had gotten underway quite smoothly, and Katie had fallen right into step as if she hadn't missed a day of teaching. She found teaching to be a pleasure; the discipline problems were minimal, thanks to Father John, because she had great support from the parents, and the kids just didn't seem to be as worldly as the ones she'd taught in Atlanta. These kids were in a bit of a time delay and weren't as current as their big city peers. She loved everything about it.

Time was getting away from her and it was hard to imagine that the Christmas holidays started Friday. Katie longed to sleep in until seven instead of her usual five-thirty wake up. Beau, her canine alarm clock, loved an early morning romp on the beach, regardless of the weather. Katie would make her coffee and take it, along with Beau to the beach. The beauty of her mornings, regardless of the color, was invigorating. Even days when the sun was opulent with its light, or days when it behaved like a spoiled child unwilling to share any of his crayons except the gray one, the beach blessed her.

But, the break was coming, bringing Christmas, which sent Katie into a mind spiral that didn't know up from down. For the first time ever, Katie had no Christmas gifts to buy. Father John had insisted that Christmas was spiritual and in the face of this economy, teachers and administrators were forbidden to exchange gifts. "Give a gift of prayer. Do works of charity. Visit the poor and the shut-ins. But do not spend money on each other." Everyone knew he meant what he said.

One thing was for certain, the girls would celebrate. Katie and the girls had invited several unrelated people over for a Christmas celebration. Mr. Sarge could come in his wheel chair, along with Lizzy, and Cat and some of her friends who were recently widowed would join them, and then Katie and Dolly. They had planned the meal and party to the nth degree making sure that they recognized the reason for the season and focused on the blessings they had all received. Katie thought it an odd Christmas for a twenty-nine year old woman, but the alternative was too sad and unbearable. These days Katie did not think of Scott very often. Dolly had finally told her about his breakdown and treatment. She felt removed from the story as if Dolly was talking about someone she didn't really know. It did make her terribly sad that the life they had tried to make together was broken before they started.

As in past years, the girls would go to midnight Mass at St. Benedicts. The church would be alit with trees decked in hundreds of tiny white lights. The crèche was waiting to have the promise fulfilled, the child Jesus. Beautiful carols echoed up and down the pews, and just before the closing prayer, all the lights were turned out and the entire congregation faced the altar and sang "Silent Night." Only the most hardened of hearts kept a dry eye.

This Christmas Eve, Katie possessed no hardened heart, but a grateful one that relished in the beauty of this night. Just as the people continued the tradition of kneeling to sing, Katie noticed someone trying to slide in next to her. She kept her eyes on the altar, ignoring the body next door. Suddenly, he leaned into her and whispered "Merry Christmas, Katie."

Katie was shocked and began to tremble. What in the world was he doing here and what would everyone say. How could she handle such an unexpected visit? She slid back onto the pew and watched the back of his head now bent in prayer. Leaning forward, he belted out the last line of the carol, turned and grinned at her like a man on the verge of losing his mind.

"Chris Martin. What in the world are you doing here?" Katie demanded although surprised at the thrill running amuck throughout her body. "How did you know I'd be here?"

"Hey, it's Christmas Eve and it doesn't just belong to you. I love midnight Mass and have been going all my life. I've been coming to St. Benedict's since I came down here on sabbatical. I've seen you more than a few times."

"Why didn't you say something to me? I haven't seen you since forever, yes when we had that almost terrible storm and we met at the grocery store. How have you been…?" Katie felt herself leaning closer to Dr. Martin as if her whispering was not passing to a more audible stage.

The singing stopped and suddenly the entire church was hushed. A beautiful stillness floated over them and the presence of the Lord was almost tangible. Heads slowly bowed in the humility that comes from a nearness of the Holy Spirit. A touch from God was the best Christmas gift ever.

Mass ended and people slowly filed out of church; the girls waited outside to visit with friends and wish a Merry Christmas to all. Katie walked out with Chris Martin and headed towards Dolly and Cat. Katie introduced them all and a hint of recognition registered with Dolly. Katie had never shared Chris' reasons for dropping her as a case, but she did share news of his sabbatical.

"Merry Christmas, Chris. Or should I say 'Dr. Martin'?"

"Chris is what my friends call me, so please, Chris."

"Well, that's settled. Now, how about joining us for Christmas dinner tomorrow? We have an almost full house, and one more will balance the table. Can we count on you then?"

Katie wanted to kill Dolly, but of course, her sweet grandmother was always the most gracious of all hosts. It would have been inconceivable to her that someone may be alone on Christmas Day. Katie just smiled as Chris jumped at the chance. He had wondered so often about Katie's girls and was secretly delighted at this gift from the Magi.

"Just tell me what time, and I'll be there."

Katie woke up Christmas morning humming her favorite oldies. She danced around the kitchen and cleaned an already spotless house repeatedly. "Are we expecting royalty?" Dolly teased Katie as she watched the genie of cleanliness obsess over the house.

"No, I'm just restless and want to get all of this out of the way before the company comes."

"Everything was already out of the way. The house is perfect, so let's go sit on the porch and have our coffee. Maybe you'd like to share why you're Cinderella just after the slipper fits."

Katie laughed at Dolly whose entire life was a metaphor. Katie inherited that dominant gene from her. It just helped people understand what they were trying to say. Words do paint the best pictures, but only when used in a proper context. Cinderella would have known all about that. As would the prince who discovered his queen all because of a shoe.

Dinnertime was high noon, and guests would be arriving shortly. The view of the beach had hold of both girls in awe of the beauty. No beach person ever got tired of the beauty; it changed every day but was somehow still the same. The colors were different; some days sharp and clear, while others were muted and fuzzy. The beach was a chameleon, changing all the time, yet always staying the same. The essence of that mass of water and sand continuously stirred the soul and refreshed the mind. The beach healed everything if given enough time.

Beau interrupted the girls from their philosophizing by dragging a large present by the ribbons binding it. After a vicious shaking and a few good growls, Beau called uncle and laid the box at Katie's feet. Of course, he could smell his box of treats, but he would have none of it until all the gifts were opened. He had been successful with killing the decorations on the tree, and more than once Katie had found a tortured angel under the covers of her bed. She would catch him sleeping so innocently by the tree and then find out the truth scattered around the house. He just didn't get the off limits thing with the tree.

Cat came over, and it was gift opening time. Beau was enthralled and dragged wrappings everywhere. He'd plop down in anyone's lap who appeared to be more interested in presents than the little prince was. Dolly handed Katie one of the last gifts. It was beautifully wrapped and certainly done by a professional. The gift had come via UPS several days before from Brandon Stewart. Dolly had hesitated to give it to Katie, fearing it might upset her and Christmas. She chose to butt out and give the gift. Katie opened it carefully commenting on how thoughtful of Brandon. She spoke too soon.

The box was large and cumbersome to unwrap. It was heavy, and as she opened it, she found several smaller gifts inside each covered in identical paper. "What in the world is all this? What did Brandon do?" Katie continued to dig into the box until she had pulled out all the individual presents. She gave each of the girls a gift to open, leaving her with two. "Okay everybody, dig in and let's see what we've got."

Cat opened hers first. Inside was a piece of paper folded down into a neat square. She opened it while the other girls watched. Cat unfolded the paper and scanned it before reading. "Ok, here we go." Suddenly, she stopped reading and looked quizzically at Katie and then at Dolly.

"Go on, Cat. Read it." Dolly urged.

"I'm not sure what this is, but I don't think we should be doing this. Let's just throw all this away." Cat began to fold the paper again following the earlier creases perfectly.

"What's the matter, Cat? Just read the paper." Katie reached over, took the paper from Cat, and started to read using a mocking, most official voice. Just as she started, she put it down and looked to the girls for help. "It's Scott's commitment papers from that night he had a breakdown. Why in the world would Brandon send this? Good Lord! This is creepy. Dolly, open your gift."

Dolly quickly stripped her box and opened it. Inside were photocopies of Scott's prescriptions while he was in the hospital. Each one had something to do with treating emotional illnesses. The girls did not understand what this was all about.

"I'm opening mine now. This could not get any stranger." Katie opened her first gift and found a picture of their house with a sold sign standing in the front yard. "I knew the house was sold shortly after Scott got out of the hospital. Why am I getting these things?" Paper clipped to the picture was an IOU for one hundred fifty thousand dollars made out to Dolly and Cat. "Why does Scott owe you all that money? What did you two do?"

Katie was starting to get very upset. She looked at the girls and demanded an answer. Dolly spoke first. "When you two got married Scott wanted to give you a dream house, which we wanted for you as well. So, when Scott found your house, he called and told us all the details. Of course he didn't have enough for a down payment, so Cat and I gladly offered to lend him and you the money."

"Why didn't you tell me? It's not like you to keep your mouth closed over anything."

Those words stung Dolly as surely as if Katie had slapped her.

"I'm sorry, Dolly. I didn't mean that. It's just that nothing with Scott was reality and to find that he lied about the down payment, and you didn't tell me, we'll, it's just another big lie. Where's the money now?"

It was Cat's turn to speak. "When Scott got out of the hospital, I met with my lawyers, Brandon and Scott. I went to Atlanta to plan the sale of the house and take care of arrangements with Scott. Dolly and I had decided that Scott could continue to borrow the down payment, with a bit more from us, in order to pay off the embezzled amount. My attorney had contacted Jim Burns, Scott's partner, and he agreed to accept fifty thousand less than Scott had stolen."

"But that's ridiculous. Why did you rescue Scott? I just don't understand." Katie was trapped in all the emotions she was feeling.

"Look Katie. Dolly and I did what we thought was best. Mr. Burns wanted to resolve this problem, we knew the house would be sold, and who knew what Scott would do with the money? We made a deal with Scott. If he would agree to stay away from you completely, and that was spelled out so that he couldn't call, write, visit, or in any way imaginable contact you. He wasn't happy about it, but he had no alternative. His father was insistent that he sign the agreement and get on with his life. Scott signed off on everything, took the money, and paid Mr. Burns. However, I don't understand for the life of me, what these gifts are all about. I will be calling Brandon Stewart shortly."

Katie said nothing. She opened the last box and found the agreement that Scott, Dolly, and Cat had all signed. Scribbled diagonally across the paper, someone had written 'null and void' in dark red marker. "What in the world is this?" Katie asked as she passed the paper around. The room stilled as the reality of the gifts hit home. Burle Ives was singing his "have a jolly Christmas" in the background. The beef tenderloin was cooking and sending out a glorious aroma. The second oven was baking broccoli casserole and some exotic dish Cat created. The kitchen sent smells wafting over them. Everything was near to perfect except the baby elephant standing in the middle of Christmas.

"I don't believe this is from Brandon. I believe these are all from Scott. In some sick way, he's striking back at you. But, you had nothing to do with this." Cat said puzzling over the mess in front of them.

"Don't be ridiculous. I had everything to do with this. Oh, I might not have given Scott the money, or had him sign these papers, but he holds me responsible for his breakdown and his financial problems. I didn't tell you about an email I got from Scott several months ago. He accused me of demanding that expensive house and putting the pressure on him. He said he'd never had embezzled the money if I hadn't been so greedy and snobby. If we'd been in a smaller house this would never have happened. He also said if I hadn't left him, he'd never had gotten sick. The killer was he said if I hadn't been so distant he would have never fooled around. I always suspected he was cheating, but I couldn't prove it. Anyway, it was disgusting to read. Everything was my fault, and he was responsible for nothing. I just deleted it. He's written a ton of times, and I just delete it every time. Now, I wish I'd known about the agreement between ya'll. But, it wouldn't have changed anything. So, what do we do now?"

"Let's start with deleting Burl." Dolly got up from the sofa and turned off the CD. She went to the ovens and checked on the dinner. She then poured each one of them a nice glass of chilled Château Puy Arnaud Maurèze, a small token of Cat's love. "Let's toast to good times to come. Then we'll toast to forgiveness and moving forward. Then we'll toast to good friends and new friends that will come to share dinner with us today. The rest we will talk about later. Cheers!"

The Christmas spread was splendid. Perfectly cooked tenderloin encrusted with horseradish was the centerpiece. It was surrounded by mushrooms stuffed with crabmeat and goat cheese. Several casseroles of similar elegance finished the buffet. Buttered rolls were offered to be the "wipe the plate clean" tool. It was a fabulous meal, and all enjoyed the wine, the food, and the company.

And when all the merriment had ended, and older ladies, sans blue hair, had had enough, the house grew less and less full. Finally, it was empty except the girls, Katie and Chris. The latter were on the screened porch, finishing the wine, and playing getting to know you again. Both were stuffed from the sumptuous meal and warm from the wine and the blankets. The roaring fire, newly poked and restocked with wood, made the perfect addition to a perfect day. Except for Scott who had managed to wrangle one tentacle into the mixture.

Chris was reclined on the love seat with his shoes off and socked feet on the ottoman. Katie sat at the opposite end and had to resist the strong temptation to snuggle up under his arm, which rested on the back of the sofa. She enjoyed the rich smell of his cologne, which was close to the best she'd ever smelled. "What cologne are you wearing?" Katie asked like a schoolgirl. All she needed was a piece of gum popping in between breaths.

"Why? Do you think I smell great?" Chris was teasing her and Katie loved it. "Yeah, it smells okay. What's it called?"

"Purple something or another. It's a Polo fragrance. Can't remember the name."

"Polo fragrance? Oh my you are a twenty first century man."

Katie laughed tossing her messy hair away from her face. The wine was making her just a bit giddy and loosening her tongue. She had never found it difficult to talk to Dr. Martin, but this circumstance and this plan were wildly different from his therapist office.

"Please tell me you are not metro sexual."

"On the contrary. I am the absence of narcissism, and I despise shopping. So what else do you call it if it's not a fragrance? Oh, never mind. I'm just glad you like it." He motioned for Katie to move a little closer. Katie put her wine glass down and started to slide over. From out of nowhere, baby boy Beau bounded over the ottoman and into the center seat perfectly situated between Katie and Chris.

"But your office is so beautifully decorated. You are a closet metro."

"My sister in law is an interior decorator. And, if you must know, she dresses me well and decorates my house and my office. Unfortunately, she and my brother just had a baby a few months back and she hasn't had a chance to redo the beach house. It can only be described as sparse."

"I kinda like sparse. So, you can't dress yourself or your house. Whatcha good for?"

"If I tell you my two deepest secrets do you promise not to tell?" Katie nodded feigning a deep interest. "If this gets out, then everyone woman on the island will be lined up at my door."

"Would that be such a terrible thing?"

"Indeed it would. Now stop interrupting, and let me tell you the secret behind Samson's strength."

"Excuse me, but who's Samson?" Katie was beside herself with laughter now and regardless of how hard Chris tried to keep a straight face, he was losing control.

"In case you haven't noticed, I'm Samson. The strength to my charisma is…" He reached over and pulled her towards him so he could whisper his secret. "I'm very handy in the house."

"That's pretty impressive. Now what's the second secret?"

"I like yard work." Chris reached over and pressed his fingers over Katie's smiling mouth. He pulled her head towards his and kissed her softly on the forehead. "Now, if you cut off my hair or tell a soul, I'll be like every other man unable to wield a tool of any sort. So keep it on the down low."

Katie and Chris continued laughing and talking until the end of the shorter winter day. The fire had been stoked and restuffed several times. Now one last log was losing the good fight and slowly morphing into the softly glowing embers. The sun was nearly gone and a chill was settling on the porch. Beau whimpered for a cover and Katie pulled hers off to share with him. Chris laughed and offered half of his warmth as well. Time suddenly flowed like sap suspended in a uniquely pleasurable pace. How silly and playful their conversations had become. They had begun to communicate on levels that surpass normal exchanges. How odd that a brush of Katie's toes against Chris' could make him smile. Or the touch of shoulder next to hers could send a thrill through her body. This day it was no sexual thrill, nor even the hint of anything other than the next level above friendship.

Katie moved Beau over and got up to light candles. "Please don't light the candles. I just want to sit in the dark with you. Are you getting too cold to stay out here?"

"No, I'm fine. Beau puts off a ton of heat. Are you cold?"

"Only when you get up."

Katie put few more logs on the fire and grabbed some wine from the kitchens. Dolly and Cat had mysteriously disappeared leaving behind a sparkling clean kitchen and only a lighted tree in remembrance of another Christmas passed. She would tease them about it later.

Katie stood at the porch entrance, by the French doors that led outside. Chris was leaning over Beau with two velvety soft ears in between his hands. Beau looked up with lids half-asleep and gently licked Chris' chin. It was a good luck omen, for Beau was impressed. As Katie walked in, Chris sat back as if caught stealing candy. "So I finally get to see Beau without his adoring fans, one of which I hope to become very soon." Chris reached down and scratched that sweet spot just above the tail and massaged Beau's sides and legs. Beau stretched out his neck and was promptly sent to seventh heaven. Katie laughed, and oh Lord, how Chris loved to hear her laugh, and started to pet Beau. There was something so addictive about petting this dog. Once someone started, everyone else needed to get a hand into it. Chris was no different.

"Katie, this is an awesome dog. I've been thinking a lot about getting a dog, and after watching you and Beau on the beach and around the island, I've decided on a Lab puppy."

"That's great. You'll love that energy ball when he's a puppy. But he will chew your house down so have lots of toys and time for plenty of walks." Katie smiled just thinking about a new puppy for Beau to play with.

Suddenly, Katie sat straight up and turned to look at Chris. "What do you mean you've seen me and Beau around the island? When did you see us on the beach? Are you now the island stalker?" Chris couldn't tell if she was really mad or just teasing.

"Well, I applied for the stalker job but was overqualified. Look Katie, I've been down here for some time doing my research and traveling. When I found out you had moved down here and were getting a divorce from Scott, I was overjoyed. But, I wanted to give you time to sort things out. I just didn't want to pop out of nowhere and say 'surprise.' You know it's a small island and you're kinda hard to miss."

"Yeah? So how come I never saw you except that one time in town and at Mass last night?"

"Okay. When I saw you, I sorta lurked in the corners or turned the other way. I just wanted you to move around without me. Didn't I do a great job?"

Katie laughed in spite of herself. "That you did. But did it ever dawn on you that maybe I'd need a friend after all I've been through?"

Beau stretched out over Chris and Katie making them a linked chain. "Yeah, I thought of that. You see, I don't just want to be your friend. So I stayed out of the picture, so to speak."

"Well, don't stay so far out of the picture next time."

They toasted over one last glass of wine. It was nearly midnight and Chris had been at Dolly's since just shy of noon. It had been the sweetest

Christmas he could remember spending in his adult years. Chris knew that he would have to take it slowly with Katie and build the foundation critical for a lasting relationship. For now, it was time to go before he overstayed his welcome.

Do not think that love, in order to be genuine,
has to be extraordinary. What we need
is to love without getting tired.

- Mother Teresa

CHAPTER 28

----------~----------

School kids live from vacation time to vacation time. Once they get back from Christmas break, they start counting down the days until spring lets them out for another nine days, counting weekends. They always count the weekends. Katie's school was no different. The top left hand corner of her white board marked the days until break, and she was as eager as the kids to lay off school for a while. Tybee Island was no spring break magnet, but being free on the beach in the early part of spring had enough pull that hundreds came to visit.

It also meant time with Chris. Since Christmas, Katie and Chris had spent a great deal of time together. They had promised each other that they would take it slow and keep the reigns in. Katie had asked for no fancy restaurants, trips, or escapes. She knew the influence of environment on emotions and had pleaded for a level playing field. All she knew was atmosphere and the right kind of soul tugging music could cover a multitude of under the skin warts. For now, if they got bored with each other living the mundane life then so be it.

Chris agreed. He'd had plenty of thrills over his lifetime and as a result of his international speaking engagements, the thought of one more plane ride made him cringe. The two would swim and take long walks along the beach. They would walk in the earliest part of the morning, often before school, and the latest part of night guided by the moon or a flashlight. They rode bikes and watched the shrimp boats come in. They created new recipes and tried them out on the girls, more times than not meeting with great success.

Chris had shown such an interest in Katie's school, that she found ways to involve him. She found Chris to be an enormously gifted speaker, and he entertained her students with all accounts of science and gore. He found time to tutor those left behind in math and science, and had even hit the tennis ball with a few.

And, everywhere they went, Beau went too. Katie couldn't imagine leaving him alone when she was having such a wonderful time. Beau was obedient and well trained. When Chris whistled, Beau stopped and came running back. He was still afraid of the water, but he did like to bark at the dead things that washed ashore. He could stay entertained by a marooned horseshoe crab, trying to rest in peace, for hours. A red rubber ball could send him into spinning frenzies to the delight of all onlookers.

It was a good life for all. Katie couldn't believe she could be this content. She had tried to explain to Chris that she wanted to avoid bliss and the happiness that felt like ecstasy. "It's not a renewable resource," she told Chris. "You can't sustain it, and when it comes crashing down, it's simply like Armageddon. Give me peace and contentment any day."

"And that's exactly what I'm trying to do. Stop being afraid of a happiness level above a two. It isn't the same as a panic level. Katie, please stop checking your emotional pulse every few minutes. We are going to be okay, and a heavy dose of happiness won't kill you."

Like opening the gauges on a steam engine, Katie dared to release some of her emotions. She dared to expand their world to something less directed and planned. She dared to dream a little, but she was very afraid that a bad dream might just escape into her good dreamland, and that was something that made her shiver at the thought.

The last Saturday before spring break ended, Katie and Chris went to Mass, had breakfast, and headed to the lighthouse to visit with Lizzy. She had been lonely without Old Sarge, but Katie had been faithful to visit them both. Since Christmas, Mr. Sarge had been failing, but was still sharp and keenly aware of his surroundings. Lizzy was overwhelmed at the thought of his passing and leaving her all alone. It was something that they had all experienced intimately.

This day Katie and Chris stopped by to see Old Sarge and take him for a stroll. The big man looked oddly stuffed into a wheel chair, with the long legs and arms overwhelming his space. His speech had gotten somewhat better, enough that Katie could understand most of what he said. As they crossed over the boardwalk, and parked the chair on the highest crest for the best view of the ocean, the three of them sat and enjoyed the beauty of the beach. Katie babbled on endlessly about the kids at school and their funny antics. Chris shared about his latest research and the latest on brain injuries from strokes. Mr. Sarge nodded when appropriate and tried to ask a few questions. It took a monumental effort to stutter out a few misshapen words. His visitors played a type of charades trying to figure out exactly what he wanted to say. After a while, he closed his eyes, laid back in his chair, and just breathed in the salty air.

It had been a peaceful time and one Katie appreciated. Time with Chris was not rushed or chaotic, nor was it impulsive and agitated. It was simply spent the way time should be. Chris' time had no wheels and it moved at a comfortable pace. Katie had learned a great deal about time controlling you versus you controlling it. It had helped her anxiety levels, so she was always cognizant of how she was spending her time. Today's time was perfectly spent.

Angry clouds blocked the sun and a summer blower was threatening. The wind was whipping up and showing off driving the three back to the home. Chris picked up Old Sarge and helped him back into his bed. He was tired and ready for an afternoon nap. His handsome, rugged face had a touch of color now, evidence of the sun's kisses. Katie tucked him in, pulled the covers up to his neck, and gave him an enormous hug and kiss. As she turned away, he reached for her with his left hand and held it on for a few minutes. He just stared into her face as if trying to think what to say. With great effort, he whispered, "Your young man. God says yes." He nodded, as if in agreement with himself, let go of her hand and closed his eyes. She kissed him once more in the middle of his forehead, took Chris's hand, and left.

"What did he say to you just now?" Chris was wildly curious.

"I'm sure it's just an old man's musings, but he said God told him that you were the one for me." Katie's eyes scanned the floor looking for anything to keep her eyes focused and off Chris.

"He's right and so is God. Katie, I've been waiting for a long time to tell you once again how I feel about you. Nothing has changed. On the contrary, I'm more in love with you than I was before. It may be too soon for you, but I see Scott Stewart as a mistake in judgment and that's all cleared up now. The church says you're free to marry, and well, that's what I'd like to do. Marry you." He grabbed her gently and pulled her into his arms. He loved to hold her, to listen to her breathing, to have her body fit so perfectly with his.

"Chris. I'm falling in love with you and there's no doubt about it. I think you'd be a great husband…just not yet. I have some issues to work on, and then we can talk about marriage. The answer isn't 'no', it's simply 'not right now.'"

"I can handle 'not right now.' An outright 'no' would be impossible to accept. By the way, I do have a little training in helping people and their issues." Chris laughed and hugged her.

"I've heard of men like you who get into the minds of wounded souls. This, my friend is an area I'll travel alone. Seriously, though, I'm struggling with forgiving Scott. Every time I think that's all behind me, I remember something he did, and I hate him all over again. I guess the worst is the lie about having kids. I just don't get how someone could deliberately do that to the person they swear they love. I guess it's just going to take time."

"Look. I want you to work through this and then move on. However, because it is impossible for me to keep my mouth shut and my opinions to myself, I just have to say something. Forgiving and forgetting are two entirely different things. When you forgive Scott, it doesn't mean that you won't remember what he did to you. Forgiveness is a choice you make to emotionally remove yourself from the hurt. Your unforgiveness doesn't hurt Scott; it hurts you. It binds you. It keeps you in the past. But with grace from Jesus, you can be free from that unhealthy attachment."

"Chris. I am not attached to Scott. That really makes me mad. You make it sound like I like how I feel. I don't. I hate it, and I hate Scott for what he did. Look at what it's cost me."

Katie was starting to walk ahead of Chris. "Slow down and let's talk for a minute. Go back over what you just said. Scott did this and he cost me that. Doesn't sound like forgiveness to me. Forgiveness isn't a feeling, it is an act of your will. If forgiveness were no big deal, Jesus wouldn't have said we have to forgive each other so we can be forgiven. Why hold so tightly, to what Scott did, when that binds you as well? See what I mean? If you don't forgive, then you aren't forgiven. Is Scott worth that?"

Katie drew pictures in the sand with her big toe. She was a doodler and needed to do something in order to stay focused on Chris' words. "This is why I'm not ready for a real relationship just yet. I'm a screwed up mess."

Chris stood up and walked over to Katie putting his big foot over her tiny, drawing one. "You're not screwed up, and you're not a mess. Ok, you are a mess, but you are a beautiful, kind, loving and amazing mess." Katie looked up at Chris and rolled her eyes.

"Okay, I guess I did just sort of slobber all over both of us with that litany of compliments. Gush, gush. Ah, school boy love."

Katie laughed and kicked sand on his feet. She turned and ran off down the sea wall until she had to slow down. They had walked the sea wall as far as it went and climbed down the rocks to the beach. The tide was low, and shimmering tide pools were everywhere. They reminded Katie so much of her childhood when she scrambled from pool to pool trying to splash into as many as she could before they dried up again. Katie resisted the urge to reenact her younger years, but Chris did promise to visit as many pools as possible on the way back home.

The pair was drenched from their thighs down, slightly winded, and definitely a bit more tanned than they should be. Turning right to head towards Dolly's private walk bridge, a man sitting low down in a neon green lounge chair raised his arm in salute. His female partner held onto her floppy hat as the wind picked up blowing sand across their bodies. Katie felt a stab of recognition cross her body; what in the world was Scott doing here?

Scott jumped to his feet and ran over to Katie and Chris. He stood there looking at her with that sheepish grin he had down pat. Tanned and obviously visiting the gym on a regular basis, he looked handsome and charming. He wore a navy swimsuit with green stripes that ran parallel to his hips. There was no doubt he was still gorgeous, but not in the same way he used to be. Katie thought he looked like a poster of himself, but something had gone missing in the translation to real life. She did not love him anymore and of that, she was sure. Yet, there was something so familiar about him that she felt tempted to connect with him. It was such a confusing thought. Her mind was on speed as hundreds of hurried thoughts raced wildly across her memory. Her hands began to tremble, but she wasn't afraid. She didn't feel anxious and she wasn't counting levels of panic. Something was just so terribly wrong.

Suddenly, Scott picked her up and swung her around as if long lost lovers had reunited. Katie was stunned and sputtering a demand to put her down. Just as Chris started to intervene, Scott rather harshly, dropped her into the sand. "What are you doing here?" Katie demanded furious that he had invaded her sanctuary once more. She brushed off her shorts and glared at Scott.

"Laura Anne and I have come to rest at the beach this weekend. It's a free beach they say."

"Of course it's a free beach, but why are you parked just outside our boardwalk?"

"It's your boardwalk? You own the boardwalk? I suppose you own the sand and the water as well?"

The conversation was utterly ridiculous. Scott was sarcastic and deliberately picking a fight. Chris would have none of it. "Scott, I'm Chris Martin, a good friend of Katie's. It's nice to meet you." Chris offered his hand, which Scott took and pumped it like an old-fashioned water well.

"Nice to meet ya, fella. I understand that you two are way more than just good friends. Things are getting a little serious I hear."

Scott's tone was ugly and surly. He'd never used words like "fella" or "meet ya." Katie just didn't understand what was going on, but Chris' warning whistles were going off all over the place. Laure Anne suddenly hopped up and came to stand beside Scott. Designer Ray Bans hid her eyes, but her body language spoke volumes. Her hair whipped across her face as she tried to stand between them. She was not ignorant of the sarcasm dripping across the air between the boys. She had seen Scott's temper on numerous occasions and was wary of what was about to happen. Scott seemed eager for a fight.

"Katie, I'm dying of thirst. How far is the nearest place to get a soda?" Everyone just stopped and looked at her as if she had asked the most ridiculous question imaginable. Katie was relieved.

"You and Scott can walk down to the south end of the beach and find lots of neat places to get something cool to drink. Scott, Chris and I have to hurry now. It was nice to see you both." Chris held out his hand to Scott, and to everyone's shock, he slapped it out of the way.

"Can't say I thought it was nice seeing you, Chris."

Katie and Chris crossed over the boardwalk and headed home. They could hear Scott shouting something from the top of the steps, but they refused to acknowledge him. In that garbled message were not so garbled threats. Scott sounded completely unhinged.

The time had come for Katie to share with Chris all about the Christmas presents, the Tweets, emails, voice mails, snail mail, and any other way Scott had tried to communicate with Katie. He had even sent emails to her at her school address sparking alarm from Father John. They were not school appropriate. Katie had also kept Dolly and Cat in the dark. Today Chris was fuming and insisted they all sit down and discuss the seriousness of what was happening. Katie was equally insistent that the girls stay in the dark about this problem with Scott. After their first argument, Chris conceded to take a short 'wait and see' attitude. But only for a brief time. A very brief time.

A week later Old Sarge passed away. Although it was not a surprise, it deeply saddened everyone. Katie hated funerals and found it took all of her courage to attend this one. There was just too much sadness, sad singing, sad words and often times, forced statements of faith. Although Katie had come a long way in her spiritual walk, there were still many issues that ran interference with her total trust in God.

Katie and Chris, along with the girls, attended the funeral. Katie went on autopilot and tried not to remember her childhood suffering and despair at her parents' funeral. At every funeral she attended, she felt as if her parents were buried all over again. She knew her inner child needed to be healed, but she didn't know how to let go of that experience. Chris had offered to help, but this one she needed to work through herself.

After the burial, Cat held a reception for the mourners. As usual, it turned out to be a time of sharing funny and endearing stories about the man the island loved. So many people shared how he had touched their lives, and so many grown-ups shared their love of a man who played with them as children on the beach. Katie couldn't share how she was feeling. She struggled to get near this area. She believed she had told Sarge all he needed to know while he was alive. She had no regrets about the gift of good times shared together.

Lizzy was the last to leave. She was so grateful that the girls had put on such a lovely spread. It took the pressure off her at a time when she had other things to worry about. "Katie, come here, and sit beside me for a minute." Lizzy patted the sofa and called to Katie. "I have something for you."

Katie kicked off her black heels, a habit that Chris loved, and sat beside her. Beau bounded from the kitchen and dove in between Lizzy and Katie. It was useless to tell him to get down and thankfully, Lizzy came from a long line of dog lovers. "Lay down, Beau." Katie pushed Beau back and tried to keep him out of the center of attention. Reaching over Beau, now fully alert and tuned in that he might not be wanted, Lizzy handed Katie a small box and laid it in Katie's lap. "Go on, and open it. There's a note inside from Sarge."

Katie could feel her hands tremble just a bit. She had kept it together through the entire funeral, but she did not expect this. Chris pulled up a chair and sat with his knees near to touching hers. He pulled Beau off the sofa and parked him under Chris' chair. Katie unwrapped the paper and slowly took off the top of the box. She peeled back the white tissue and gasped. Inside, shined and polished, was W.C. She picked it up and smelled the utter sweetness of the tobacco. It flooded her senses with memories of Mr. Sarge.

"There's a note under the pipe. He wrote it a few months ago when he told me he wanted you to have this." Lizzy dabbed at her already swollen eyes. "He did love you so much."

Katie read the letter aloud. "Katie, girl. Me and Lizzy never had a little girl of our own. I always sorta felt that you got to be ours after your parents died. I know I ain't never been a substitute for your daddy, but I sure have loved being in your life. This old pipe here, W.C., means the world to me. You know the story so no sense rehashing it now. I want you to keep it for always, and maybe pass it on to somebody else who can understand its meaning.

It ain't magical or nothing like that. It's just a time when I needed some strength and the pipe reminded me of where I needed to go. I never told you what connected us, the pipe and me. I read that Churchill once said this quote that I used for the rest of my life when listening to God: 'I am always ready to learn although I do not always like being taught.' Katie, you may say you want to hear what God's got to say, but most of the time you don't like sitting still long enough to learn it. When you used to see me rubbing my pipe and thinking, I was asking God to keep me wanting to learn and asking him to show me how. I didn't always like what he had to teach me, but I knew I had to learn it. Take this old pipe and let it remind you of how you got to ask for learning and then learn to accept what you're being taught. I think you know what I mean.

Thanks, Katie, girl for being in my life.

Mr. Sarge

Katie held on to the pipe and hugged Lizzy. Chris got up and gave a group hug, which made everyone laugh including Beau who was leaping up to get into the action. "Thank you for this sweet gift. I am so touched that I find myself at a loss for words. And, we know how unusual that is. Maybe I'll have a child I can pass it onto some day. Lizzy, thank you so much for all that you have given me. I love you."

Chris walked out to the porch and looked out at the ocean. He was close to becoming overwhelmed with love for that chatty, goofy girl sitting on the sofa. Even though styles had changed and rules of etiquette had unfortunately become relaxed, Katie deferred to time honored traditions and chose black for her funeral dress. She looked so refined and self-assured sitting there wearing a linen sheath, a-line style, topped with a string of Dolly's pearls. She bespoke of a simple refinery, elegance, and respect. Chris's chest swelled with his love for her.

Katie was an amazing woman who had touched the lives of so many people. Living near her at the beach and getting to know her history confirmed how special she was. At this point, their relationship could go anywhere, but regardless of the direction, he understood the depth of his love for her and that he would follow her to the ends of the earth. He would slay dragons for her and free her from imprisoning towers. He would climb mountains and swim shark infested waters. She made him feel strong and invincible, valued and cherished. He was seriously and completely in love.

The gem cannot be polished without friction,
nor man perfected without trials.

- Chinese proverb

CHAPTER 29

S chool was out for the summer and Katie wondered about her plans. Elizabeth's baby was due any day now and she desperately wanted to be with her. Shortly after 'Lizbeth got married, Scott and Evan had a terrible argument in front of far too many witnesses. The fallout was devastating, causing Evan to sever all relationship ties with Katie and Scott. Rumors had been flying about Scott, and Evan wanted no part of his life infiltrating theirs. He couldn't stand Scott, so this gave him a perfect opportunity to shut the door on him forever.

Katie was crushed, but she understood that 'Lizbeth would never go against Evan's wishes. Katie missed her terribly. She had been Katie's best friend for half of eternity, and Katie felt a deep loss without her. Hopefully, with Scott out of the picture, Evan would reconsider.

Katie opted out of teaching summer school and going on for a higher graduate degree. But the thought of just hanging around the beach all summer was not as appealing as she had once thought it would be. So much had happened over the past three years or so: marrying Scott, divorcing Scott, getting the marriage annulled by the church, teaching school again, and finding Chris as a friend and not a therapist. If it weren't for the lulls in between each event, Katie would have had a hard time believing it had all happened to her.

Dolly and Cat were on a two-week pilgrimage following the footsteps of St. Paul. Their itinerary included Athens, Rhodes, Pompeii, Patmos, and Thessaloniki. The trip was by land and by cruise ship, and the girls were exhilarated to be tracing the steps the great disciple of Jesus traveled. Katie declined her invitation despite much well intentioned urging; she chose to stay behind and work on her life. Plus, somebody had to watch Beau. He was always a great excuse when Katie didn't want to do something. She was aware that at times, she exaggerated the need to include Beau in everything, but she had to deal with that later. Whatever she was doing to cope and get well was working. She was afraid to discount anything.

Chris had put on a brave front about Katie traveling. He really thought it was a great idea even if he dreaded the thought of her absence. Yet, he had been without her for months at a time and survived. Now with Scott acting berserk and skulking around the island popping up at the strangest places, Chris thought an out of town experience had multiple positive outcomes: independence and protection. Who knew what Scott would do next? Right now, he was just obnoxious and obtuse. He actually showed up at a Sunday morning Mass. Katie, Chris, and the girls sat in the second to the last pew. Mass was drawing to a close and everyone was kneeling except Katie. A skinned knee kept her in her seat. Suddenly, someone was kneeling behind her and started breathing into her hair whispering a reminder that good Catholics are always guilty and must always kneel. When Katie turned around, she saw that it was Scott. Before she could speak, he got up and left the church. Katie walked out after him, but only saw a black Mercedes with Atlanta plates pulling out of the church parking lot.

Chris had called the island police, but they were ill equipped to deal with anything like this. The problem was, when you gave voice to it, it wasn't really anything. Of course, it was to Katie and Chris, but to an outsider it was just childish and immature behavior from a jilted husband. As a psychiatrist, Chris knew Scott was in behavioral trouble, and like an embedded tick, would have to be dealt with eventually. If only Katie would go on the trip.

Post cards came daily from Dolly and Cat. Katie was convinced the girls mailed the postcards from the airport before they left. Each note expressed some exciting detail of their trip: feeling the presence of the Holy Spirit, visualizing Paul preaching, wondering exactly where he was when the prison gates flew wide open.

"I guess I wanted to go more than I realized. Maybe we can take a trip like that someday."

"Who? You, me and Beau?"

"Nah. Next time Beau stays with Dolly." Beau perked up when he heard his name. After deciding he had not been in trouble, he grabbed Chris' flip-flop and took it on the porch to destroy. It was a bad habit, but at least it was just a flop that had lost its flip. Beau had chewed many an item but had miraculously learned to spit things out. However, Katie checked his mouth thoroughly during the massacre.

Katie and Chris had packed a lunch and grabbed a cooler then headed to the beach. A nice midmorning swim and lunch would make the day near perfect. After noon, storms were sparking nearly every day so the beach was more crowded than usual.

"I can't believe all the people who are here. The beach is crowded. I really don't like it this way. What's going on?"

"Katie. Your brain is schoolteacher summer mush. It's the Fourth of July weekend and by tomorrow afternoon this beach will be standing room only." Chris laughed as he unfolded their low to the ground beach chairs, put up the blue striped umbrella and opened the cooler for a drink. "Let's sit for a while, and then we'll swim. How's that sound?"

"Umhmmm. Sounds perfect." Katie took the soda from Chris, opened it and aimed for the cooler top, and missed it by inches. The sand slurped all of the remains. "Katie. What's the matter with you today? Are you paying any attention to what I'm saying?"

Katie looked over at Chris and stared at him for a moment. She reached in her beach bag, down by her feet, and handed Chris an envelope she'd found taped to the screen porch door leading to the beach. Opening it, Chris found a picture of a dead yellow lab, very similar to Beau, lying on top of a vet's metal exam table. There were no words, no obvious wounds, and no hint of where the picture had been taken or by whom. It was totally disturbing on every level.

"It's not the first bizarre thing I've gotten from Scott. I know it's from him. This is the last in a series of dead animals. You see, he started with little puppies and gradually progressed through the life cycle of a dog. I know what he's trying to do, but it isn't going to work."

"What's he trying to do?"

"When I had such bad panic attacks, Scott liked to think he helped me get through them. He was always so kind and gentle helping me breathe and stop the adrenaline from spiraling. You know he wasn't always evil. So, I think he's trying to push me to the edge. He doesn't know how far I've come in dealing with the anxiety or how few and far between the attacks are. Plain and simple, Scott's trying to drive me back to him." Katie raised her hand to stop Chris. "I know it sounds crazy, but I'm telling you, that's what he's doing."

"He's twisted and sick, but I do believe you're right. So, what are we going to do about it? Confront him? Beat him up? We've already tried the police. Frankly, Katie, I'm at a loss right now."

"First things first. We are not going to tell Dolly. Agreed?"

"Nope. I don't think it's fair to her to have this nut case stalking you, and she's being kept in the dark. No. I can't go along with that. She needs to know that if he comes around the house, she should call the police. No...we'll tell her today."

The last bit of power Katie had was in protecting Dolly. Now that it was gone, she broke down and started to cry. She had been so terribly brave through all of this, but when it came to putting Dolly in danger, she lost it. "Maybe I should move away, go back to Atlanta. All of a sudden, I'm scared, and I can't put my finger on it. Will he hurt Beau? Is that what these pictures mean? Will he try to hurt you or me? He's right you know. He can drive me back into full blown anxiety attacks."

Chris stood up and pulled Katie up with him. He hugged her hard in the midst of the minions milling around them. Strands of shiny, chestnut hair had escaped their ponytail binder and were blowing across her face. She had the face of a small child; eyes wide open, mouth slightly parted, pale cheeks.

"Listen to me, dammit. Scott can't make the panic come back like before. You're well, and if you have a small attack, or hell, a big one, you can handle it. Don't give him that power in your life. Put that out of your mind, now." His words were stern and sharp intent on penetrating to her deepest level of understanding.

"I want everything Scott's sent you, and I'm going to the police. They won't be able to do anything, but at least they'll have a record of what's been happening. Let's pack up and head back up to the house. When I get back from the station, we'll sit down with Dolly and fill her in on all the details."

Before they could finish packing, a voice wafted over the beach. "Hello, you two. What's the hurry this morning?" Katie and Chris turned around to the direction of the call and saw Laura Anne and Scott.

It was bizarre. "Why are you going up in such a hurry? The morning is still young."

"Katie," Chris whispered. "Do not say a word about those pictures. You are to play ignorant. Be friendly and welcoming. Don't buy into any of his anger triggers. As much as I hate to say it 'be cool.'"

Laura Anne was stunning in her barely-there black bikini. It looked like it belonged on some private beach where only the rich and famous sun. A black floppy hat covered her blonde hair and a sari hung low below her navel, and a slit ran up the thigh. Nothing was left to the imagination. Scott was dressed in black beach shorts with a pink Polo shirt. His tan was nearing perfection. Why did his looks spark such feelings in her? The thoughts troubled her.

To Katie's surprise, Chris started to unpack and invited the couple to set up with them which they obligingly did so. Katie thought he was nuts, but if he could play this game, then she could as well. After checking the cooler, Scott decided to make a beer run and offered to spice up the meager sandwiches still in storage. *Have at it, Scott. Katie thought. Now, this was typical Scott. Always the entertainer, the showman, controlling all the action.* Seeing him like this gave Katie a certain peace; she knew this man and this familiarity gave her boundaries. She had seen all of this before.

The beer flowed and the couples actually laughed and poked fun at each other. Scott kept it light and airy, giving no hint of the disturbing things he'd done. With a beer or two under her belt, Katie felt the tongue loosen and knew she'd have to be careful. "So, you two. How long have you been together?" No one skipped a beat or blinked an eye. Laura Anne, on her fifth beer of which only Katie was counting, giggled, "Well, since the cat's obviously out of the bag, we were seeing each other-oh, wait! Remember when we saw you at Pappadeaux's that night? You caught us, right, Scottie? Yep, the pull was too strong. Anyway, your marriage was already broken." She chugged down the rest of her beer and grabbed for number six. No one stopped her.

Katie put her beer down and searched everyone's faces. She needed a reality check. Laura Anne just admitted to an affair and no one even choked on their beers. Scott was having a side conversation with Chris and only nodded in Laura Anne's direction. No one acted like a giant bomb had just exploded obviously landing only in Katie's lap. "I'm going for a swim." With that, Katie got up and then jogged around the sunning bodies and into the ocean. The wind was whipping the water into little white caps and the clouds were beginning to spoil their day. The weatherman had promised a pass on Hurricane Barbs, but offered she would mess up the weather for a few days. No fun for the Fourth of July. Although Barbs was a little early in the season, she would do some damage towards the Outer Banks. It looked as though Tybee Island would dodge another bullet.

Katie swam out waist deep and slumped down to cool off her shoulders now a rose that was darkening by the minute. With the addition of Laura Anne and Scott, which seemed so strange to say those two names as a couple, Katie had been unceremoniously pushed out from under the umbrella. In her fear to say just the perfect things, she kept mum about her place as odd man out.

Katie heard her name called and turned to practically collide with Laura Anne. "Oh, this water is so cold. And I think I'm a little tipsy." She giggled like a schoolgirl who was much farther along than tipsy. "It's so nice out here, and we're having such a good time. This is our first vacation together. Katie, I hope you don't mind that we came here. Scott's always loved the beach and of course, you and I go way back to the days of playing out here. When he suggested we start coming here, I felt like I was going home again. Oh, I loved Atlanta, but this is where I really want to be."

"You said 'loved' Atlanta. Don't you love it anymore?"

"Silly, you didn't know? Scott and I have gone into business together and started a catering business in Somerville. Scott was over Atlanta and wanted to get closer to the water. We're planning on getting a big ol' boat. Why, just yesterday we were looking at some forty footers. That just sounds so funny that you'd call a boat a footer." Laura Anne was moving into the drunk phase causing Katie to start inching her way out of the water.

"So, you've moved to Somerville?"

"No, we've moved to Tybee Island. We don't mind spending the thirty minutes or so it takes to get into town. Why in Atlanta it could take me thirty minutes just to get to Malmasion. Now, that's what I miss, rich brides starting their lives in debt. Scott and I decided to leave the bride business to someone else while we cater the food.

Katie didn't hate many things in life, but a slurring, sloppy drunk did top her list of most obnoxious and annoying things. Katie took Laura Anne's arm and pulled her stumbling from the water. "I wanna go swimmin'. Let me go swimmin'." Laura Anne was getting louder and sounding like a spoiled child. Katie wanted to slam her to the ground and mess up that perfect hair sitting under that perfect hat. If she could have seen her perfectly painted eyes under those designer glasses she might have been tempted to flick a nail or two across them. *Scott picked you over me. Doesn't bode well for me.*

A great rumble rolled across the sky followed by higher winds and pushier gray clouds. Disappointed bathers gathered up their treasures and wares and headed in straggled lines towards their cars and homes. The rain was coming sooner than expected, but everything was unexpected when it came to beach weather. Katie was continuing her interior dialogue with Laura Anne, Scott, and Chris. She was having a one sided argument with all of them and she was coming out on top. She thought Laura Anne was a drunken fool. She despised Scott for his adultery and lies. As for Chris? She had no use for him right now either. She knew they were playing normal because of Scott, but Katie didn't know Chris had won Oscars in the past. This was beyond ridiculous. *If he asks them back to the house, Dolly will die, and then I'll kill him. Or if he invites them back to his place, I'm not going. Then his life will be over for sure.*

He didn't deserve to die that day. Chris skillfully directed the players to go their separate ways, with an admonishment that Laura Anne hit the hay for a nice long nap. He promised to call Katie later, and then sent everyone home. Katie was rehashing her kill skills.

By the time Katie got back to the house, kicked off her sandals and washed the sand off her feet, the phone was ringing. "I'm going to the police and tell them what has happened. I don't want to talk about today, or what anybody did, or said. I know they've moved to the beach, and that's why I'm going now to the police. You get cleaned up, and I'll be over after I've done the same. Check the weather, and see what's going on. Things are sure getting ugly outside. I'll call you later."

All business. Dit. Dit. Dit. Katie didn't know why it annoyed her so much. She was desperate to share what she had learned in the water, but

Chris would not discuss it. He had muzzled her, and she hated the way it felt.

"What are you fuming about this afternoon? I can hear you slamming things from back in my room." Dolly walked over and pressed down on Katie's sunburned shoulders. "That has a pretty nasty 'over-done' look to it. How about some aloe?"

"Dolly, I am just furious. Please sit out on the porch with me. I can hardly speak."

"The day you could hardly speak passed about twenty-seven years ago. Now, what's bothering you?"

If an alien wanted to see a picture of the meaning of "split gut", he only had to watch Katie in action. All the creepy things Scott had done, the "surprise" meetings on the beach, the whispering in her hair at church, dog pictures, and Laura Anne's scandalous admission of an affair with Scott oozed out. Dolly thought it would make a great soap opera should anyone be so inclined to watch one. Her reaction surprised and disappointed Katie. She had hoped for some indignation, some ire, at the very least some commiseration. But all she got was the forgiveness speech. *Here it comes again. No matter what somebody does, I have to forgive that person. No matter how heinous the act, how cruel, thoughtless, life altering, I'm the one who has to do something. That stupid, sap-producing, forgiveness. Hi, I'm a doormat, so do whatever you want to me, and I'll forgive you. I'll take you back into my life so you can do it again. How many times are you kicked in the teeth before you get smart enough to walk away?*

The front door opened and Cat came in bringing a large box of peaches. "I'm making peach ice cream if anyone wants to help." She looked at the faces of her two best people and started to laugh. "What did I walk into? Wait. Don't tell me. Let's peel peaches and have some fun."

Chris came home to girls pouring buttermilk, adding ice to the ice cream maker, measuring rock salt and sugar, and making sure the peaches had optimum taste. It was quite a production. "Does this family have a taste testing rule? Our family rule is if you can taste without getting caught, have at it."

Dolly passed him a spoon and the three girls turned their backs to the ice cream. "Let us know when we can turn around." Chris knew he was always going to love this family. "I now officially love peach ice cream."

"How'd things go at the police station?"

"I thought we agreed you wouldn't tell them until I was with you. 'fess up, you already told everything, didn't you?"

"I couldn't help it, honestly. Once I opened my mouth, a sludge of sewer refuse came out. It was disgusting. Dolly wants me to be holy and forgive everyone. I'm still fuming over that."

"My dear. You come from a long line of forgivers. It's in your genes, your Christian genes that is. There is no escaping it. It is the only wise thing to do. You know the routine. Struggle for a while, pout and get mad with God, tell him how unfair it is and how innocent you are. Tell him you understand why so many people don't like him. He's heard it all. Then, ask for the grace to forgive and keep on asking until you stop taking back the forgiveness. Would somebody pass me a spoon and then all of you turn around?" Cat laughed as she got her taste. "Delicious. Let it freeze for a few hours in the downstairs freezer and we'll have heaven for dessert."

No one wanted to hear about the police or what Chris had to say. Dolly turned to Katie and Chris and said, "Put it on the altar. Either God is in control or He's not. Either way you believe, there's nothing you can do about it now."

I am not afraid of storms for
I am learning how to sail my ship.

– Louisa May Alcott

CHAPTER 30

M eteorologist Danny Sandler was going into spasms on the television. After years of near misses and abuses hurled from under umbrellas as pedestrians weathered an unpredicted thunderstorm, the big one was approaching. The set background was overly busy with charts, graphs, swirling clouds, and ominous looking radar screens.

It seems Tybee Island was about to watch the toddler time of a very large hurricane born two weeks ago. All the factors were falling into place: warm ocean water producing enough heat, warm moisture into the overlying atmosphere, enough evaporation, and wind patterns near the surface that will drive the hurricane. Mix these altogether, and you've grown a hurricane.

Usually hurricanes plod along like drunken sailors unsure of their left from their right. However, this hurricane, she knew her business, and she seemed to have it in for the island and its neighbors.

Sandler was ecstatic. It looked like a hurricane four and that meant serious winds and lots of damage. Why, it would even mean a mandatory evacuation. Old timers, those who had seen many an evil storm, would refuse to leave, but the newer kids on the beach block would gas up and leave at the first hint of the order to evacuate. Katie left it up to Dolly while Chris was packing the car anxious to beat the crowd. He was stunned to walk into to Katie's house and see them watching T.V. and eating dinner. "Hey, why aren't you guys packing? We need to get on the road. I don't want to be in bumper to bumper traffic."

Dolly put down her fork and looked up at Chris. "Dear boy. We don't run from hurricanes." Chris didn't think it was funny at all. "Seriously, Chris, this house is far enough from the ocean to be spared the waves, and the house is hurricane proof to a level four or one hundred thirty mile an hour winds. We also have a room that was especially prepared for such an occasion. We have a generator, emergency supplies, and all the food we might need. We'll be fine. Honestly, a hurricane hasn't hit this beach in over one hundred years."

"Has anyone told this hurricane that she can't come? Let's don't tempt fate, and I'll treat for hotel rooms. Come on. Chop, chop! Let's get moving." No one moved.

"Chris, it's futile. She's not budging, and I'm not leaving her. If you want to go on that's fine. We'll be okay. If you hurry you won't be trapped in traffic." Katie smiled and walked towards Chris with open and inviting arms. "I really mean that it's okay if you leave."

"I know you are kidding me. I'm not leaving you guys here, but I don't want to stay either. Guess this is the old rock and a hard place. Anybody willing to reconsider? Anybody?"

They ignored him. Katie sent Beau to his crate and secured him. Dolly asked Katie to check the tacky yellow tubs under each bed. She asked Chris to pull the cars farther into the driveway and lock the garage gates. Next, they were to move the screened porch furniture into the den and lock down the shutters.

"Don't forget St. Francis out in the garden. He'd hate to be flying during this storm. Just put him in the garage. He won't mind for a while."

Chris suddenly plopped down on the sofa and started to laugh. He laughed harder and louder until he couldn't catch his breath. Katie sat beside him and laughed at his laughter while Dolly stood watch over them lest either one explode. "We can laugh later when the house is proofed. Come on. We've got more work to do."

The front door bell rang and Katie opened it do find a crying Laura Anne Stapleton. She was not looking her usual glamorous self and appeared to be soaked to the bone. "Come in, come in." Dolly handed her a towel and offered her a kitchen chair. "What in the world are you crying so hard about? Who died?"

"No one died, Dolly. Scott and I had a fight because he won't leave the island. I'm scared to death that this stupid hurricane will kill all of us, but he won't leave. He says he's riding it out. He doesn't know a damn thing about riding out a hurricane. I'm just so scared. Oh, God, we had such a terrible fight."

Katie offered Laura Anne a room and a good meal if she wanted to stay with them. She could not look more horrified if Katie had offered her a kiss with a cobra. "Why in the world would I stay here if I wouldn't stay with Scott? I want you to make Scott leave. We aren't staying down here." Her tongue was biting and sharp and her voice was shrill. Katie was glad she was scared out of her wits.

"Chris, go get Scott and tell him to leave. We just can't stay here. I'm not staying down here, and I want him to leave. Chris, please go get him." Katie was just waiting for Laura Anne to stomp her foot as she ordered Chris to obey her.

"Scott is a grown man and has the right to make his own decisions. You need to decide what you're going to do and then get on with it. Maybe Scott will follow later."

"You're an idiot. How many cars do you think we have down here? This is the only car. My car and I'm driving it back to Atlanta. Coming here was the biggest mistake of my life. You people are dumber than Scott." She stood up and threw her towel at Katie. "No wonder you left him. He's down at our rental throwing back the booze. I never knew he had a drinking problem on top of every other problem under the sun. Hey, maybe you can go talk some sense into him and get him to leave. Will you go?"

"Sorry. I'm just a stupid idiot, and I can do nothing for you. Whatever you decide, we need to finish readying the house. Pull the door tightly behind you." Katie walked back into her bedroom and sat on her bed. She wrapped her cotton blanket around her and bent her head down on her knees. She was never that ugly to anyone, not that deliberately anyway. Good Lord, she couldn't stand that woman. But, she was troubled about Scott. Suppose he died during the storm and she hadn't done anything to help him. She knew he wasn't well and hitting on all cylinders. She would have to do something. She grabbed her keys and headed to the door.

"He's already gone. He said you'd do something stupid like try to help Scott. You are not to leave this house. Chris will try to get him to leave with Laura Anne or to come stay here. But again, you are not to get involved. Clear enough?"

"Dolly, how did things get so screwed up again? Can't we just have a good blow without worrying about Scott? And, what can Chris do? Scott hates him. Oh, God, do you think he'll hurt Scott? I've got to go down there."

"Katie. Stop this nonsense this instant." The tone of Dolly's voice stopped her dead in her tracks. "You are not super human, nor are you God. Leave this alone. Now, go pick up Lizzy and Cat. Neither one of them wants to evacuate. Make sure you call Sergeant Hendrix and let him know who will be staying with us. No sense people looking for people when people are perfectly safe. Go on now. And, don't go looking for Chris. Katie, I'm as serious as a heart attack about this. Trust Chris to do what he was trained to do. Go on and get back as soon as possible. Sandler just said the hurricane is gaining speed as it comes over the warmer coastal waters."

Rain bands of pelting beads slapped the island. Katie couldn't believe how hard it was raining. Even with the wipers on full speed, she could see only shadows. Lizzy was ready at the door and ran out to the car. They sat for a moment and took a last look at the small two storied home Lizzy and Mr. Sarge had lived in for over forty years. "I'm afraid she won't be standing when this is all over. Then what will I do?" Tears fell down her face and Lizzy just let loose. "What is going to happen to me?"

"Nothing. If the house goes swimming or follows the wind, you'll come live with Dolly and me. Lord knows we've got enough rooms. Please don't worry about that now. Anyway, this one will change course just like all the others ones have. Let's go get Cat."

Cat got in the car and had her official list. She had already called the sergeant and had given him the necessary information. She had picked up potent potables to help strengthen the nerves during the storm and to aid in recovery once the storm blew over. The spaghetti casserole was cooked and wrapped in her brown tote. Brownies, heavy with pecans, sat tucked in tins to survive the storm. Stove popped corn was packed in zip lock baggies and bags of fruit needed to be picked up from inside the garage. "I'll get them and then we need to hurry home. Chris has gone to find Scott and crazy Laura Anne was at the house."

"I know dear. Dolly has already called me. Please be kind. Remember, you were a bit crazy while you were married to Scott. Practice a little empathy."

They all started to laugh. It was good and deep laughter. All of Dolly's friends had spent many an hour on bended knee praying for Katie and Scott. Katie had come back to the Lord and was once again practicing her faith. Scott was lost literally and figuratively. Only the Blessed Mother knows how many rosaries were sent heaven bound.

For now, prayers were going up all over the island. St. Benedicts began ringing its bells in the predetermined warning signal to evacuate Tybee Island. Emergency personnel drove up and down the streets shouting unnecessarily through megaphones stating matter of factly that everyone was to leave now. But, if there was no urgency in the men's voices, there was an equal calm and deliberation for the beach people. Too many times the warning had gone out and too many times the result was a false alarm. For people living by the ocean, well, they just didn't frighten easily.

Laura Anne, on the other hand, was hysterical. The darker the sky got the more hysteria spewed out of her. Chris had been unsuccessful with his attempts to get Scott off the island. As usual, the reality of the situation was confused with Scott's desire to control and his aversion to be being controlled. It was the epitome of a stalemate.

"Scott, I'm leaving. I don't have a dog in this fight, so I don't really know why I'm here. Leave or stay, it's up to you." Laura Anne slumped to the floor blocking Chris from leaving the beach house. "Good Lord, you are a drama queen. Try the theatrics on Scott." Chris bent down and gently pulled her away from the door, sliding through the small opening, and heading out to his car. He didn't blame Laura Anne one bit for being afraid; he was afraid. There was nothing left for him to do here.

Chris left one chaotic scene and walked into the flip side at Dolly's. Beau was howling out to escape his crate. Katie was vacuuming the den carpet. Cat was piddling in the kitchen, and Lizzy was napping in one of the quest rooms. It was eerily calm, all except for Beau who demanded his release as soon as he saw Chris.

"I take it this is the calm before the storm?"

"Did Scott leave? What happened to Laura Anne? Tell me, Chris." Katie toe tapped the vacuum and pulled Chris into the nearest chair. "Tell me everything."

"There's nothing to tell. Laura Anne's hysterical. Scott's been drinking although he's not drunk. He's belligerent and won't evacuate. And that's that."

"That's that? You mean you aren't going to do anything else? Chris, what's the matter with you?"

Chris stood up furious. "What's the matter with me? What the hell's the matter with you? A hurricane is coming and will probably hit us, we people, those nuts standing here arguing instead of leaving the beach. I have three old ladies and a crazed girlfriend, oh yeah, and one spoiled dog I've got to worry about and I come home to find you vacuuming the house? Are we all in denial here?"

"Don't you dare yell at me! This is how I deal with stress. I'd like to leave too, you know, but Dolly isn't going. What am I supposed to do? Leave her? Leave Lizzy and Cat? I can't. And I can't help that I'm concerned about those nuts down the street."

Dolly had been standing in the doorway and heard their exchange. "No one needs to worry about this old lady. I appreciate your concern, but I will be just fine. You two need to decide to stay or decide to leave, but make the decision soon or the choice will no longer be yours to make. We might take a direct hit, but we will be okay. You have five minutes to change your collective minds and then I'm done with this conversation." She turned and went to her room, grabbed her Bible and began to read.

No one needed to say a thing. The reality was the gates were closed, and nobody else was leaving the island. The merging of high tides, high winds, and blistering rains had sealed the island in a ring of water. The marshes were flooded and had submerged the causeway in several feet of water. The electricity, which had threatened to depart several times, had given up the good fight. It was dark so you couldn't see the color of the sky and maybe that was a gift.

A badly behaved monster was outside making noises that didn't seem possible coming from wind and rain. It was as if a child, locked in his nursery, were having a temper tantrum. Tossing trains, stepping on dollhouses, ripping apart plush animal toys sending their innards across the room. Nothing in the room was untouched. Just like the beach.

The hurricaners said grace and ate a dinner of Cat's divine spaghetti. She'd left the oven on warm planning to eat as soon as they'd lost the power. They lit candles and kept the conversation small and distracting, away from the storm. "I wonder what happened to Scott and Laura Anne." Katie just couldn't help herself. She was edgy and nervous. She was beginning to play "what if" games with her mind. *What if I have a panic attack? What if I suddenly lose my mind? What if Scott drowns?*

Chris put his hand over hers and squeezed tightly. "Leave it alone, Katie. Now's not the time to dredge up old memories either for you or for Scott. You're fine, we're all fine. Let's finish dinner."

Katie knew she loved this man and his calm, reassuring ways. Being with him tonight was the greatest blessing as she was not strong enough to weather this or any other storm without him. She silently offered a prayer in thanksgiving for her second chance and one for her first chance that had ended in such a disaster. Chris, however, was living proof that God restores the years the locust have eaten.

It was bad, no question about it. The beach house was sturdy and well built, worth every extra dollar in hurricane proofing that Dolly had spent. The shingles were glued down; the shutters were drawn and locked; the hatches battened down. Each and every door had been blessed with holy oil and prayers had been said over the house and its inhabitants. The storm's rage seemed to have endless energy. It would run its course, but at what cost?

During the eye of the storm, when things were not as they appeared, Beau began scratching at the door leading down the back steps into the garage and the rooms on that level. "Katie, why don't we let him roam around downstairs? I think being cooped up like this is getting to him."

"If you're sure you locked the garage, then you can let him go downstairs."

"Yes, I got the question you were asking. I did lock the garage. Come on, Beau."

Beau was ecstatic to be freed from the calm restraints of the room. Chris opened the door, and Beau flew down the steps tail wagging in ecstasy. It had been a few hours since the lights had departed and Chris had a sad thought that the ice cream might be melting. The generator would not turn on until later, but the freezer was supposed to keep things cold for several hours. Taking the chance, Chris went to the freezer and grabbed the ice cream. Beau was barking at something in the corner underneath the chair and cooler storage area. It's probably some critter coming in out of the storm. Beau won't hurt him, maybe just annoy the fool out of him for a while. Chris decided not to look.

The eye had passed and hell's furies were at it again. It was hard to imagine what drove the hurricane to such sustaining winds. Although Dolly's house was solid brick, the rafters and windows still rattled and protested against the storm. Based on the ferocity of the winds, they were all pretty sure the new pier would be swimming with the fishes. They debated over some of the new homes built practically on the water's edge; they figured those chances were slim. The little market should be safe, probably all the brick buildings would be okay. The old houses built along the back river would sustain some terrible damage; what the wind didn't destroy the rising river just might.

In the midst of all the sad reverie of dying homes, Beau continued to bark. Suddenly he let out a terrible yelp alerting everyone that he was hurt. Then there was silence. "Good Lord, Chris, what happened to Beau?" Katie jumped up from the sofa and flew to the back door. Chris beat her there and stopped her. "Look, something might be down there. I don't know maybe a snake or something. I saw him poking around and thought it was an opossum or something. God, help me, maybe it was a snake. You stay here, and I'll go check."

Taking the stairs two and three at a time, Chris was stunned to see Beau on his side motionless. "Beau, I'm coming buddy. Hold on boy." Chris called out to him offering a soothing voice. He shined the flashlight on him and nearly fell to his knees. A deep cut ran across his chest and bright red blood was oozing from the wound. That was no snakebite.

Beau's tail began to beat ever so slowly as Chris approached. "Hang on, Beau. Hang on." Chris checked for broken bones and then swooped the wounded dog, now whimpering softly, into his arms and headed back up the stairs.

Katie waited at the top of the stairs frozen in fear and not obedience. She screamed when she saw him. "Put some towels on the kitchen table and let me look at him there. Dolly, ya'll grab some water and something to clean this wound. I'll need something to bandage him with and hands to restrain him. Hurry now!"

The wound was certainly no snakebite. It was a clean swipe of a knife blade running a good seven inches across his blonde chest. It ran from his neck down towards his shoulder but was not as deep as Chris had first thought. Beau lay very still. He had lost a good bit of blood but not enough to worry about at this point. His gums were nice and pink and his breathing was regular. Parts of the wound were deeper than the others were and would require stitches. In the middle of this hurricane, Chris was left to rely on his medical skills; he would have to stitch up Beau.

"Katie, anyone have any Valium in the house?"

"I do. The doctor gave them to me when Mr. Sarge died. I've never taken them, but I like to keep them with me just in case. Now, when this storm was coming, I thought I'd better put them in my purse and-"

Chris interrupted her rambling thoughts. "Go get them, please. Valium will hopefully knock him out enough so I can get some clean stitches." Chris was petting Beau while keeping an eye on Katie who was shocked to see her dog like this. "He'll be fine, I swear. Just keep talking to him and Cat, can you find me a needle and thread? Find one and sterilize it over the candle. Dolly, get some alcohol and hydrogen peroxide for me quickly." She looked at him briefly as if not understanding his command. "Remember now, you said we had all the supplies we needed to ride out this hurricane. Well, I need these now. Please go to wherever you keep Band-Aids, and bring me everything you have. Now, please."

In less than thirty minutes, Beau was stitched and sound asleep. Candles flickered around the room and all the guests sat near each other for comfort. "Poor Beau. What do you think happened down there?" Lizzy had been so upset about Beau. She cried when he was stitched as if she were lying there instead of him. "Chris, what did Beau get into?"

"I don't think he got into anything. I think someone is down there hiding, just coming in from the storm. But that's a knife wound and Beau didn't hurt himself."

Katie laid her head on Chris' shoulder. "How could anyone hurt such a sweet dog? I feel terrible that I let him go down there. Poor baby Beau." The garage doors slammed back against the house. Everyone sat straight up and looked at each other. The doors slammed again and again weakening in the wind. "I'll go close those. Katie, you come with me in case I need help. Do we have any rope?"

"Downstairs on the right side of the garage. There's a whole wall of hoses and things like that." Dolly offered to come show them. "Forget that. I think I'll be hungry for some of that popcorn when I come back. Who knows, maybe we'll play charades in the dark. I stink at that game so no one will want me on their team."

Katie and Chris walked down the stairs. Holding a large, black flashlight lantern, Katie led the way. She was keeping up a constant barrage of chatter that was Annoying Chris supremely. Everyone's nerves were on edge. Something just did not feel right.

Katie heard a loud grunt from Chris and turned to see him slumped on the floor. She screamed, dropped the lantern, and bent over him. A nasty bump was already rising on the back of his head. "Chris! Chris! What happened? Chris, wake up!" She turned him over but he was still knocked out. "Chris!"

A mocking voice, like that of the wicked witch of the east, mimicked Katie. "Chris. Chris. What happened? Chris. Please wake up. I love you, Chris. I need you, Chris. Ooooh, Chris." Katie would know that voice anywhere. She grabbed for the lantern and lit the direction of the sound. "Dear God, what are you doing in here? Scott. Tell me."

"Tell me, Scott. Ohhh, order me around, Katie. Tell me, Scott." He walked over to her and grabbed her roughly by the back of the hair. "What am I doing here? I'm taking you home where you belong- with me." Scott used the point of his knife to touch his chest. "Me. Me. Do you hear me, me? I don't want to be without you anymore. I have a beach house now, and we can go live there." Someone cracked open the back door. "Katie? Chris? Are you down there? Is everything okay? Should I come down there?"

"Everything's just fine now, Dolly. We are going home now. Just leave us alone, and we'll be fine."

"Katie? Katie answer me. Who was that talking? Katie." Dolly's voice was riddled with anxiety. "Where's Chris?"

"He's down here, knocked out. Not much of a man to drop with that little tap I gave him. Dolly, it's me, your favorite grandson in-law. Your best girls' husband. It's meeeeee. Scott. Come see me, Dolleeeeeeeeee."

Dolly started down the steps, and Katie screamed for her to stop. "He has a knife in his hand so please don't come down. I'll be okay."

"She's right there, Dolly. I won't hurt the only thing in this world I love. Now her ex-lover might be a different story."

"He's not my lover, Scott. And, he isn't my ex. Put that damn knife away. What is wrong with you?"

"I get it. He isn't your lover like we weren't lovers before we got married. I get it. You're playing that game with Dolly so she'll think you've become a virgin again? Toss the act, Katie. I know you're lovers. And, heh, in case you haven't noticed, I'm calling the shots here. Hear me; he ain't gonna be your lover again." Scott pulled her roughly towards him and smashed his face into hers. The brutality of his kiss shocked her. She could feel the blood seeping from her mouth where his teeth had cut her lip.

"Remember when you used to like that, baby girl? Remember all those nights that we couldn't get enough of each other? No girl has done it for me since you abandoned me. Why'd you do it? Why'd you leave me when I got so sick? I stayed by you all the time. Katie, why?"

"I never liked that because you've never done that to me before. I just don't understand what's the matter with you! Why are you talking and acting like some gangster?"

"You're all I've got left. I'm penniless, and my reputation is ruined. I'm stuck with a loud, bossy, conceited cow I can't stand. So you see you are really all I have left."

"Scott, you don't have me. We are divorced, and our marriage has been annulled. We aren't together anymore, and we never will be."

"We'll see about that." Scott took the rope off the garage wall and tied it around Katie's waist. She just stared at him incredulously. "What are you doing?"

"I already told you, we are going home. We're gonna walk on the beach until we find our house. If I tie us together then our weight will keep us safer. If you start to blow away I can save you. Now let's go." He pulled hard on the robe dragging her two steps at a time into the den. "We have to go out the screen porch door. A big tree's blocking our way to the beach. Come on, Katie, don't fight me."

The girls were horrified to see Scott pulling Katie across the floor. He ordered them to sit down or Katie might get hurt. They did not speak or move. Interiorly, however, they were interceding for Katie and Scott, asking God for a miracle. Scott had clearly broken with reality.

They walked past the kitchen table where Beau was still sleeping. "Glad to see you got him all fixed up. Damn dog just wouldn't quit bothering me. He was jumping on me and making all kind of noise. I didn't mean to hurt him, I just wanted him to stop, and he wouldn't. He's gonna be alright isn't he?"

Katie swirled around catching Scott off guard. "You cut Beau? You hurt my dog. What kind of crazy fool have you become? You could have killed him!"

"Yeah, but I didn't. I couldn't have you crying all through our honeymoon. Let's go."

The storm still had lots of fight left. No man or beast should be out in the storm let alone one man whose mind was lost. Scott kicked opened the porch door and watched it slam back against the house. He took one last look at the three old ladies sitting on the sofa praying. "Superstitious old fools. Prayer isn't gonna help you or them."

Dolly's voice played through Katie's memories. The times she had begged her not to marry Scott. The days she had shared how the Holy Spirit had warned her about Scott. That terrible day she picked Scott over Dolly. Now she had placed everyone in danger. *Dear Lord, please take care of my family and Chris. Heal Beau too, Lord. Deliver Scott, and set me free. Please, Lord.*

They were tied together now, tightly around the waist. Scott was pulling Katie down the boardwalk stopping just at the crest of the walkway. The ocean was mad. Simply mad. The waves were six feet above normal crest, and they were a powerful and frightening sight. Water was washing over them stopping them just in the middle of the bridge. Katie could see the ocean water forging just inches from the bottom of the bridge, which stood eight feet above the sand dune. In no time, they would be washed out to sea.

The wind knocked Katie off her feet several times, and each time Scott dragged her back up again. He'd look her straight in the eye and scream at her for falling. Scott was two hundred pounds; Katie was one hundred thirty-seven. She could not possibly fight the wind and survive.

Suddenly, a giant rogue wave swept over the boardwalk pulling Scott off his feet and forcing him face down on the planks. He was stunned for a minute and tried to shake the stupor from his head. As he grabbed for the railing, Katie kicked him in the groin as hard as she possibly could. This man was no longer the Scott she had once known and loved. This man was out to kill her, and she was going to have to fight with all of her strength.

He grabbed his privates and fell down again, rolling and moaning, calling out obscenities towards her. For a split second, she started to run back to the house, but everything she loved was there. No, she would have to do it another way. Katie had doubted her ability to fight someone who threatened her life; now she knew that she could, beyond a shadow of a doubt. Blood was still flowing from her mouth and her lip was bruised and swelling. It felt like a giant goose egg and it hurt like a mule had kicked her. Scott slowly got up and moved towards her. She had no escape. The house wasn't an option nor was the ocean. There was no beach, no light, no place to run.

Slipping off the tether holding them together, Katie tried to climb over the boardwalk. Maybe she could swim under the boardwalks and hold on until the hurricane blew on. She could hardly stand against the power of the wind, but she knew she'd have to do something now. She fell again and saw a chance to slide under the bridge. It was her only chance. Just as she was halfway off the bridge, Scott caught her by her hair and snatched her back onto the boards. She lay on her back staring up into the face of this crazy man. She could hardly breathe from the rain pelting her face. Scott got down on one knee and put his face just inches from hers. "You can't treat me like that, Katie. I'm your husband-you must honor and obey me. Now, get up and don't try any of that again or we'll both die."

Out of nowhere, a yellow blur flew past Katie and into Scott knocking him over. He nearly slipped off the bridge and was hanging on by one hand. Beau was actually biting him and biting him hard. Scott was howling. Poor Beau, he couldn't stand to get wet, and here he was in the middle of a hurricane, biting his old master and saving Katie's life.

Scott was cruel. He took his free hand and punched Beau in the chest knocking the breath out of the dog. Beau laid on his side gasping for breath and reeling from the pain of his incision. He looked up at Scott with those magnificent sad eyes as if asking *why, what happened to you?*

246

Scott rolled back onto the bridge and walked over to the dog. He picked up his booted foot to stomp the dogs head. He was laughing and told Katie to watch. "This dog will never bite me again." He pulled the knee up higher, going for more power and advantage. The knee came down and Chris fired. He had aimed for the knee but instead missed sending the bullet clean through Scott's calf.

Scott grabbed his leg and rolled and rolled, screaming at the top of his lungs. But, with the high winds and rains, only Chris and Katie could hear Scott.

"Katie, take Beau and go back into the house. Lock the doors and do not let anyone in unless you can see me through the screen. I will come up the back steps, just the way we came out. Go now. Come on Beau, go with Katie."

In perfect obedience and without a single protest or question, Katie struggled to help all ninety pounds of precious Labrador retriever to the house.

The waves were unleashing a power that was unimaginable. They moved in every direction all at the same time. Katie struggled to hold on to Beau's collar and the boardwalk. Beau was crawling commando style, moving forward and making some progress. Katie was drowning in adrenaline. This hormone she had feared most of her adult life was now a lifeline coursing through her veins giving her a strength she did not know existed. Repeatedly Katie called out to the Lord. She couldn't form a prayer, just utterances of Jesus, Jesus, Jesus. She was single-minded, determined to get to safety. The water slammed her into the rails, while actually pushing her closer to the house. She refused to look back at Scott and Chris; She knew they were in God's hands now.

Scott's hands were bleeding badly from Beau's attack. He was going into shock from his bullet wound. His eyes had a glazed look and Chris knew Scott had succumbed to a psychotic break. All his defenses had failed him. All of his charisma and charm had failed to keep Katie in his life. He was clearly a sociopath who tripped up and actually, truly fell in love. Scott had nothing left, absolutely nothing, making him extremely dangerous.

"Why don't you go ahead and shoot me? I know that's what you want to do. Do it. Shoot me." Scott's voice was raspy as if screaming from an infected throat. The blood poured from his leg wound and mixed with the water swirling around his calves.

"This isn't a movie, pal, and I'm not going to shoot you again. I want to take you back to the house so we can all be safe. In the morning, we can get you some help. Believe you me, the last thing I plan on doing is seriously hurting someone." Chris tried to make his voice sound friendly and reassuring, but he had to scream over the wind to get Scott to hear him. Scott was beyond discerning subtleties in sound.

The waves were racing towards them, each one slightly taller than the last one. "Look, Scott, we've got to go in now or it'll be too late for both of us. I don't want to die out here, and I'm sure you don't want to either. I'll hold out my hand, and you can let go of the railing. We'll get there."

"Why are you being so nice to me? You think I'll give you back Katie if you're nice to me? I won't, Chris. She's mine." Scott slipped out of the rope and let it slip over the side and into the dark water. He began to step backwards towards the steps and the brewing ocean.

"Come on buddy. Scott, listen to me. We can work this out. You can have Katie. You can have whatever you want. Just come with me." The wind whipped Chris right to his knees making him bang his head on the second hand rail. He had a powerful headache and that last blow stunned him. Shaking his head to unrattle his brains, he looked to see Scott walking in the knee-deep water and heading towards the ocean. "Don't do it Scott. It's just about the only thing in life you don't get a second chance on."

Scott looked strangely calm. His black hair was soaked and plastered to his head. Rivers ran off his arms and legs and his clothes clung to his body. He had a strange, but peaceful smile on his face, and he no longer looked frightened. "She's yours, old boy. Tell her I really am sorry. I really, truly am." Scott appeared as sane as any other man standing on a boardwalk during a hurricane was. Now he was lucid, and he was making peace with Katie and Chris. "Ask her to forgive me, I mean really forgive me. And then, Chris, can you hear me? Please get it right, okay? Forgive me, Katie girl. I really loved you. Forgive me and pray for me." Scott trudged through the water and grabbed onto the last inch of the handrail. "Chris. Remind her, please. You know what JB said- 'No fishing allowed.'"

Suddenly a branch flew across the bridge and sideswiped Chris. Taking advantage of the moment, Scott lunged at Chris, grabbing for the gun barely visible in the raging storm. Arms swung wildly as both men missed their mark. It was pointless to fight one another with the hurricane pounding them to a pulp. With the strength possessed by a mad man, Scott grabbed Chris by the throat and began to choke him, pulling him down onto the walkway. With both men underwater and struggling for air, there were no bets on who would come out ahead.

Yet, Chris found a way to push off the boardwalk, knees first and then to feet, dragging Scott up with him. Leaning against the rails, both men gasped for air and slippery arms tangled in a weak attempt at fighting. Then the wave came washing over them, sending Chris up towards the door while Scott slipped off the steps with his rope still tied to his waist. The rope that would bind him to Katie would now be his demise. The twin wave followed, more furious than the first, and with an unimaginable power sucked Scott off the bridge, rope trailing behind him, and moving too quickly for Chris to do anything to help.

Suddenly, he was gone. Chris tried to get closer but it was no use. He would never find him in the water and if he did, he wouldn't be able to do a single thing for him. Scott had disappeared, never to be seen again.

EPILOGUE

F ather John held up the babies with the help of Deacon Lambert. "Help me to welcome our newest baptized members, Ashley Elizabeth and John Christopher Martin." As usual, those who hung around Katie and her family knew to have a box of tissues somewhere close by. Katie smiled at the small gathering of close family and friends. Chris was the proud and over protective father. He adored Margaret Mary, the first baby, and loved calling her name in a sing songy way that delighted her. Katie doubted any little girl could suffer from hero worship more than Miss Maggie did.

Dolly sat in the first pew holding Margaret. Her blonde curls were loosed, but framed her head. She was beautiful and looked a great deal like Dolly did as a child. Cat sat next to Laura Anne and whispered promises that her turn was coming soon. Lizzy was, as usual, all grins, and morphing daily into the Aunt Bea of Tybee Island. Thanks to the goodness of Father John's heart, and his deep love of animals, Beau and Bella lay under Dolly's feet while the babies were baptized. Bella, sweet Bella, Lizzy's contribution to the newlyweds, was the top rated wedding gift. Part two of the gift was in the successful house training just in time to celebrate Maggie's conception.

The twins were beautiful and healthy and an unexpected addition to Margaret Mary who, at just a hair over a year old, was delighted to have two new friends to play with. Forget the old adage that you cannot get pregnant while breastfeeding. Katie and Chris were a bit shell shocked, but there were many loving hands to help raise all three of these sweet babies.

Cat was helping Laura Anne with her new bridal shop in Somerville; without Scott, the catering business seemed a bust. Laura Anne had just made it off the island in time. She was devastated about Scott, but she did get some counseling and was coming around to giving Jesus a chance. She had sent Katie a beautiful note after Maggie was born. The note begged for forgiveness for her affair with Scott and her rude and demanding behavior. "I've dropped the 'Anne' from my name and am just going by Laura. It is the new me, and a way to distance myself from the old one. I adore Cat and cannot believe how much she is teaching me. I am opening a new circle of friends, and I hope I can count you and Chris as members. As it stands today, I do not have a circle or any friends. Interested?" And they were.

Although a search and rescue mission was thoroughly carried out, Scott's body was never found. A sad and depressing memorial service was held with very few in attendance. Katie and Chris got married as soon as they could after the storm. All the tragedies had made them realize that waiting made no sense.

Yes, the lighthouse and Lizzy's cottage were still standing. They had been right about the new pier and the houses on the back river. The clean up would take some time, but Tybee Island would be restored to its original beauty. Dolly's house was indeed hurricane proof.

Made in the USA
Charleston, SC
06 August 2014